THE GLENCOE LITERATURE LIBRARY

Fallen Angels

with Related Readings

Glencoe
McGraw-Hill

New York, New York   Columbus, Ohio   Woodland Hills, California   Peoria, Illinois

Acknowledgments

Grateful acknowledgment is given authors, publishers, photographers, museums, and agents for permission to reprint the following copyrighted material. Every effort has been made to determine copyright owners. In case of any omissions, the Publisher will be pleased to make suitable acknowledgments in future editions.

Fallen Angels by Walter Dean Myers. Copyright © 1988 by Walter Dean Myers. Reprinted by permission of Scholastic Inc.

"Catharsis," by Denise Kusel. *Southwest Art*, July 1994 (Copyright © 1994, CBH Publishing, Inc.). Reprinted by permission.

"The Home Front" by Steve Hockensmith (Chicago Tribune Magazine, August 6, 2000). Reprinted by permission of the author.

From "Ernie Pyle Writes of a Dead Man and of Mules" Copyright © 1998, 36th Division Association. Reprinted by permission of the Texas Military Forces Museum.

"The Gift in Wartime" by Tran Mong Tu. Reprinted by permission of the author.

"Zebra," copyright © 1998 by Chaim Potok, from *Zebra and Other Stories* by Chaim Potok. Used by permission of Alfred A. Knopf Children's Books, a division of Random House, Inc.

Cover Art: *Distant Shudder*, 1991, John Keane. PVA and Crayon on Paper, 76 x 51 cm. Angela Flowers Gallery, London, UK/The Bridgeman Art Library.

Note: *This novel is the story of young Americans engaged in battle in Viet Nam. Such a story can be told honestly only by including the graphic and often disturbing language and emotional responses of the young people caught up in the war. Some words, references, and situations may offend certain readers.*

Glencoe/McGraw-Hill

*A Division of The **McGraw·Hill** Companies*

Send all inquiries to:
Glencoe/McGraw-Hill
8787 Orion Place
Columbus, OH 43240

ISBN 0-07-826331-X
Printed in the United States of America
5 6 7 8 9 026 10 09 08 07

Contents

Fallen Angels

Continued

Contents *Continued*

Fallen Angels

Walter Dean Myers

Chapter 1

Somebody must have told them suckers I was coming."

"Told who?" I asked.

"The Congs, man. Who you think I'm talking 'bout?"

"Why you think somebody told them you were coming?"

" 'Cause I don't see none of 'em around here. They don't want their butts kicked."

"Yeah, okay." I looked at the guy's name tag. It read "Gates." "Hey, Gates, I'll tell you as soon as I see some Congs."

"I'm going on in the bathroom," he said. "Make sure they ain't none in there."

"Right."

I watched him wade through a sea of GIs, stopping now and again to talk to one of them.

"Does he really think we're in Vietnam already?" Specialist, Fifth Class Judy Duncan looked sharp in her dress uniform as she leaned against the Coke machine. Most of us were in fatigues, the army's work clothes. I had been sitting next to Judy on the flight from Massachusetts. She had brought along an assortment of snacks to eat on the plane and was now digging into a bag of potato chips as we waited for the plane to refuel in Anchorage, Alaska, on our way to Vietnam.

"He's just a clown," I said. "On the plane he asked a captain to wake him up when we reached Cong City."

"Where you say you were from?"

"New York," I answered. "You?"

"I tell most people I'm from Dallas," she said. "But I'm really from Irving. That's right outside of Dallas. I don't think anybody is really from Dallas anymore."

"You took advanced training at Fort Devens?"

"Unh-uh. Sam Houston, in Texas. I did basic there and then went right into medical school. I got assigned to the hospital in Devens, but it got boring."

"Now you going to see the world?"

"Something like that," she said. She had a nice smile. "I think somebody figures if I see Nam first, everything else is going to look good to me."

The plane had been half empty coming from Massachusetts to Anchorage. We picked up about fifty more guys in Anchorage, most of them infantry from Fort Lewis. There were a few nurses with the group, too, and Judy went and sat with them.

We were served dinner shortly after we were airborne, but I wasn't hungry. I usually can't eat when I'm nervous, and going to Nam made me nervous. The only reason I was going anyway was because of a paperwork mess up. At first my unit was scheduled to go to Nam, but a doctor at Fort Devens had said that my knee was too bad for combat duty. I was assigned to a supply company while I waited for new orders. But then my old company didn't go to Nam, they went to Germany instead—which was cool because there wasn't any fighting going on over there—and I got orders for Nam.

"Look at it this way, Perry," the captain had said. "The only reason you're going to Nam is that it takes forever to process a medical profile. Once it catches up with you, you'll be headed home. In the meantime you'll get to Nam, they'll put you behind a desk in some headquarters company, and the worst thing that'll happen to you is that you catch a social disease in downtown Saigon that'll rot your twinkie off."

I hadn't been too worried about going to Nam. From what I had heard, the fighting was almost over, anyway.

Our next stop was Osaka, Japan, and I slept most of the way. We landed at a commercial airport because of some kind of disturbance at the military facilities. There was supposed to be a change of planes, but they didn't have another plane available until the next morning. A tall, square-shouldered first lieutenant gave out meal tickets, and we were told we could use them at the airport cafeteria. The people at the cafeteria were civilians, and they didn't want any part of our meal tickets, even though a sergeant tried to explain to the head of the cafeteria that the U.S. Army would redeem them. Two corporals made some noise about taking the cafeteria over. What finally went down was that we all bought our own dinners. Typical army.

We spent the rest of the night sleeping on benches in the airport. A lot of Japanese civilians gave us the once-over. I bought a few souvenirs to send home, a little parasol for Mom and some Japanese comics for my brother Ken. By morning the cafeteria mess was straightened out, and we ate anything we wanted. I talked with Judy at breakfast, and she told me how she had wanted to be a garbageman when she was a kid.

"The trucks were just the best things I had ever seen in my life," she said. She had an order of scrambled eggs and bacon, and a small mountain of toast that was disappearing quickly. "When I found out I couldn't be a garbageman, I settled for being a movie star, but it was definitely second-best."

She asked me what I had wanted to be when I was a kid, and I told her that most of the time I had wanted to work in a drugstore and wear a white coat with the buttons on the shoulder.

"Yeah?" she shook her head approvingly. "That's what I like about you, Perry, you know all the good stuff. And buttons on the shoulders are definitely the good stuff."

When the plane took off for the final hop to Vietnam, the conversations got quieter. Everybody who could was looking out of the windows.

"Okay, listen up!" A sergeant stood in the aisles with a clipboard. "We're scheduled to arrive at Tan Son Nhut, the ree-public of Vietnam, at 1400 hours. When you deplane, you will form four ranks in the area designated by Lieutenant Wilson. There will be no grab-ass, no excessive running off at the mouth, and no wandering around. Is that clear?"

"Yes, Sergeant!" came the familiar chorus.

"You will have your gear ready to deplane the moment we touch down. Is *that* clear?"

"Yes, Sergeant!"

I had to go to the john. I thought about it for a while and looked back toward the plane's johns. Too late. The line already stretched halfway down the aisle. It was 1320 hours, twenty minutes past one o'clock civilian time. We'd be in Nam in less than an hour. I thought of writing Mom and took out my paper. All I could think of was the date: September 15, 1967.

"Hey, Perry." Judy was leaning over my shoulder.

"How's it going?"

"Okay. Look, I just found out the nurses are going right to Chu Lai. I just wanted to wish you luck."

"Hey, thanks." I shook her hand. "Where's Chu Lai?"

"Who knows?" she shrugged.

Hot. Muggy. Bright. Muggy. That was the airport at Tan Son Nhut. We deplaned, followed Lieutenant Wilson across the field into an area in front of some Quonset huts, and started forming ranks. It took a while. The sergeant with the clipboard came along and tried to encourage us as best he could.

"You faggots can't even line up straight, how you gonna fight?" he shouted.

He kept on yelling and Lieutenant Wilson started yelling, and we finally got in order. Then a captain came out, and we were turned over to him. The sergeant's clipboard was turned over to him, too.

"Medical personnel assigned to the Sixty-seventh Group or the 312th or the Twenty-third Battalion fall out and get in those buses over there. Everybody else stand at ease."

When the medics fell out, Judy waved to me again, and some of the guys around me told me to go give her a kiss.

"That's what they do in the war movies," one guy said.

I didn't really know Judy, and I probably wouldn't have had the nerve to kiss her in front of everybody, even if I did. We watched the medics go toward the buses while the rest of us stood in the sun. I checked my watch, and it was 1430 hours.

The next time I checked my watch it was 1530 hours, and we were still standing in the sun. Once I had figured that of the seven months I had spent in the army, four of them had been standing around waiting for something to happen. Vietnam might have been a different place, but the army hadn't changed.

Vietnam. There were mountains in the distance. A helicopter hovered over the far end of the field, tilted at a crazy angle, and then flew off. I watched it until it was almost out of sight.

Most of the guys around the landing field were in fatigues. No different than Fort Devens, except that half of them carried their rifles around with them. There were a lot of pistols, too. You didn't see many pistols stateside.

There were Vietnamese soldiers around, too. They were smaller than I thought they would be. I tried not to stare at them. A rumbling noise off to my left sounded like distant thunder. We knew it was artillery. My stomach felt queasy. Guys started looking at the ground. This was Nam.

We had a roll call. I listened for the sergeant to call my last name. When he did, I responded with my first name: Richard. Two marines—they had obviously been in Nam awhile—came over and stood near the sergeant and looked at us. They were unshaven. Their uniforms looked worn, darker than ours. One of them was wearing a necklace of some kind. The other one had a peace symbol painted on his helmet. They were old-looking guys, older than any of the guys just coming in.

We went back to waiting in the sun. We waited until 1600 hours. Then the trucks came.

I was assigned to the Twenty-second Replacement Company. That's where I met Gates again, the guy who had been looking for "Congs" in Anchorage. We bunked next to each other.

Gates was brown-skinned, but he had reddish hair and freckles. I thought I was going to like him.

"You see any Vietcong?" I asked.

"Yeah, you see that girl come in here a moment ago?"

"The one cleaning the barracks?"

"Yeah, she's a Cong, man."

There were three or four Vietnamese civilians around our barracks. Two were painting the decorative rocks around headquarters, the kind of thing that we all did stateside, and the other two were cleaning inside.

"They're not Vietcong."

"Who told you that?"

"It figures," I said. "We're fighting the Vietcong. You don't fight some-body, then hire them to clean up."

"I remember back home this boy come into a poolroom—"

"Where's back home?"

"Chicago." Gates was lying on his back on his bunk. "Anyway, this dude come into the poolroom, and he knowed he was a good pool shot, see? So he hustled this other dude into a pool game for twenty dollars and beat him."

"Yeah, go on."

"Well, he figured he was supposed to get his money," Gates said. "But the boy he beat didn't want to pay him so he shot him in the stomach."

Gates stopped talking and started taking his boots off.

"So what's the end of the story?" I asked.

"That the end. The dude that did the figuring done figured wrong. That's why you shouldn't be figuring that chickie that be doing the cleaning ain't no Cong."

Right.

I started writing home. The Vietnamese cleaning lady came in again. She started dusting around the bunks. I looked over at Gates, and he was looking at me. He smiled.

"Hey, Gates," I said, "I know you're wrong."

"Don't be calling me no Gates," he said. "You call me Peewee."

"Okay, Peewee," I said. "You're still wrong."

"I can prove it to you," Peewee said. "Watch this."

"Hey, you!" he sat up and called to the Vietnamese woman. "Mama Cong!"

The woman looked at him, shrugged, and then turned away.

"Mama Cong!" he repeated, louder.

"She probably doesn't even understand English," I said. A couple of other guys had turned to see what Peewee was doing.

"Watch if she don't split," Peewee said.

The woman turned again and looked at Peewee. Then she left.

"See!" There was a big smile on his face. "She's a Cong, that's why she left. She know Peewee got her number."

"If you talked crazy at me," a heavy, red-faced guy called over to Peewee, "I'd leave, too."

"That's cause you probably a Cong," Peewee said. "And you a ugly-ass Cong, too."

The guy stood up. He seemed twice as big standing as he did sitting. He came over to Peewee's bunk and put his foot on Peewee's bed.

"Boy," he said, "I just finished seven months of ranger training, learning how to kill little people like you. So why don't you just shut up?"

"Yo, you, what's your name?" Peewee called over to me.

"Perry."

"Perry, did this peckerwood just call me 'boy'?"

"I think you'd better leave him alone," I said.

"Yeah, but did he just call me 'boy'?"

"I can answer for myself," the ranger said. "Yes, I did call you 'boy,' Boy!"

Peewee turned and looked as if he were going to put his feet on the floor. Instead he shot both legs into the ranger's crotch. The big man doubled over, and Peewee punched him on the side of the head. Then he laid back, put his hand under his pillow, and pulled out a knife, which clicked open with a flick of the wrist.

"Now you can get up and start beating on me if you want," Peewee said. "But if you do, I'm going to cut your damn throat soon's you go to sleep."

The ranger got up, looked at Peewee, and started sputtering something about if Peewee didn't have the knife what he would do. I put Peewee in the letter to Mama.

Chapter 2

A SERGEANT CAME IN and put the lights out. Then he made a bunch of stupid remarks about what we should and shouldn't do in the dark.

"Hey, Perry!" It was Peewee.

"What?"

"What did you do back in the World?"

"Just got out of school," I said.

"You didn't finish, either?"

"I finished high school."

"No lie?"

"No lie."

"Then why you come in the army?"

"Seemed like a good idea at the time," I said.

I finished high school, but I hadn't gone to the graduation exercises. It just hadn't made sense anymore.

"You can go to City College," the guidance counselor had said. "Your grades are good enough."

I told her I'd think about it. What I was thinking about was that I had to get up every morning and dry the clothes I had washed the night before by putting them on the oven door, to have something to wear to high school. How was I going to get the clothes for college? How was I going to get clothes for Kenny so he would stay in school? Mama had said that she'd see to it that Kenny stayed in school if I sent the money for clothes for him. I wasn't saving any money, the way I figured I would when I first got into the army, but I figured that might come later if I made sergeant.

I thought of writing a letter to Kenny. He would dig getting a letter from Nam. I remembered once he was involved with a pen-pal program and got a letter from some kid in Logan, West Virginia. He had looked at me with his wide, bright eyes and smiled like he couldn't believe the great thing that had happened to him. The night before I left for the army we had sat and talked about what we were going to do in the future. No matter what I said, I knew he was sorry that I was leaving.

"Richie," he had said before he went to sleep, "when you get to Vietnam, I hope you guys win."

The Monarchs, the neighborhood team I played for, had just lost a tournament the week before. It had bothered me a lot. I had done well, and Kenny had said that it wasn't my fault. I had given him a big speech about basketball being a team sport, and that my doing well didn't matter.

"Either the team wins or the team loses," I had said.

I had wanted to win badly. I knew I was going into the army, but for me that was a kind of defeat. My plans, maybe just my dreams really, had been to go to college, and to write like James Baldwin. All the other guys in the neighborhood thought I was going to college. I wasn't, and the army was the place I was going to get away from all the questions. I wanted to win the tournament, to walk away from the streets I had been raised in with my head high, a winner.

That night I kissed Kenny good-night. It was the first time I had kissed him since we were both small.

Peewee and I had breakfast together. I asked him if he liked the army, and he said it was okay.

"You got all this chickenshit to go through," he said. "And I don't like that. But this is the first place I ever been in my life where I got what everybody else got."

"What does that mean?"

"Back home when everybody got new sneakers, I didn't get none," Peewee said. "Either Moms didn't have the money, or she had the money, and we had to get some other stupid thing, like food. When everybody got a bike I didn't get one 'cause there was no way we could get the money for a bike. But anything anybody got in the army, I got. You got a gun, I got a gun. You got boots, I got boots. You eat this lousy-ass chip beef on toast, guess what I eat?"

"Lousy-ass chip beef on toast," I said.

Peewee's grin just about filled the mess tent.

Most of the day was spent sitting around. Some of the guys were talking about how hard they had had it in basic training. They all had the same stories no matter where they had taken basic. I thought the stories were probably part of the training.

There were a lot of black guys. I didn't think there would be so many. Some of them stayed off to themselves, but one guy was making the rounds of all the other blacks.

"The way I figure it, we got to stick together over here." He had three rings on the hand he waved in the air. "I can't trust no whitey to watch my back when the deal go down."

"So what do you want to do?" I asked.

"We got to make an oath or something," Rings said. "You know, mingle some blood. That's symbolic of what we going to be about over here in this strange land."

The dude was serious. I watched him take out a pocket knife and cut his wrist. Then he handed the knife to Peewee.

"You got to be out your mind!" Peewee said. "You sitting there cutting your own damn self, you don't need nobody watching your back!"

"You don't understand," Rings said. "This is symbolic of our common African blood."

"Yeah, all that is cool, but I want my common African blood in my common African veins," Peewee said.

"You ignorant!" Rings pointed at Peewee.

"Maybe I am, but I ain't bleeding."

Rings shook his head and slid the knife across the table to me.

"I got hemophilia," I said. "If I cut myself, I won't stop bleeding."

"You a Uncle Tom, what you is," Rings said. "If you had some damn hemophilia, they wouldn't have you in no army!"

He grabbed his knife, got up, and walked away. I watched him go.

"That fool is crazy!" Peewee said.

"I don't know, he might have something," I said.

"Well, whatever he got, he can sure keep it. Set up the checkers."

We played checkers until it was time for chow, the same way we had the day before. Then we ate chow and played checkers in the afternoon.

Another black guy, a specialist, fourth class, came over and joined me and Peewee. He asked where we were from, and we told him.

"I'm from Monroe, Louisiana. You ever hear of it?"

"No," Peewee said.

"Ain't much to it," he said. "How long y'all been in country?"

"You mean *this* country?"

"You don't have to say nothing," he said. "You just told me."

"How long you been here?" Peewee asked.

"I been here nine months. I got sick, and they sent me to the hospital over in the Philippines. You ever been in that hospital?"

"We just got here," Peewee said. "How we gonna get in the hospital?"

"You just getting here don't mean nothing," the spec four said. "I seen a guy drop dead getting off the plane from Hawaii. The plane come down and landed just as pretty as you damn please. He come out, took him a good look around, and dropped stone dead."

"What kind of outfit were you in?" Peewee asked.

"I was with the Twenty-fourth Transportation Battalion, but I put in for a transfer 'cause I had a run-in with my commanding officer."

"What kind of run-in?"

"I was high on guard duty," the spec four said. "My pal brought some smoke from Saigon, and we all got stoned."

"So what you doing now?"

"They give me a choice, transfer or court-martial," he said. "So you know I got to transfer, because I can't stand no jail time."

"You been in any fighting?" Peewee asked.

"They didn't have no fighting around Cam Ranh Bay," was the answer. "They had more fighting in a juke joint outside of Fort Eustis than I seen all the time I been over here."

It sounded good. Peewee and the spec four played checkers for a while and then he played with an Italian from Connecticut. We told him what the spec four had said about not seeing any fighting.

"I heard it was over anyway," the guy said. "They're supposed to be signing a truce or something in Paris."

"That's 'cause they heard I was here," Peewee said with this real serious look on his face.

The Italian guy looked at me and looked at Peewee and shrugged. I was getting to like Peewee.

They showed a movie in the day room and passed out some beer. Three guys from each hooch, which is what they called the barracks, had to pull guard duty and the ranger volunteered for it. They had beer in the day room and a Ping-Pong table. There was a line for the Ping-Pong table, so we watched the news from the States. They didn't mention anything about Nam.

The next morning about half of our hooch got their orders. Most of them were going to some place called Cu Chi. The rest of us sat around or played three-man basketball.

"Let's go to town," Peewee said.

"Where's town?"

Peewee went into the HQ hooch to find out where town was just as they were looking for somebody else to pull guard duty, and he got put on. I went back to our hooch and wrote my first letter to Kenny. I told him that I had heard that there was going to be a truce, and there wouldn't be any more fighting. I also told him I would bring him back a souvenir if I could.

Saturday. My ninth day in country. The army paper *Stars and Stripes* was full of the truce talks in Paris, but the war was still going on. In the distance F-100's streaked across the sky. I saw a lot of planes, mostly jets and helicopters, and all ours. I didn't see any enemy planes. I didn't even know if they had any.

"Yo, Perry!"

"What?"

"When they going to get us into this war, man?"

"We have to get orientated first," I said. "I heard that the orientation officer broke his ankle playing basketball."

"He probably a damn Cong," Peewee said. "You ready to get into it?"

"Yeah."

"Damn straight!" Peewee said. "We got to get into it before it's over."

I was less nervous than I was when I first got in country. We were in Nam to stop the North Vietnamese from taking over South Vietnam. I didn't feel really gung ho or anything, but I was ready to do my part.

One of the new guys who came in was from Fort Dix. He looked like one of the characters from an Archie Andrews comic, but he was so scared it wasn't funny. He told us his name was Jenkins.

"What's it like so far?" he asked Peewee.

"Ain't nothing to it," Peewee said.

"You been here long?" Jenkins asked.

"Eight months," Peewee lied. "I got to kill eight more Cong before I get my quota. Then I can go home."

"How many you kill so far?"

"A hundred and thirty-two," Peewee said. "I weigh a hundred and forty. Whatever you weigh, that's how many you got to kill to leave early."

"I never heard of that," Jenkins said.

"That ain't for regular rotation," Peewee went on. "That's just so you can leave early."

"Oh." Jenkins took it all in.

"Air force guys can get their quota in one or two days," Peewee said.

"What did you do, machine gun most of them?" Jenkins' eyes were wide.

"No, man," Peewee shook his head. "They issue you so many bullets per week, see? But each one you turn back in you get a quarter for. So mostly I sneak up on the suckers and cut their throats. That way I save my bullets. Way I figure, by the time I get back to the World I have me enough to buy a little Chevy."

"None of that is true," Jenkins said. He was pissed at Peewee for pulling his leg.

The sergeant came in and picked three guys for guard duty. The ranger volunteered again, and they got Jenkins and one other guy. Jenkins was shaking when he left the hooch.

"Don't forget to save your bullets!" Peewee called out to him.

That night the mosquitoes ate us up. I had bites all over my body. Back home I thought mosquitoes never bit black people. Not as much as they bit white people, anyway. Maybe Vietnamese mosquitoes just bit blacks and whites and didn't bite Asians.

We finally got the orientation lecture. This young-looking lieutenant showed us a slide of a map of Nam. Then he showed us where we were.

"You are not in Disneyland," he said. "The little people you see running around over here are not Mouseketeers. Some of them are friendly, and some of them have a strong desire to kill you. If you remember that, and manage to kill them before they kill you, then you have a good chance of getting through your year of service here.

"Take your pills. Once a week for malaria, twice a week if you're too stupid to remember the day you last took them.

"Stay away from the women. They got venereal diseases over here that eat penicillin for breakfast. Three quarters of the women over here have it.

"They got crabs over here that line up every morning to get a shot of DDT. It wakes them up, gets their day started right.

"Stay away from the black market. Anything you buy that's worth a damn will be taken away from you, or you'll lose it.

"Stay away from dope. There's only two kinds of people in Nam. People who are alert twenty-four hours a day, and people who are dead.

"If you see anything else they got over here that we don't have at home, stay away from it. What these people use on a daily basis will kill you as fast as an RPG."

"What's an RPG?" a guy in the front asked.

"That's a rocket-propelled grenade. Stay away from them, too. If you have any more questions, ask your unit commanders when you reach them. Good luck."

When we got outside, the mosquitoes got us. The lieutenant hadn't even mentioned them, but we had been given a supply of insect repellent.

Orders. Me, Peewee, Jenkins, and another guy were assigned to the 196th. We were going to Chu Lai. I remembered that was where Judy Duncan was assigned.

"What's that like?" Jenkins asked the sergeant in headquarters.

"That's First Corps," the sergeant said. "All you do up there is look around for charlie, and when you see him you call the marines. Light stuff."

"Charlie?" Jenkins looked toward me and Peewee.

"Charlie is the bad guy over here." The sergeant put his arm around Jenkins' shoulders. He was obviously enjoying himself. "Sometimes we call him charlie, sometimes we call him Victor Charlie, sometimes we call him Vietcong. That is, unless he sends us his business card with his full name and address on it."

We packed our gear and lined up outside, waiting for the truck to the airport. We were going to Chu Lai in a C-47. I thought guys from other hooches were going, but there were only the four of us.

"I bet I kill me a Cong before you get one," Peewee said.

"You can have them all," I said.

"You scared?"

"Yeah," I said. "You ain't scared?"

"No, man, I'm just surprised," Peewee said. "I didn't think they was going to have no real fighting in this here war."

"How come?"

"I tell you how I got in this mess?"

"Unh-uh."

"Me and this dude I used to hang with sometimes was out in front of the projects where I lived, and he said to me he was gonna join the army. So he said to come on down to the recruiting office with him." Peewee was sitting on his gear, picking out his hair. "So we go on down, and the recruiting sergeant ask him if he ever got into any trouble. Stick, that was this guy's name, said yeah. He already done shot him four or five people.

"The recruiting sergeant said he can't get in no army 'cause they don't be taking no rowdy dudes like him. I figure if they don't take no rowdy dudes, the army had to be pretty cool. If they really meant to be doing a whole lot of killing and carrying on, they should go get them suckers from the projects, 'cause that's all they like to do, anyway."

"So you joined up?"

"Yeah," Peewee said. "But I think I got tricked."

Peewee looked out over the trucks, which were mostly packed with crates of rations and supplies. The land beyond them was flat as far as we could see in one direction. In the other direction, where we thought the action would be, there were mountains shrouded in haze.

"Hey, at least I ain't rowdy," I said.

Peewee looked at me and smiled. "Yo, you remember that brother wanted to mingle our blood and stuff?"

"Yeah?"

"Maybe we could do that stuff with some spit or something," Peewee said.

He spit on his hand and held it up. I spit on mine and we exchanged fives. It felt good.

Peewee didn't say much after that and neither did I. I was scared. My mouth was going dry, and I could see that Peewee was scared, too. Jenkins was crying. It made me feel a little better to see him crying like that.

"Load 'em up!"

Me and Peewee got on the trucks between boxes of peanut butter, and started to the airport and to wherever the hell Chu Lai was.

Chapter 3

Most of the flight to Chu Lai was over water. A sergeant with us said that the plane swung out over the water to avoid anti-aircraft fire. Chu Lai was cooler than the area we had come from, but not much. It was still muggy. They had expected us earlier, and the lieutenant who directed us to the truck that would take us to our units seemed pissed.

"We can't hold these trucks up any longer, so you guys are going to have to chow down at your units," he said. "When I call your name, get right in the back of the first truck. Keep your hands and arms in the truck, and leave that netting up. You don't want to be sitting in there when some slant throws a grenade in the back."

The lieutenant was sharp, his brass belt buckle and insignia were shined, and his uniform was creased in all the right places. Chu Lai seemed less frantic than Tan Son Nhut.

I was looking around, trying to figure out what Chu Lai was like, when I heard my name.

"Any of you guys know this Perry?" the lieutenant was asking.

"I'm Perry," I said.

"Well, wake the hell up, soldier!"

"Yes, sir."

"Well, get on the damn truck!"

"Yes, sir."

When I got in the back of the truck, Peewee was cracking up. I laughed with him. Jenkins started imitating the sergeant, and he had his voice down perfectly.

"Hey, are you an actor?" Peewee asked.

"No, I can just . . ." Jenkins' voice trailed off.

"Do it again!" Peewee nudged Jenkins' foot.

Jenkins did it again, and Peewee cracked up again. I thought Jenkins was going to be fun after all.

Peewee pulled the net over the back end of the truck and tied it down. Then we started off. The back of the truck was like an oven. We started off reasonably slowly, and I got my first glimpse of the base. It looked okay. The movement cooled the truck off a little, and I thought the ride wouldn't be bad. Then we went through the gate and an outer checkpoint, and the driver picked up speed. We were bounced around the back of the truck like crazy. I had to hold onto the sides and keep standing. Sitting in the bouncing truck was impossible.

We arrived at headquarters company a half hour or so after we left the main base at Chu Lai. The captain who greeted us was wearing a flak jacket, the heavy vest that was supposed to stop bullets and shrapnel. There were big rings of sweat under his arms and a pool of sweat in the hollow of his neck. He glanced at each of us and checked our names off on his copy of our orders.

The GIs I saw at Chu Lai looked sharp enough to be in a parade; these guys looked as if they had just come in from a hard day's work, a damn hard day's work. Most of the guys who had come with us from Chu Lai were assigned to one of the row of hooches behind us. Me, Peewee, and Jenkins were told we would be going out to Alpha Company.

A chopper was supposed to take us and one other guy out to the company. In the meantime we had to load a pump onto the truck we came on. The pump wasn't crated, and it was hard to get a grip on it. Peewee and Jenkins were on one side of it, and I was on the other, but we couldn't get it up on the truck. Then an officer sent another guy over. His name tag read Johnson. He was black and as tall as I was, but bigger.

"We're supposed to—" Peewee was pointing to the pump when Johnson reached down and grabbed it. He grunted, rocked backward, and brought the pump to his knees. He grunted again, lifted the pump onto the back of the truck, turned slowly, and walked away.

"Amen!" Peewee called out behind him. "Amen!"

"Sir?"

"What is it?"

"Did you notice that I had a medical profile?"

The captain looked at his clipboard, looked up at me, and then back down to the clipboard.

"I don't see anything about a profile here," he said. "What's your name?"

"Perry, sir."

"You got a lot of pain?"

"No, but every once in a while the knee sort of gives way," I said. "That's why they gave me the profile."

"You get to your company commander, mention your profile to him."

"The officer at the replacement company said. . . ."

He was already walking away, and I had the feeling that he wasn't particularly interested in my profile.

We were told by a corporal that Alpha Company was "In the Deep."

"In the Deep *what?*" Peewee asked.

"In the Deep Boonies," was the answer.

We were supposed to get to the "Deep Boonies" by chopper. We waited for three hours for one to come and get us, but none came. We found a mess hall and ate. Jenkins didn't feel like eating. I could tell he was still scared out of his mind.

"What were you trained for?" I asked him.

"My MOS is infantry."

"You went to advanced training for infantry?" Peewee looked up at Jenkins.

"Yeah."

"You look like a clerk-typist or something like that," Peewee said.

"My father's a colonel," Jenkins said. "He wanted me to be infantry. He's got this thing, he calls it his game plan. First I volunteer for the army, then I volunteer for infantry and take advanced individual training in infantry. I serve my time over here, then I go to Officers Candidate School."

There were Vietnamese people working behind the counter. They looked peaceful enough, and so small. I was six-three, and many of them seemed a good foot shorter than I was.

Johnson, the guy who had lifted the pump onto the truck, turned out to be going to Alpha Company with us. He brought his gear over and sat with us.

"Where you from?" Peewee asked Johnson.

"Savannah."

"Savannah, *Georgia?*"

"You ever been there?"

"No, and I don't want to go to there, either."

"How you know what it like if you ain't never been there?" Johnson was eating his second dish of ice cream. He was about as black as a human being could get and as thick as he was wide. Even the whites of his eyes were dark. When he wasn't talking or chewing, his mouth sort of hung open. It hung open as he stared across the table at Peewee.

"I ain't never been to hell," Peewee said. "But I heard enough about it not to want to go there for no damn vacation."

"Where you from?" Johnson was pissed at Peewee for dumping on Georgia.

"Chicago."

"Chicago ain't nothing."

"Neither is your daddy," Peewee said.

Peewee didn't raise his voice when he said it, and he didn't smile. What he was saying was that he didn't care how big Johnson was. I glanced over at Jenkins, who was looking down into his food.

"You kinda little to be talking about somebody's daddy." Johnson pushed the words out through thick lips.

"No shit?"

"You guys think we should stay in here or get back outside in case they come looking for us?" I asked, hoping to cut off a confrontation.

They both looked at me like I had said something wrong. I was in the wrong war.

We finished eating and went back out to the pickup zone where the chopper was supposed to be. We asked around to see if anybody had been looking for us.

"You guys waiting for a lift to Alpha Company?" A short guy wearing what I thought was a flight suit came over to us.

"Yeah," Johnson said.

"I'm looking around for some smokes," the short guy said. "You guys wait here."

He started off toward some low Quonset huts off to the left. It was getting cooler, but the humidity was so high I was dripping wet. We found some shade, dropped our gear, and Johnson and Peewee went off looking for a latrine. Jenkins sat on the ground with his head in his hands, and I asked him how he was doing.

"I think I'm going to die over here," he said.

"You're not going to die," I said. "Most guys over here won't ever fire their rifles. I mean, they won't ever really shoot at anybody."

"Who told you that?"

"A major I had at Devens," I said.

"He probably wasn't ever over here," Jenkins said.

"Hey, it won't be that bad, man."

"Thanks." He looked up at me and forced a smile. Jenkins acted as if he didn't want to talk anymore and so I didn't talk, either. Peewee came back from the latrine.

"Where's Johnson?"

"That country fool?" Peewee sat on the ground between me and Jenkins. "He in there, sitting on the john, trying to figure out how to shit."

"You better leave that guy alone."

"He better leave Peewee alone," was the answer.

The chopper pilot got back an hour after sunset and said we'd have to wait until morning. You could smell the booze from three feet away. He was so high he couldn't stand straight. I figured the guy must have been a career guy. A lot of the career guys drank heavily. It took us two more hours to find a place to bunk for the night.

In the middle of the night I woke. I thought I was hearing thunder. Then I realized that it was artillery. I went outside and looked around. In the distance someone was shooting off flares. In a way it was beautiful, like brilliant white and red flowers against the dark sky. They left behind puffs of colored smoke that drifted away like tiny fairy clouds.

Johnson slept naked on one side, snoring. Peewee lay on his back, arms and legs spread, eyes not completely closed. Jenkins had his head under the blanket.

Morning. The chopper pilot came to get us. He was bright-eyed, shorter than I thought he was the night before. We piled our gear on and climbed on. It was my first chopper ride. I had missed that part of training when I got the medical profile. No marching. No prolonged field duty. No combat. I had seen the doctor at Fort Devens sign it. He was supposed to have sent it to the company.

The chopper trembled and rattled. Then it lifted slowly, tilted, and jerked into the air. It was the noise I hated. More than the wind through the open door. More than the slow speed, or the sitting still in the air waiting to fall, I hated the noise.

I looked over at Johnson. The one expression he had in the world was on his face. Peewee was busy looking out the door. Jenkins had his eyes closed and his knuckles were white from holding onto the seat.

"Which one of you is Perry?" We had reached Alpha Company in the boonies and were sitting in the commanding officer's hooch. A stream of tobacco juice oozed from the side of the captain's mouth.

"I am."

"You supposed to have a profile or something, right?"

"Yes, sir."

"Well, they got it listed that you're concerned with it," the captain said. "You got any pains or anything?"

"Not right now," I said. "But I got a bad knee."

"You been wounded in the knees?"

"From playing basketball," I said.

"Yeah, okay," the captain looked me up and down. "I'm sending a radio message through to look up your medical records. In the meantime I'll just let you stay with the squad. You'll be okay."

"Yes, sir."

"Fact is, all you guys better go on over and stay with the squad for a few days. I got word this morning that we'll probably be moving down to Third Corps and then ship over to Hawaii from there."

"Hawaii?"

"Yeah, looks like this thing is about over," the captain said. "What I want you boys to do is to listen to your squad leaders and try to keep yourselves alive."

We got weapons. Me, Peewee, and Jenkins got the usual M-16 rifles. Johnson, who had had machine-gun training, got an M-60. It was a big, wicked-looking weapon that made the M-16's look almost fragile in comparison. Johnson signed for it, took it by the handle, and walked away without even looking at it. They fit each other.

We were asked if we wanted anything else. Peewee asked for and got a pistol in addition to his M-16.

"You want a pistol?" the armorer asked me.

"What for?" I asked.

He didn't answer. I didn't want to be close enough to anybody to shoot him with a pistol.

"Make sure you keep those M-16's clean," he said. "Don't go believing that stuff about how it's going to work no matter what happens to it. You don't clean that piece, charlie is going to clean your ass."

We were assigned a hooch and found bunks. I wondered what had happened to the guys who had had the bunks before we got them, but I sure as hell wasn't going to ask anybody.

"Okay, listen up!" A soft-voiced lieutenant stuck his head into the tent. His name tag read "Carroll." "I'm your platoon leader. You guys have any problems, you let me know through your squad leader. Anything really heavy, and you can come right to me with it. This is a book platoon. We do everything by the book. You new guys better listen and learn. That way you get to be old guys.

"Everybody's talking about Hawaii. There's plenty of time to think about getting out of here and getting to Hawaii when we're at the airport on the way out. Until then, keep your mind on your work. That's all and good luck."

The rest of the squad was outside playing volleyball. We unloaded our gear and picked out bunks to lie on. There was gear on some of the other bunks. An M-79 grenade launcher lay across one. There were copies of *Playboy* on another.

"Hey, Johnson, bet you didn't have nothing this good down in Georgia, huh?" Peewee said.

"You really need to die young, don't you?" Johnson grunted the words out.

"What you do in Georgia, anyway?" Peewee said.

Johnson got up on one elbow and looked over at him. I thought he was mad, but he just grinned at Peewee. "If the man give me a job back home I wouldn't be doing this job over here," he said. "Guess you didn't know that, huh?"

They kept at it for a while, Peewee agitating until I felt that for him it was just some kind of sport. Find somebody big and mean-looking to mess with and then push your luck.

I started writing a letter to Mama. I hadn't written much during basic training, but now I wanted to, and I really wasn't sure why. I started writing about the trip over, remembered that I had already written about that, and started again. The second start was about how I was glad that the war was in Vietnam and not home, but that didn't sound right, either. I was looking for things to say but everything sounded lame.

The track over the gym in Stuyvesant High School was so small you had to run around it nearly fifteen times to go a mile. As I ran around that day I could hear Mrs. Liebow's words echo in my ears.

"You have to get out of yourself, Perry," she had said. "You're too young to be just an observer in life."

I was fifteen, and painfully aware that I was "just an observer in life." I didn't want to get into what was going on at home, about how Mom seemed to be falling apart, and how I couldn't think about much else than keeping us together.

Being an observer hadn't been so bad in Stuyvesant. There was always a way to frame things, to put them into a romantic setting, that made you feel good. Even the loneliness I felt sometimes was okay. I could break the loneliness, the feeling of not belonging to the life that teemed around me, by going to the basketball courts. I was somebody else there: Mr. In-Your-Face, jiving and driving, looping and hooping, staying clean and being mean, the inside rover till the game was over.

But sometimes even that didn't work. Sometimes, when I was tired and the competition was really rough, things would change for me. There would be a flow of action around me and it would seem as if I were outside of myself, watching myself play ball, watching myself trying to establish a place for myself on the hard park courts. It was then that I would feel a pressure to give in, to let a rebound go over my head, to take the outside shot when I knew I had to take the ball inside. I told Kenny about the feeling, and he hadn't understood it. I told Mrs. Liebow, my English teacher, and she said that it was what separated heroes from humans, the not giving in, and I hadn't understood that. It was a weakness in my game, not about being a hero.

Peewee said something that pissed Johnson off, and Johnson started to get off his bunk. Peewee pulled his M-16 across his body.

"Come on," he said. "I got something for you, Georgia Boy."

I wanted to say something to Peewee but thought better of it. It came to me that Peewee could be crazy. I caught Jenkins looking at me and shrugged.

The squad we were assigned to came in. They were arguing over who won a volleyball game. They saw us, and one guy beckoned for me to get up.

He looked around, and then pointed to another bunk. I got up and moved my gear to it, and he laid on the bunk that I had been on.

"You the cherries?" A tall, thin-faced sergeant.

"We're the new men," Peewee said.

"What's your name?" the sergeant asked.

"My friends call me Peewee. You can call me Mr. Gates."

"Uh-huh. Well, my name is Simpson and I'm the sergeant of this here squad. I'm gonna tell you guys something," the sergeant was black with a high voice that seemed to get higher with every word. "I ain't got but one hundred and twenty days left over here. If we go to Hawaii, then I ain't got that. Now I ain't about to let neither one of you fools kill me, you hear?"

"We look like Congs to you?" Peewee said.

"You look like cherries!" the sergeant said. "I'd rather go out and mess with a whole bunch of charlies instead of y'all cherries. That the truth, too!"

I made believe I was scratching my forehead so my hand would cover my face. The guy was strange. Thinking we were going to kill him when we were fighting a war with the Communists was weird.

The rest of the squad consisted of one black guy and four white guys. They played cards in the afternoon, and asked us if we had heard anything more about Hawaii. Later we played volleyball against another squad and won. Sergeant Simpson said that our victory was a good sign.

We checked our gear and watched television in the afternoon. The television was hooked up to a small generator, and we got more noise than picture, but that was okay. We watched a game show that had been taped. I knew most of the answers and impressed everybody.

It started to rain. A lieutenant, not our platoon leader, came in and spoke to Sergeant Simpson. He nodded and then, when the lieutenant had left, told us to pack up our gear. We were going on patrol.

A chopper came in quickly from just over a stand of trees. We were airborne less than a half minute after the chopper had touched down. We skimmed over the treetops for a little under ten minutes before touching down in the landing zone, or LZ, as Simpson called it.

It was exciting, a little scary. This is what I had been trained for. I thought about my knee, if it was going to be okay.

"You could get into surveillance with your test scores," a lieutenant had said. "Maybe even army intelligence."

An officer at the classification center had told me that if I could play ball I could always find a post to play for. I chose basketball. I was assigned to the infantry with the understanding that I was going to play ball for Fort Devens. Two good games led to a write-up in the post paper. Then I started dreaming again. Enough write-ups sent to the NBA, and who knew what might happen?

Then there was the game against Fort Monmouth. A quick move at the top of the key, drive through the middle, leap, leap, twist, and jam the ball through the hoop. I had come down amid a mass of sweating bodies, had landed on a sneaker instead of the floor. My knee had twisted. The pain burned through the joint into the thigh. My season was over.

"Perry, wake the fuck up!"

I looked at Sergeant Simpson and saw that he looked genuinely pissed.

We were going past a flat area. Off to the right there were short trees with wide trunks. A quarter mile off to our left there was a wooded area that ran halfway up a small hill. Even from where we walked I could see that near the top of the hill the trees were just charred sticks. On the very top they were black silhouettes against the sky. I looked from side to side, telling myself not to daydream again.

The regular guys in the squad walked differently. They seemed to do a kind of slow lope, lifting their feet more than they had to. I thought it must have been because of all the mud.

Monaco, a sweet-faced Italian kid who looked as scared as Jenkins, was on point-out in front of the squad. The regular squad guys took their positions, leaving me, Peewee, Johnson, and Jenkins in the middle. Simpson said that a plane had spotted two guys with what looked like surveying instruments.

"They could be laying out some kind of assault plans," he said.

For the first ten minutes I had to wipe my right hand on my fatigues at least a dozen times. I kept imagining VC popping up and me not being ready to fire. We were on flat ground going along a row of small rice paddies. I didn't see anything. Nobody saw anything.

We walked or, it seemed, wandered for nearly an hour before Simpson called in the chopper to take us back.

We went to a pickup zone that was different from where we had landed and squatted in the knee-high grass. Simpson and this corporal named Brunner kept us covered while we mounted the chopper. Then they were in and the chopper was off. Then we were back to our base area.

"Y'all looked okay out there," Simpson said. "You got to stay alert like that all the time."

We started back toward the camp. It was less than a hundred yards. We had been told that there were mine fields and trip flares planted around the perimeter. Sergeant Simpson had a map of our way back in. The path we had to walk up was covered by a brace of M-60 machine guns. The guys manning them looked bored.

There could have been a whooshing noise, I wasn't sure. I just heard Sergeant Simpson yelling for us to stay on the path. The other regular squad guys were already down.

I was in the dirt. My eyes were closed. I could hear somebody screaming. "Oh, God! Oh, God! Oh, God!"

Noises. Somebody saying that it was a booby trap. Sergeant Simpson talking into the radio. I opened my eyes; everybody else was up. I got up as quickly as I could.

Some of the guys were looking around, their weapons moving, shaking almost as if they were alive, looking for an enemy to fire upon.

"Keep those pieces still! Keep 'em down!" Sergeant Simpson's voice had changed. He barked commands. "Get into the camp! Get into the camp!"

Brunner was dragging somebody. I looked behind me. I couldn't see anything. It was light out, but all I could see was a few feet in front of me. My vision didn't go any further.

We got back to the camp. Two sergeants opened the barbed wire fence. They pulled the wounded man in. I looked.

There was a shard of metal protruding from Jenkins' chest. The blood gurgled out of the wound it made and sprayed along the concave metallic surface. He tried to bring his hand to it, to touch it. A medic had reached him and pushed his hand away. Jenkins' face was white and twisted as he struggled to look down at his wound. There were bubbles on the wound as he struggled for a final breath, and then that, too, stopped.

Chapter 4

YOU GOT THE TAGS?" The supply guy had a long face and his mouth twisted oddly when he spoke.

"How many bags you got there?" There was a neat stack of dark bags on the shelf.

"Enough," he said, handing me the heavy plastic bag. "What he do, step on a mine?"

"Yeah."

"That's what happens," he said. "They sneak in and plant a mine on your path, and you don't know where the hell to walk."

"Oh."

I took the bag out to where Simpson and Lieutenant Carroll waited. They lifted Jenkins by the shoulders of his uniform. Sergeant Simpson used a first aid patch to pick up something that had erupted from the hellish wound on Jenkins' chest and fallen on the ground near him. He placed it in the bag at his side.

I thought I would throw up. I stood along with the other guys in the squad until the bag had been zipped up. We started back to the hooch. On the way I looked back at the body bag again. Sergeant Simpson and Lieutenant Carroll were talking together, the body bag was at their feet. I turned away and went to the hooch.

Monaco came over and sat on the edge of my bunk. For a while he didn't say anything. Then he put his hand on my shoulder.

"You know him?"

"No," I said. "I just met him at the replacement company."

"Sometimes it goes like that," Monaco said. He started to say something else, then shrugged it off and left.

I wanted to say more to him. I wanted to say that the only dead person I had ever seen before had been my grandmother. I wanted to say that when I saw her I was ready, walking into the darkened church with the family and sitting in the first pews. But Jenkins was different. Jenkins had been walking with me and talking with me only hours before. Seeing him lying there like that, his mouth and eyes open, had grabbed something inside my chest and twisted it hard.

The neat pile of body bags was waiting for the rest of us. There were enough there—the supply clerk had reached for the top one without even looking—to know that they expected that many of us would be going home in them.

I didn't know what to think about what had happened. I didn't know what to feel. I touched my fingers to the palm of my hand. I could feel my fingers. It was only inside that I was numb.

Lieutenant Carroll, our platoon leader, came in. He was a quiet guy, with dark hair and dark, calm eyes and an uneasy smile. I never felt that he was comfortable with himself. I hadn't had a chance to talk with him yet, but sometimes I would see him drift off into his own daydreams and be embarrassed when we caught him at it.

When the old guys—the guys that had been through it before—saw him, they put their cards down, and their magazines, and gathered around him. I got up and nudged Peewee, who was lying facedown on his bunk.

Lieutenant Carroll took off his helmet and bowed his head.

"Lord, let us feel pity for Private Jenkins, and sorrow for ourselves, and all the angel warriors that fail. Let us fear death, but let it not live within us. Protect us, O Lord, and be merciful unto us. Amen."

In the morning, in the mess tent, I asked Lieutenant Carroll why he had called Jenkins an angel warrior.

"My father used to call all soldiers angel warriors," he said. "Because usually they get boys to fight wars. Most of you aren't old enough to vote yet."

"How old are you?"

"Twenty-three," he said.

"How come you're not retired?"

Lieutenant Carroll stayed in our hooch for a while and helped check our supplies. He asked if we were short or anything, and Monaco said we could use some more three-day passes.

"I got a letter from Virginia Union." A brother we called Brew sat on a footlocker next to Lieutenant Carroll. His real name was Brewster, so I could see where Brew came from. "They said I can probably get into the theology school there but they can't accept me formally until six months before my admission date."

"Did you write to that school in New York I told you about?" Lieutenant Carroll asked.

"No," Brew grinned. "From what I've heard about New York, the temptations might be too great for me."

"If the Temptations don't get you then you got to look out for Smokey Robinson and the Miracles," Peewee called out.

"You know"—Lieutenant Carroll had spread all the extra first aid packs on the floor in front of him—"my brother went to theology school and I almost followed him."

"You can still go," a guy called Walowick said from his bunk. "It's good for a priest to be older."

"I might have too many doubts, now," Lieutenant Carroll said.

"If you turn to God, He'll take away your doubts," Brew said.

"I don't have doubts about God," Lieutenant Carroll said. "I'm just not that sure who I am anymore."

He gathered the first aid kits together and asked Brew if he would give them out. Then he got his weapon and said he would see us later.

"He don't look like a priest," Peewee said after Lieutenant Carroll had left.

"He used to act more like a holy guy or something when he first got over here. He never cursed or anything like that." Walowick was putting powder on a rash he had. "Then one day we were trying to clear a road and some guys got trapped in a ditch off to one side. We were on the other side of the road, and we could see them but we couldn't get to them. It was getting dark, and we knew they couldn't last. Charlie was throwing everything at them. Then Lieutenant Carroll just went wild and stormed across the fucking road. We went after him. We were shooting at guys maybe three or four feet from us. We finally wasted all of them and cleared the road. He hasn't been the same since, but we all found out what kind of a guy he was that day. When the chips were down, he put his ass on the line for the guys."

"You get the guys out of the ditch okay?" Peewee asked.

"Unh-uh." Walowick shook his head. "That's why you guys are in the squad."

I wrote Mama a letter all about how Jenkins had got killed. Then I tore it up and decided not to tell her about it. It would only get her upset. Instead, I told her more about Peewee. I didn't want to tell her about Jenkins for another reason, too. I didn't know how I felt about it. In a way I was really sorry for Jenkins, but there was a small voice inside me that kept saying that I was glad that it wasn't me that was killed. I didn't want anybody to see me putting that in a letter.

They brought a VC into camp to question. They questioned him, and then they took him into a hooch they used for storage while they decided what they were going to do with him. Peewee had been in there to get extra clips earlier and thought he might have lost his comb there. He went into the hooch to look for his pick, and the VC was sitting in there and started a conversation with him.

"Sucker spoke better English than I did," Peewee said.

"What was he talking about?" Brunner asked. Brunner had a thick neck and short blond hair. He also seemed to have a chip on his shoulder.

"Ask me where I was from and stuff like that," Peewee said. "I thought he was a friendly, you know."

"You tell him where you were from?"

"Yeah, and he told me he used to go to the flicks down on State Street and even asked me if I knew some chick named Thelma."

"Then what happened?"

"Then he asked me for a cigarette, and we was sitting there smoking when the captain come in. That's when all hell broke loose. The fool jumped on me and tried to get my pistol, and the captain run up to him and punched him in the face."

Then they had tied the VC up and threw him in the back of a jeep to take to an intelligence unit, and the captain gave Peewee hell for giving information to the enemy.

Peewee said he was glad he gave him some information.

"How come?" Monaco was cleaning his rifle again.

" 'Cause if the Cong ever get to State Street, I want to be on their side," Peewee said.

Walowick, a Polish kid with dimples who looked like he had more teeth than he needed, looked up from his magazine, flashed a smile, and went back to reading.

"By the time we get out of here there won't be any Cong left," Brunner said.

"We'd get out of here a lot faster if we took them all to Hollywood." Lobel was tall and a little pudgy. His hair looked as if he had given himself a perm or something. He was almost as tall as me but soft-looking. He didn't look feminine or anything, just soft.

"What are you going to do with the Vietcong in Hollywood?" I asked.

"Look what they did after World War II," he said, getting up on one elbow. "We made a hundred war movies, and we brought all the Germans over and gave them nice little bit parts, and they were very happy. We brought the Japanese over and gave them little bit parts, and they were happy. Now all we have to do is to stop this silly war and start making the movies right away. We take all these little slant-eyes over to Universal, give them SAG cards, and put them to work."

"That is a fag solution, only capable of coming from the mind of a fag," Brunner said.

"Hey, Corporal," Lobel got up on one elbow. "Just because I don't have my serial number tattooed on my genitals does not mean I'm a fag."

"You wouldn't have enough room for more than three numbers, anyway," Brunner said. He looked around to see who was laughing. Nobody was.

We got mail call and I didn't get anything. I had to find somebody to write to beside Mama so I would get mail. I couldn't depend on Kenny to write.

There was something happening up north the next morning. For about an hour we heard artillery. Simpson was in our hooch, talking about squirrel hunting outside of Petersburg, Virginia, and Monaco was getting on his case.

"You call that sport?" Monaco asked. "I mean, there you are, you gotta weigh two hundred pounds, and you got a rifle, and you're against a squirrel that weighs maybe two or three pounds, and he ain't got nothing."

"Man, it's a damn sport!" Simpson protested. "You know what a sport is?"

"Do I know what a sport is?" Monaco pointed to himself. "I played football and baseball for Marist High School in Bayonne. I made All-County. That's sport. I don't have to shoot no little animals."

"You had you a rifle," Peewee said. "You could have made All-World."

"The way I figure it," Monaco went on, "if you hunt a squirrel with a rifle, what do you hunt a bear with? Artillery?"

"Call in some white phosphorus on him," Brew said. "That'll get his attention until the jets zero in."

White phosphorus, or Willy Peter as they called it, was an artillery round that burned the crap out of anything it touched.

"You don't know nothing about no hunting!" Simpson was getting pissed. "You don't know what hunting is!"

"What he's trying to say,"—Lobel was flat on his back; there was a can of Coke on his chest—"is that the white phosphorus is enough. After it burns the bear's ass off, then the good sergeant will finish him off with a couple of frag grenades."

"Lobel, y-y-you are a faggott!" Sergeant Simpson got up and left the hooch.

We had to go to a village and do what sounded like public relations work. We were supposed to pass it around that anybody who was a Communist and who wanted to change and be on our side was welcome to come. The program was called "Chieu Hoi," but Peewee called it "chewing the whores."

The village was a good ten minutes away, and everybody seemed relaxed. I wasn't. I was scared.

I had never thought of myself as being afraid of anything. I thought I would always be a middle-of the-road kind of guy, not too brave, but not too scared, either. I was wrong. I was scared every time I left the hooch.

On the way to the chopper I found myself holding my breath. I kept thinking of the noise I had heard when Jenkins got it. By the time we took off I was panting.

When we landed, another squad was already at the landing zone. They told us that all the women in the village were either under six or over six hundred.

The village stunk. You could smell it as you got near. There were huts laid out about fifteen meters from each other. Some were fairly large. There were people in the village walking around, some were building a pen of some kind. Like the guys had told us, they were either very young or very old.

"All their men is either in the VC army or the ARVNs. The ARVNs is the South Vietnamese army, and they suppose to be on our side. The VC is the enemy. This is like the Civil War," Simpson said. "Sometimes one brother go to the VC and the other brother go to the ARVN. After a while the brother who fighting with the VC either gonna get killed or want to leave and join the ARVN."

"They don't care what side they fight on?" I asked.

"They would if they got time to think about it," Simpson said. "But the ARVN kick they butts if they catch them in the village and they ain't fighting for the ARVN—"

"—and the VC kick they butts if they catch them and they ain't fighting for the VC," Peewee said.

" 'Bout the size of it."

There was a jeep with medical supplies on it. There were aspirins, a few malaria pills, and some Band-Aids. A captain was giving them out to the squad.

"If you give them malaria pills, make sure they take it on the spot," he said. "We don't want this stuff falling into the hands of the VC."

"So why we giving it to them?" Peewee asked.

"To make them love us," the captain said. He had a smirk on his face.

When we got to the village, some of the people ignored us while others came up and begged for C rations and whatever else we would give them. Lobel and I gave chocolate bars to a Vietnamese woman. A small girl clung to the woman's legs, and Lobel asked her name. The woman told us the girl's name was An Linh. She was about seven, maybe eight. She was small, like all the Vietnamese, compared to us Americans. She looked like a little doll with dark black eyes that dominated a round, brown face. She could have been black, maybe Puerto Rican.

Lobel gave her some candy and carried her around on his shoulders. I shook her hand, and she seemed to want to hold on to my fingers, so the three of us went around the village. Sergeant Simpson let a young boy wear his canteen.

We broke out more C rations, the canned stuff the army passes off for food, and shared them with the kids. Me and Lobel ate with An Linh. A woman, her head too big for her small body, brought us some rice, and Lobel took some.

"Not bad," he said.

I didn't want any rice. It smelled okay, but I was afraid of being poisoned. My mind went back to Jenkins and how he had been afraid of dying. We hadn't mentioned his name since he got it. I wanted to ask Lobel about that, but I didn't.

"If I owned this village," Lobel was saying, "I'd make it into a real jungle scene."

"It is a real jungle scene," I said.

"No, to make it real you have to have one side of the huts open so you can shoot inside," Lobel said. "Then you have to get some artificial grass so it stays the same color throughout the whole picture, and finally have to get a wind machine so you can make the grass sway."

"Why not just shoot it naturally and save the money?" I asked.

"Aren't you from New York?" Lobel squinted at me.

"Yeah."

"I thought black guys from New York were supposed to be smart?" he said. "Nobody pays to see anything natural. You pay to see unnatural things look *almost* natural."

"Oh."

"Would you want to see Doris Day or some natural-looking girl with pimples on her forehead and heat rash on her chest?"

The Vietnamese woman who had brought us rice squatted at the edge of the bush to take a leak.

"See, you couldn't have any of that," Lobel said. "People in Hollywood don't pee."

We gave An Linh as much of our C rations as she could carry, and Lobel gave her a new name. "She'll never do anything in Hollywood with her name," he said.

We decided to call her Arielle. Lobel said that as soon as we got her to Santa Monica we had it made.

Peewee spent most of the time sitting down in a hut until Lieutenant Carroll made him walk around the village. He found a bottle of wine in one of the huts and tried to buy it for four American dollars. The people in the hut said that he could take it for nothing, but Lieutenant Carroll said not to. He finally paid two dollars for it.

"Suppose it's poisoned or something?" I asked.

"Then I'm gonna die," Peewee said.

"You taking it back to the base?"

"Nope."

He borrowed a corkscrew from the woman he had bought the wine from and opened the wine and drank some of it. He made an awful face, then drank some more.

"That bad?"

"Yep, but that's one thing I got done."

"What is?"

"That's the first time I ever drank wine from a bottle with a cork in it," he said. "Now all I got to do is to make love with a foreign woman and smoke a cigar."

We stayed around the village for the rest of the day, and then it was time to leave. The choppers came in and lifted us out, and we were back at the base before we knew it.

"Those gooks will probably be having supper with the VC by the time we sit down to chow," Brunner said.

"How come when you say 'gooks' it sounds like 'nigger' to me?" Johnson asked.

"You hear what you want to hear," Brunner said.

"What I'm hearing is what you saying," Johnson said.

"Y'all shut that shit up," Sergeant Simpson looked from Brunner to Johnson and back again.

We had roast beef, mashed potatoes, carrots, carrot cake, and milk for supper. I sat under a tree with Peewee, eating. A bug crawled over his leg, and he put some mashed potatoes on his knee in the bug's path, but the bug turned and went the other way.

"You think he's saying something about the chow?" I asked.

"He probably want some of the roast beef," Peewee said. "He know it Sunday and everything. But he ain't getting none."

"Sunday? It's not Sunday, it's Wednesday."

"Bugs is four days behind people," he said matter-of-factly.

Sergeant Simpson saw us and came over. He sat down and asked us how we were enjoying ourselves.

"I've seen places I'd rather be," I said. "Times Square, Lenox Avenue, Fifth Avenue, you name it."

"I loves it here," Peewee said. "I ain't never seen no place in the world better than this place right here. You know what I love the most?"

"What's that?" Sergeant Simpson was amused by Peewee.

"The bugs," Peewee said. "You go to sleep at night they right there. You wake up in the morning, they right there. They better than a damn dog."

"So what you guys think about this outfit?" Sergeant Simpson asked.

"It looks okay to me," Peewee said. "I might have to straighten a few things out, though."

"Like what?" Sergeant Simpson asked.

"Like Brunner," Peewee said. "That boy got a quick lip on him."

"Uh-huh." Sergeant Simpson looked away. "He might got him a quick lip, but Captain Stewart is the one eligible."

"Eligible for what?"

"For major," Sergeant Simpson said. "And his best chance of making it is while he over here. His tour is up the fifteenth day of March."

"That's his problem," Peewee said.

"If he don't pick up his body count soon," Sergeant Simpson started to get up, "it's going to be your problem."

Chapter 5

THE TALK ABOUT US going to Hawaii was stronger than ever. Me and Peewee decided to save our money and have a blast in Hawaii. I also thought about taking some courses at the University of Hawaii.

I got a letter from Mama at mail call. Peewee got a letter from his girl-friend, but I don't think he liked it. He crumpled it up and threw it in a butt can. Then he got it out again and reread it.

"Peewee, my mother says you shouldn't eat any native food over here," I said. "She says it'll give you the runs because of the heat and everything."

"Where was she when I needed her?" Peewee answered. He had spent the better part of two days on the crapper.

"How was that wine, anyway?"

"How I know?" Peewee turned over on his bunk to face me. "The only other wine I had in my damn life was some 'Bird back home."

"How old you got to be in Chicago to drink?"

"Old enough to carry some money to the man," Peewee said. "What else your moms got to say?"

"You wouldn't be interested," I said.

"How you know?"

"You want to hear about how her feet swell up when she walks?"

"My mama's feet used to swell like that," Peewee said. "She went to four doctors, and they couldn't do shit for her. Then she went to a mojo lady who gave her something to soak her feet in."

"That work?"

"Yeah, she can walk all day now."

"My mother's a Baptist," I said. "She wouldn't go to a mojo lady."

"My mama's a Baptist, too, but she what you call a sore-feet Baptist. Your feets get sore enough, those mojo ladies start looking pretty good."

Walowick came in pissed off because some motor pool guys were over from Chu Lai to play poker and one of them was smoking pot.

"You know what this guy is?" Walowick was stripped down to his drawers and helmet. "A damn white hippie."

"A what?"

"A hippie!" Walowick said.

"Yeah, but you said he was a white hippie before," Peewee said.

"Well, he is white," Walowick said.

"All hippies is white," Peewee said.

"No, they're not," I said. "You got to come to New York, and you can see some black hippies."

"Everybody in New York is white," Peewee said.

"Perry is from New York, and he sure ain't white."

"Yes, he is, he passing!"

"You know, we had something like you back in Galesburg," Walowick said. He spoke carefully, as if he wasn't sure of the language. "We cut it up and put it in formaldehyde."

"Didn't that leave your daddy lonesome?"

"What's that got to do with my daddy?"

"Nothing, Walowick," I said. "Peewee's just running off at the mouth."

"He's a crazy dude," Walowick said. He got his towel and went out to our makeshift showers.

The next day we got a new film in. It was something about how Julie Andrews wasn't going to be pushed around anymore. We watched it once and then we watched it again with the reels mixed up, just to be different. Johnson wanted to get the kids from the village up to the base, but a captain said we couldn't do that, so Johnson and a guy from Delta Company worked on a way to get a generator down to the village so we could show the movie to them.

For two days we didn't do anything. Nothing. We didn't have any formations, patrols, nothing. Beautiful.

A new supply of insect repellant came in. Lieutenant Carroll said that it was good for making Molotov cocktails. Peewee wanted to know how come he was thinking about making Molotov cocktails when we had all the explosives in the world right in camp. Good point.

Lieutenant Carroll was a decent kind of guy. He talked a lot about Kansas, which is where he was from. His parents had a farm near Hays and his father was proud of him being an officer in the army. He'd told us that, about his father being proud of him being an officer, twice. It was like he didn't know what to make of it.

For Sunday chow we had roast beef, mashed potatoes, peas, carrots, carrot cake, and milk. We seemed to be having that quite a bit.

After chow we put the television on, but nothing was on. Nothing at all. All we got was static. Brew wrote a letter to President Johnson saying that if he wanted us to fight, he'd better send us some good televisions, and we all signed it. Then we threw it away.

Then we watched the movie again without the sound, and we all had parts to play in it. That was the best showing of the movie, especially with Peewee as Julie Andrews.

We listened to the news on the radio and heard about peace talks in

Paris. There was a lot of talk about how we were kicking the living crap out of the Communists, too.

"Turn that up loud as you can," Peewee said. "Make sure them Congs hear it."

We heard stories. Stories about fighting in Dak To, and down south in Pleiku, but we weren't doing any of it. I thought about it, though. I wanted to know how it felt to shoot at a Cong. The way I thought about it, mostly, was thinking of what I would say when I got home. Maybe even what I would say to Kenny.

Kenny always looked up to me. He couldn't play ball as well as I had when I was his age, and he didn't do as well in school. Maybe it had something to do with Dad leaving when Kenny was four. He saw all the fights between Dad and Mom, and I think it hurt him more than it did me. I had basketball, and I was good in school. Later, with Mom drinking so much, all Kenny had was me. I wanted to tell him that I did something in the war.

I couldn't sleep most of the night. When the rats weren't running around in the dark, the mosquitoes were after you. Peewee said that the mosquitoes ran patrols for the rats and afterward they split up their catch. I had to go to the bathroom, but I didn't want to go out to the outdoor latrine. In the first place it stunk too bad, and in the second, as soon as you pulled your pants down after dark the mosquitoes bit your ass.

For breakfast we had eggs, coffee, buns, bacon, and grits. Peewee complained that he missed the roast beef.

"You getting that for lunch," the cook said.

"If you serve any more of that damn roast beef you better bring a rifle with it because I'm going to put a hole in your ass for every slice of beef I see." Brunner said it like he meant it, too.

The cook, a short blond guy with a tattoo on his right arm that said "Mother" and one on his left arm that said "Linda," spit in a cup and slid it down to Brunner. "There's your lunch, skinhead."

Captain Stewart, our company commander, came over and asked what was wrong, and Brunner told him what had happened.

"We can only fix what they send us, Captain," the cook said.

"I'm sure the corporal realizes that, soldier," the captain said. "But men who go out and risk their lives every day would like a little more respect."

"I didn't ask to be no damn cook!"

"Watch your mouth, soldier," the captain's voice assumed captain's status.

Two jets swept by and started hitting a target less than five miles away. They must have made a half-dozen passes before they were joined by two more. We went outside and watched them, our food still in our hands.

"They must have got a convoy," Brunner said. He said it to Captain

Stewart, and he had his sucking-up voice on. Behind him, the cook was spitting in Brunner's coffee and stirring it up. Lobel smiled when he saw it, and turned away.

"The VC are trying to get in position for the truce," Captain Stewart said. "They'll try to get into as good a position as they can and then negotiate to hold those positions."

"If the war is going to be over, they can have the whole damn country," Peewee said. "I don't want the sucker."

"That's not why guys are out there humping, soldier." The captain pulled out a pad and pen. "What's your name?"

"Gates, sir," Peewee said. "That's G-A-T —"

"I can spell, Private. Are you a cook, too?"

Just then a guy came from HQ tent and called Stewart. Two more minutes, and everybody was running around except Lieutenant Carroll.

"I think they want all the officers in the HQ tent," I said.

"They want me, they know where to reach me," Carroll said. "Or they can just leave a message with my secretary."

There was a sadness about Lieutenant Carroll, something that you didn't notice at first, but it was there just the same. Even when he made jokes it was there. I watched him walk toward his hooch.

The choppers. They made a noise like the heartbeat of a machine gun as they came in. My stomach knotted for a second, and I told myself to relax. I had a feeling, a sense that something important was going to happen.

"Alpha Company, let's go!" Sergeant Simpson started yelling.

Alpha Company started lining up. Sergeant Simpson started checking out our squad, making sure we had the right gear.

"What's up?" Lieutenant Carroll had to raise his voice to get over the noise of the choppers.

"Charlie Company is pinned down over there," Simpson said. "They were going to send some marines in to get them out but they sent the marines up to Khe Sanh. They expect some heavy stuff up there. They got reports of battalion-size movements."

"A *battalion* of VC?" Carroll looked at Simpson.

"That's what they said," Simpson said.

Lieutenant Carroll went off toward HQ tent.

"Okay, you guys, this is what's happening. The air force is gonna try to clear the LZ and then we'll secure it. Third platoon's responsibility is just to protect the left flank of the LZ. We move in and push out one hundred meters. First platoon will clear the area of hostiles along with second platoon. Fourth platoon gets the right flank. We shouldn't have any problems unless the VC want to stand and fight a whole damn company."

"You hear anybody going out last night?" Peewee asked me.

"Unh-uh."

"Then Charlie Company must have been out there all night," he said.

I hadn't heard of any company going out at night before.

Lieutenant Carroll came running back with another lieutenant. He spoke a few words to Sergeant Simpson and Simpson nodded.

"Okay, you guys, make sure your pieces are on safety. Do that right now!"

I ran my finger over the safety catch of my M-16. It was on.

"I don't want no rounds in the chamber until after we hit the area," Simpson said. "We hit the ground, me and Lieutenant Carroll will mark off the squad assignments. And don't go shooting at nothing until you see something to shoot at! Let's go!"

My legs felt heavy as I ran toward the chopper. Lieutenant Carroll was at the door, checking us in. I banged the shit out of my knee getting in. My bad knee, too.

I looked at Peewee. There was a smear of blood across his face. Simpson noticed it, too.

"What the hell happened to you?"

"This dumb fucker hit me with his rifle," Peewee jerked a thumb at Brunner. "Simple-ass farm boy!"

"Shut your mouth!" Brunner came back.

I had to grab Monaco to keep from falling toward the door as the chopper jerked into the air.

"When we hit the zone, keep your distances! Don't bunch up!" Lieutenant Carroll called out. "We shouldn't get any resistance, especially at first. When we dig in, make sure you're dug in behind something solid."

"How about my daddy's pickup truck?" Walowick asked. "I wouldn't mind going home and getting behind that baby."

I couldn't see a thing outside the chopper. The door gunner was reading a comic book. He looked cool. I thought of saying a prayer, but I couldn't think of one. I didn't know one prayer. Under my breath I apologized to God.

"Yo, Peewee!"

"What?"

"We get back to the base, remind me to memorize a prayer."

"I know one," Peewee said.

"What is it?"

"Flying into combat, 'bout to have a fit, Lord, if you listenin', Please get me out this shit!"

"Just say a Hail Mary!" Monaco yelled.

From where we were at the base the action looked like it was just a few miles away. We were in the choppers nearly ten minutes and still going.

I didn't know we were even getting near until the door gunner put his hand on his headset, as if he were listening to something, then moved to his gun, pointed it down at the lush green jungle below us, and started firing. The .50 caliber started spitting, and the shells came out at an enormous rate. They were flying back into the chopper and banging around. I dropped my rifle. Monaco pushed it back toward me with his foot.

We didn't just come down, we damn near fell down. I was grabbing for the sides and shaking. I thought the chopper had been hit.

"Get ready!" Sergeant Simpson called out. "Monaco, you go first. Don't none of y'all shoot Monaco!"

Monaco had his eyes closed, praying.

"Now!" the machine gunner yelled over his shoulder.

Monaco went out in a flash, and Lieutenant Carroll was right behind him. Johnson jumped out next and fell. I was next in the door, looked down, and saw that we were still about ten feet off the ground.

"Jump, shithead!"

I jumped and landed across Johnson's legs. I got up first and started to help him up just as two more bodies landed on top of us. We started crawling away from under the chopper.

"Let's hit it! Spread out!"

We spread out and started moving toward the trees. I kept as low as I could, bent over at the waist. We kept moving ahead, with Monaco running like he was crazy or something. There was no fire, and we stopped in a pretty dense area.

"Stay down, stay alert!"

We didn't move for a while. I looked up and saw the choppers in the distance. Then they were gone. Even the sound was gone. The only thing I could hear was the heavy sound of my own breathing. We were on our own.

Simpson started going around, placing the squad. Johnson was off to one side with the .60 caliber machine gun. Brew was his feeder. I gave Johnson the thumbs-up sign and he gave it back.

The air in Nam was always hard to breathe; it was heavy, thicker than the air back home. Now it was harder. I opened my mouth wide and sucked in as much air as I could, but it didn't seem to be enough.

We waited ten minutes. Nothing. Then we began to hear small-arms firing off to our right. I looked, but I couldn't see anything. You could smell it, though. You could smell the stink of gunpowder and hear the distant burping of the machine guns.

We waited twenty minutes. Nothing. The sound of gunfire subsided. The smoke didn't. It drifted our way like a gentle mist through the tall trees. Behind us the choppers were coming in again. They went back into the landing zone. Then they were gone again.

We waited. Forty minutes.

"Brunner! Back up!"

We started out, moving less quickly than when we came in. The landing zone, without the excitement, the fear, was a longer distance away.

We reached it finally, and I was near enough to Carroll to hear him call the choppers in. We were on the choppers and out in minutes, with Simpson screaming at us to get our weapons on safety.

We got to the base area, and I remembered Jenkins. I was behind Brunner and followed the path he walked.

We got back to the hooch, and Simpson came in.

"How did Charlie Company do?" Walowick asked.

"They lost nine people," Sergeant Simpson said. "One platoon lost one man, got six wounded."

"How many VCs were out there?" I asked.

"They don't know, but what they do know is that they didn't have on no damn pajamas. They was North Vietnamese regulars."

"They still talking about us going to Hawaii?" Walowick asked.

"Yeah, they talking about bringing some Lurp teams up here, too," Sergeant Simpson said. "That the stuff I don't like."

When he left, I asked Walowick what a Lurp team was.

"It's a long-range surveillance team," Walowick said. "They don't fight if they can help it. They just go out and see what's out there."

"Why does Sergeant Simpson think that's so bad?"

"I don't know," Walowick said. "But he didn't live to be a short-timer by being stupid."

Lieutenant Carroll came and asked me about my profile. He said that he saw that I had mentioned it when I first got into the company. I told him how I had hurt the knee playing ball.

"It bother you too much to go on patrols?"

"Not so far," I said. "I just don't want to get messed up because of the knee."

He looked at me for a long time without saying anything. Then he looked away for a moment and back at me. "Perry, I don't want to take you into combat if the knee's really bad," he said. "It's not just you, I mean. Everybody in the squad depends on everybody else."

"I guess it's not really that bad," I said.

"Look, I don't want to avoid the issue," he said. "If you tell me you can't go on patrol, I'll see if I can get you transferred to another outfit. If you tell me that you can go on patrol, then we'll just wait until the profile comes down and take a look."

"I'll wait for it," I said.

"I don't like putting you on the spot," he said. "I really don't. But we're all in this mess together."

"Sure."

When he left, Peewee asked me what the conversation was about and I told him.

"Don't go being no fucking hero," Peewee said.

"What would you have said?" I asked him.

"Probably the same thing you did, but I would have been pissed off at myself," he said.

"I'm a little pissed," I said.

I really wasn't pissed, because I knew the real question wasn't about my knee. I thought the knee would be okay. The real question was what I was doing, what any of us were doing, in Nam.

Chapter 6

I GOT GUARD DUTY with Lobel. Sergeant Walcott from Bravo Company was sergeant of the guard, and he gave us a pep talk. We were on from eight to midnight.

There were sandbags around the shallow foxhole we had to sit in. At Fort Devens a four-foot-deep hole was plenty. Now it didn't seem so great. It was about seven feet wide. I had my M-16 and Lobel had his and an M-79 grenade launcher. There were sandbags piled in front of the foxhole, with a place to shoot through. The perimeter of the camp was marked by intricate patterns of barbed wire barriers. The wire itself had razor-sharp protrusions as well as trip flares planted throughout. Lobel and I had to watch about sixty meters of the wire to make sure that no VC broke through.

"Perry, you okay?"

"Yeah."

"You look a little uptight."

"I feel a little uptight."

"What's the matter?"

"Still thinking about Jenkins, I guess," I answered.

"Who's Jenkins?"

"The guy I came in with. You remember, he stepped on a mine."

"Yeah."

"Nothing can get through that much wire," I said.

"Nothing can get through it without getting messed up," Lobel answered. "But they try."

I didn't answer. For all the talk, the war was still far away. All you had to do was to be careful, and you'd be okay. Jenkins hadn't been careful.

"You know, Perry, if I was going to make a movie over here, I'd make it a love story," Lobel said dreamily.

"How come you always talk about movies?"

"Because they're the only real thing in life," Lobel said. He slumped down in the foxhole. "You didn't think any of this was real, did you?"

"Look, Lobel . . . why don't you get up and watch the wire with me?"

"You scared?"

"Yeah, man."

"Oh, okay." He got up, just like that.

There were things chirping out beyond where I could see. I remembered going to the old cowboy movies and seeing the cowboys sitting around a campfire and the Indians sneaking up on them and making noises like owls and stuff. I looked over toward Lobel, who was looking out toward the wire.

"Hey, Lobel, I didn't mean anything," I said. "I guess I'm just a little nervous."

"No sweat." He wore his helmet down low over his eyes and the top part of his face was in shadow. "I'm a little nervous, too. I'd be real nervous, except I know none of this is real and I'm just playing a part."

"What part you playing?"

"The part where the star of the movie is sitting in the foxhole explaining how he feels about life and stuff like that. You never get killed in movies when you're doing that. Anytime you get killed in a movie, it's after you set it up."

"You play a part when we were on patrol?"

"That wasn't a patrol," Lobel said. "That was a firefight."

"I thought a firefight was when you shot at something."

"Anytime anybody is getting shot at it's a firefight," Lobel said. "Anyway, I was playing Lee Marvin as a tough sergeant. That's my best part."

It got quiet again, then I heard somebody's radio. It sounded a little like Wilson Pickett.

"What do you think the VC are like?" I asked. "I mean really like?"

"Who knows?"

There were two radios on. In the distance I heard what sounded like a chopper but could have been a generator. The shadows were deepening. I didn't want to say anything else to Lobel.

There were lights on towers behind us that played on the wire. I saw something furry scurrying just outside the wire. The damned thing scared the crap out of me. I could see that it was a small animal. I knew it was a small animal. And yet it still scared me being out there in a place I was supposed to be watching.

A bug crawled on the back of my hand. I decided not to move. I had to get used to the bugs, I told myself. I felt him crawl over the back of my hand and start up my wrist. I slapped him away.

"What's your favorite movie of all time?" Lobel asked.

"I don't know," I said. "*Shane*, maybe."

"You ever see foreign movies?"

"I saw a Japanese movie I really liked once. I don't remember the name of it."

"What was it about?"

"This guy was a farmer. He and his wife use to carry water up a hill all day. . . ."

"*The Island*. That's the name of it," Lobel said. "The kid gets sick and he has to go get a doctor. . . ."

"Then the kid dies. . . ."

"Right. *The Island*, good flick." Lobel put down the grenade launcher and sat down in the foxhole again. "If you like that flick and you liked *Shane*, you probably qualify to be a real movie freak, like me."

"You see a lot of movies?" I didn't turn toward him, hoping that he would stand up again.

"My uncle's a director," he answered. "I've dated more starlets than you can imagine."

"You got drafted?"

"Unh-uh. Enlisted."

"How come?"

"Long story," he said.

"Oh."

I looked at my watch. I still had three hours to go. I had time for a long story. I hoped that Lobel didn't fall asleep. I swept my eyes over the gate, the way they had showed us to on night maneuvers back at Devens.

I thought about Mama. I worried about her. She had hoped that when I finished high school I would get a job and help her keep the house together. When I told her I was going into the army, she cried.

"I might as well get it over with," I had said, sitting in the tiny kitchen. Over the stove the old electric clock was five minutes early. Kenny always set it early in the mornings, knowing that by evening it would be late.

"You don't have to go," Mama had said. She didn't say it as if she meant it. She said it like a little girl hoping that I wouldn't leave. There was liquor on her breath. I had bent over and kissed her cheek, and she had put her arm around me.

I wouldn't have joined if I had seen anything else to do. When I figured I couldn't afford college, I just didn't want to be in Harlem anymore.

There was an old woman who used to sell the *Daily News* outside of Sydenham Hospital. She was the first person I told about going into the army.

"Why you want to go off to war?" she asked. She was short and dark with eyebrows turned white with age, although her hair was only lightly streaked with grey. Her voice was high and wavered uncertainly as she spoke.

"Got to get away from here," I said. "See something new."

"What you want to get away from here for?" she asked. "You got your peoples here. They ain't got this many black folks no place else in the world, 'cept maybe Africa and Haiti. You ain't going there, is you?"

"No, ma'am."

"Then stay on around here!" she said, a smile lighting her face. "You ain't doing no better than us, child."

"Perry, what the hell you thinking about?" Lobel looked up at me.

"An old black woman in Harlem."

"No market," Lobel said.

"What?"

"No market for old black women," Lobel went on. "If we're going to make a fortune on the silver screen, we got to figure what's going to sell. What we need is young girls. You got a girlfriend?"

"No."

"How come?"

"Didn't think that much about them," I said. "Between playing ball and school I filled my time up pretty good. I wish I had one to write to now, though."

"You worried about it?"

"Worried?" I looked at him, he was looking out toward the wire again. "No, I'm not worried. Just wish I had somebody else to write to, that's all."

"You want to write to a starlet?" Lobel asked. "I know one who can just about read, she might know how to write."

"I mean a real girlfriend," I said.

"There you go again," he sighed, stood up, and picked up the grenade launcher. "You're really hooked on reality. It's a bad scene, Perry."

"You got a girlfriend?"

"Nope, and I'm worried about it, too."

"How come?"

"Because I'll be twenty on the third of May and I'm still a virgin."

"Big deal."

"What do you mean, big deal? I could be playing the part of the baby-faced virgin who gets killed and all you see is a pan shot of him near the end of the flick. You think I want that?"

"I thought you were playing Lee Marvin," I said. "Don't you know what role you're playing?"

"No, not for sure. You know what role you're playing?"

"I don't know," I shrugged. "What roles you got?"

"The role you got to stay away from is the role of the good black guy who everybody thinks is a coward and then gets killed saving everybody else. That's a bummer. You can't be the romantic lead."

"Why not?"

"You don't have a girlfriend, you just said so."

"I met a nurse on the plane coming over here."

"White or black?"

"White."

"No good, then it becomes one of those noble flicks about interracial love, and they kill you off at the end so they can show it in Georgia."

"Shit."

"That's why I keep saying we should make this whole war into a musical. A big Busby Berkley number. Thousands of little VCs running up and down stairs in their little black PJs. We won't even have to pay them scale."

Captain Stewart came around with a television crew, and we were all filmed. First they got us cleaning our weapons. Then they asked each one of us why we were fighting in Nam. This is what everybody said:

Lieutenant Carroll said that we had to demonstrate that America stood for something, and that's what we were doing.

Sergeant Simpson said that we were trying to free the South Vietnamese people to do what they wanted to do.

Brunner said he was fighting because he hated Communism.

Walowick said that he was fighting because his country asked him to. I liked that.

Lobel said something about the domino theory, how if Vietnam fell to the Communists then the rest of Asia might fall.

Brew said the same thing about the domino theory. I think he was just repeating what he had heard Lobel say.

I said that we either defended our country abroad, or we would be forced to fight in the streets of America, which everybody seemed to like.

Then the news team got to Peewee and asked him why he was fighting in Vietnam.

"Vietnam?" Peewee looked around like he was shocked or something. "I must have got off on the wrong stop, I thought this was St. Louis!"

The news guys just walked away from him, and then they started talking to Brunner, who talked a good five minutes. Captain Stewart watched Brunner, and I could see he liked what Brunner was saying. He left for a few minutes and then came back and told Lieutenant Carroll that we had to go on patrol. Captain Stewart said that the television guys were coming with us.

Lieutenant Carroll looked over at Simpson and Simpson looked away.

We got into the Hueys—big, mean-looking choppers—at 1200 hours and headed north. Part of the squad was in the first chopper and the rest in the second. The news guys were filming everything, We landed in a sandy area about two kilometers from the sea.

Simpson put Monaco on point again, but this time he told Johnson to be the trailer. Johnson looked at me, and I could see he wasn't happy to be the last man on the line.

The news team was in the middle. We walked along a trail for about twenty minutes with the television guys photographing us, and then headed back toward the Hueys.

We were in sight of the landing zone when Monaco opened up.

"Hold your fire! Hold your fire!" Sergeant Simpson had ducked behind a tree.

Carroll moved toward Monaco, who was still firing, and yelled something to him. Monaco stopped firing and yelled back.

Carroll put his back to a tree, pointed to his eyes, and held up one finger.

"What's that mean?" Peewee asked.

"He means he saw one VC," Brunner said.

We stayed low for a while, then the cameramen started getting up and easing forward.

There was another burst from Monaco, and then I heard Lobel yelling. "There he is! There he is!"

I didn't see anything. I looked, but I didn't see anything. Monaco was firing on a stand of trees and soon the whole squad had opened up. Simpson was crawling back, and I saw him grab Johnson and turn him around. He wanted Johnson to watch our rear.

I looked to see what they were shooting at, but I still didn't see anything. I decided to shoot anyway.

I looked closely at where the others were shooting, then thought I saw something move. I lifted the sixteen and pulled the trigger. Nothing happened.

"Cease fire! Cease fire!" This from Simpson.

Simpson, Monaco, and Walowick moved out. Lieutenant Carroll was telling everybody to hold their fire.

They found the guy. Walowick dragged him out of the trees. The newsmen went to take his picture while Simpson was posting us around the LZ. My hands were sweating. I looked at my rifle, wondering why it hadn't fired.

"You okay, Perry?" Lieutenant Carroll came over to me.

"Yes, sir."

"Soon as you fire off a clip put a new one in," he said. "We got better supplies than the VC, we have to use them. Got that?"

"Yes, sir."

I looked at the rifle after he had left. Then I shoved in a clip. I had forgotten to load the damn thing.

The newsmen were on the chopper first, then the rest of the squad. Brunner threw on the VC before he got on.

I didn't want to look at the VC. I knew, by the way that Brunner had thrown him on, that he was dead. The news guys were getting still photos of the dead VC. Brunner took out a cigar and lit up.

We got back to the base, and they took off the VC first. They must have called ahead because there was a jeep waiting to take the VC back. Carroll went with the news team in another jeep. The rest of us walked from the chopper pad to the huts.

We got back, and they had laid the body out on the ground. The arms were out, and the legs were crossed at the ankles. I walked by him. He wasn't any bigger than Kenny.

We went directly to the mess hall. They had saved lunch for us. The news guys were buzzing around, checking their gear and everything. They must have taken a hundred pictures each of the dead VC. They even put a weapon down by his body and took a picture of him with that. Simpson came over to the new guys and made sure that we all had our weapons on safe.

We had baked chicken, carrots, mashed potatoes and giblet gravy, and rolls for lunch. And strawberry ice cream.

I sat with Peewee and asked him what he thought.

"I done seen two VC over here so far," he said. "One captured sucker and one dead sucker."

"I didn't even see where he was hit," I said.

"Fool had 'bout twenty holes in his ass," Peewee said. "I don't know where you was looking at."

Neither did I. I couldn't tell if there was too much to see, or if my eyes were getting bad. Maybe I just didn't want to see some of the things I was seeing.

Lieutenant Carroll came over and said that we had done a good job.

It wasn't real. We were eating baked chicken, and all I could think of was that it was pretty good. We had gone out to the jungle and seen one VC and killed him. Then we came back in time for lunch. Maybe Lobel was right. Maybe it was just some kind of movie.

Sergeant Simpson came to our hut and brought some magazines. I asked him if they had found a rifle or anything near the body.

"Perry wants to make sure the dude was a VC," Brunner said. He still had his cigar in his month.

"He wasn't no VC," Simpson said. "He was a North Vietnamese regular, from one of their big units, the 324th. They found his papers on him."

"What's that mean?" I asked.

"How I know?" Simpson said. "All I know is my time is getting short. I'm going to go take me a short nap because I ain't got time for a long one."

Monaco wanted the squad to practice volleyball. He had bet twenty-five dollars on our squad versus the Blazers, a team from Charlie Company.

"We can't beat them," Brew said. "They beat us six times already."

"You know that tall guy with the big hands?" Monaco was flossing his teeth.

"Yeah," Brew was putting salve on his feet. "He's the one that spikes all the time."

"Well, he got hit the day before yesterday," Monaco said. "He ain't playing."

Chapter 7

JAMAL, THE MEDIC, came by with malaria pills. I took one, and he sat on the edge of the bunk.

"I see you people got three VC today," he said.

"Three?"

"That's what the report says," Jamal said.

"We got *one* VC," I said.

"All I know is what I see on the reports," Jamal said. "They put three down on their reports, I send three in to Regiment."

"I don't believe they put down three when everybody saw that we only got one."

"You'll get used to what goes on over here," he said. He had a singsong way of talking, like a child in a man's body.

"Did Captain Stewart see the report?"

"Who do you think *gave* me the report?" He left some malaria pills on Peewee's bunk and split.

"Thanks," I called after him as he left the hooch.

One of the correspondents had left a *New York Times* behind and I went through it. Mostly it was the same old garbage. The Knicks had drafted some guy from Southern Illinois I never heard of, and they were still losing a lot of games.

There wasn't much about the war. A lot of VC were killed north of Saigon, and President Johnson was saying that the United States was ready to come to the peace table if the Communists were.

It wasn't even Thanksgiving yet, and the weather was already cold in New York. I imagined the brothers hustling down Lenox Avenue trying to get away from the wind. Howard, a guy I used to play ball with, crossed my mind. He was somebody I could write to. He'd probably write back. Three years before, he had pulled a robbery in midtown and been sent up to a prison in Stormville, New York. I had written to him the whole time he was up there. He used to tell me how much he appreciated the letters. Maybe he would answer my letters from Nam.

Mail call was hard when you didn't get any mail. I thought that what I needed was to have something more in the World than I had. I remembered what Lobel had said about the starlet, but it was silly. I needed something real. It didn't even have to be something that was going on at the time, a plan for when I got back would have been fine. I couldn't think of anything and felt depressed.

An image of the VC we had killed flashed through my mind. I wondered if he had a family? Had he been out on a patrol? When did he know he was going to die?

What was worse than thinking about him dead was the way we looked at him. At least we had cared for Jenkins, had trembled when he died. He was one of us, an American, a human. But the dead Vietnamese soldier, his body sprawled out in the mud, was no longer a human being. He was a thing, a trophy. I wondered if I could become a trophy.

"We won." Walowick came in after the volleyball game and sat on the edge of the bunk. "They're paying us off in beer."

"Way to go," I said.

"You okay?"

"Yeah."

"Seeing that dead gook mess you up some?"

"A little," I said. "Maybe even more than Jenkins."

"Who's Jenkins?"

"He was the guy—" I couldn't believe that Walowick didn't know who I was talking about. He had been on the patrol when Jenkins was killed. I looked into his face, and I saw that he was for real. "Jenkins was the guy I came in with. He stepped on a mine."

"Oh, yeah. Sorry about him," Walowick said. "You play chess?"

"A little, you got a set?"

Walowick went to get his chess set, and Jamal came back in. He had a clipboard and he put it in front of me. He pointed to a figure. It read "3." I looked at the column it was in and it was listed "Confirmed Kills." I looked up at Jamal, but he was already on his way out.

"You know, that guy is a little. . . ." Walowick held his hand out, palm down, and turned it from side to side.

"It takes all kinds," I said. Walowick had put the chessboard on a box, and we started setting up the pieces.

"How many VC were killed today?" I asked.

"One, I guess," Walowick said.

"The report said three," I said.

"You shoot a VC, and they take the bodies and run off with them," Walowick said. "That's so you never know how many are killed. You can't even find shells when they shoot at you. They take those, too."

"Then how do you know how many were killed?"

"Long as it's them and not us," he said. "Take the white pieces."

As soon as I crossed Manhattan Avenue I knew something was up. The street was quiet except for a radio that blared from behind a window with its shade pulled down. I stopped on the corner and looked down the street. A small girl, too young to be out past eleven, came out of a hallway and peered around a mail collection box.

"The Rovers down there," she said.

"Who?"

"The Rovers," she repeated. "They're from Brooklyn. They looking for somebody."

I wasn't about to go down the street. I had heard too many stories about gangs looking for someone who they had to "deal" with. A lot of them were getting out of the gang thing and into a Black Pride thing, but the gangs were still there.

A car, I hadn't noticed it before, had eased onto the block. Suddenly it picked up speed, wheels squealing, lurching from one side of the narrow street to the other. The Rovers came out and threw rocks and bottles. Then I heard the shots and flattened myself against the wall. The Rovers started running from down the block. A minute later the street was empty again. Then came the police sirens.

"Here's one!"

It startled me at first. Then I went over to where the woman was pointing. I saw the kid's frightened face; the eyes wide, as the neon lights from Joe Walker's restaurant turned it alternately green and red. He had been shot. The police cleared the corner. It was safe to walk up to Morningside, and home.

The next day in the West Indian store I heard two teenagers saying that the kid had died.

Brew came in and put his radio on. He had cupcakes and tossed me one and Walowick one. The radio was playing something about going to San Francisco with flowers in your hair. A nice tune.

We played two games of chess, and I won both of them easily. Walowick didn't seem to mind. His idea was just to capture as many pieces as possible. If it led him to a bad position, he would just lose. I was glad the game wasn't hard. I didn't want anything hard to do.

When I tried to sleep, I kept seeing the VC, just the way he was laid out in front of the company. I pushed my mind away, forced myself to think about other things. I started thinking about Kenny. There was a kid in his class who used to bother him a lot. The kid used to call him a punk and push him around. Kenny wasn't a punk, but he wasn't a fighter, either.

Sometimes we used to imagine traveling around the world together.

We'd have imaginary trips around the world. I would imagine just the two of us, but Kenny would always include Mama. That was the difference between me and Kenny. He could get other people, mostly Mama, into his dreams easier than I could. He was the bridge between me and Mama, and I liked him for that.

I woke up in the morning, about 0400 hours, with the worst pain I've ever had in my life. I thought I was having an attack of appendicitis. I was doubled up in bed and had to crawl out of the bed to get to where Peewee was sleeping. I shook him, and when he opened his eyes I told him I needed help. He got up right away and went to get a medic.

Jamal came over and saw me doubled up on the bed.

"You got the shits," he said.

"No, man, I feel like I've been poisoned."

"Hurts worse than anything else in the world, like it's burning for a while, and there's a sharp pain for a while?"

"Yeah."

"You got the shits."

"What he got to do?" Peewee said.

"He don't have to do nothing," Jamal said. "After a while he's going to go to the latrine and shit his lungs out, that's all."

"He gonna feel better, then?" Peewee asked hopefully.

"No." Jamal put some pills on the table and some Kleenex. "Every time you go to the bathroom, take two of these. Sometimes it helps, but usually it don't."

Then he started to leave.

"Yo, faggot, you got to do more than that," Peewee said.

"Don't be calling me no faggot," Jamal said. "You don't know me that well."

I threw the box of Kleenex at Jamal and told him where to shove them. He picked them up, shrugged, and left.

"I see where I'm gonna have to kick his ass before long," Peewee said. "You want some water or something?"

"No."

I remembered that after the orientation the old-timers started telling us about the diseases they said the lieutenant overlooked.

"They got one kind of thing they call the Damn Nam jungle rot. It rots you from the insides out. By the time it gets to your skin you're dead meat."

I didn't believe it, then.

"They got guys on an island out in the middle of the Pacific that can never go home again."

I didn't believe that, either.

"And if that don't get you, the stuff they spray on the trees will eat your liver up."

I was beginning to believe it all as I lay on the end of the bunk.

It was almost 0500, and the company was usually up and around at 0600. I would go on sick call then.

0510. I could hardly stand I had so much pain. I went to the latrine. I crapped out most of my insides. The cramps were worse. When I got back to the bunk, my hands were shaking.

0520. I crapped out the rest of my insides. I was getting nauseous from the stink. I was sweating.

0541. I tried to hold off, but I couldn't. I didn't have anything left to crap out so I just crapped out water.

0555. Again. I stopped off at Jamal's hooch and got the Kleenex.

0630. Again. This time Peewee came with me to the john. He sat on the john next to me and asked me if I thought Jimi Hendrix was for real. I said I thought he was okay.

"You know, I can play some blues," Peewee said.

"You can?"

"I ain't as good as Jimi Hendrix," he said, "but he play them citified blues, anyway. I'm thinking about writing a blues number for you. I'm gonna call it 'The Serious Stink Blues.' "

"Peewee, go die."

0800. The squad went on patrol. Jamal came by and I asked him if he had any softer Kleenex. He told me not to bother wiping.

I was still weak the next day, but getting around. At any rate I wasn't in the bathroom every five minutes. Jamal gave me potassium tablets. There was a lot of excitement in the camp. A sergeant from Charlie Company refused to take his squad out on patrol. He said the war would be over as soon as the truce went into effect and he didn't want to be the last guy to die in Nam. I stayed in bed all day and read a supply of *Ebonys* that Peewee got for me. Everybody was talking about the possibility of a truce before the holidays were over.

Johnson and Walowick got into a fight. Johnson wanted something from Walowick, I think it was a cleaning patch, and called Walowick a farm boy. Walowick threw Johnson the patch and called Johnson a cootie.

"What you call me?" That's what it sounded like Johnson was saying as he flew across the room.

He hit Walowick and sent him reeling across the floor. Then it was on. I had never seen human beings hit each other so hard. Everybody else in the hooch was trying to get out of it. There was blood everywhere. I got out just behind Peewee, and we both stumbled over Lieutenant Carroll trying to get in.

I thought about going back in to help Lieutenant Carroll stop the fight, but by the time I turned around, Lieutenant Carroll came hurtling through the doors. Then Johnson came out with Walowick around his middle. They went about three meters, hit a patch of mud, and went sliding into some crates of ammo. It took six guys to break them up.

Okay, the worst part of the fight was that Lieutenant Carroll got a broken tooth. His back tooth on the left side split right down the middle. He showed all of us. Also, it bled around the bottom and his jaw was swollen. Johnson and Walowick got called to the company commander's office. Then I got called as a witness.

"Tell 'im what he called me," Johnson said. "Tell 'im."

"Before you open your mouth, Private," Captain Stewart was chewing on the end of his cigar, "make sure you know what you're talking about. I don't want any rumors starting anything around here."

"He called him a cootie, sir."

"A what?"

"That's what he called me," Johnson said.

"What the fuck's a cootie?"

"It's a bug," Walowick said.

"That's like calling me a nigger," Johnson said.

"Is that a racial thing?" Captain Stewart looked at Walowick.

"A cootie's a cootie," Walowick shrugged. "He shouldn't have called me no farm boy. If he calls me a farm boy, I'm gonna call him a cootie again."

That's when Johnson hit Walowick again, and the fight started again. This time Lieutenant Carroll got out of the way. When the fight was over, Captain Stewart told them both to stop talking to each other. That was that.

Peewee asked me to write a letter to his girl for him. I had been right about her writing him a Dear John letter, and it really messed him up.

"Every time I get ready to write the damn thing I get messed around," Peewee said.

"Peewee, I can't write a letter to your girl for you," I said.

"Hey, if somebody in Chicago is doing my night work for me, you can write a letter," Peewee said.

We had some gung-ho stationery, the kind with a picture of GIs jumping out of a chopper on it. The picture was in light blue and you could write over it.

"What do you want me to say?"

"Say, 'Dear Two-Timing Slut.' "

"What's her name?"

"Her name Earlene."

"Okay, so I'm writing, 'Dear Earlene.' "

" 'How can you leave me for that old, fat Eddie Thompson when his feet stink, he ain't got no hair, and he got breath that smells like a polar bear what done died from eating too much garlic?' You got all that?"

"Wait a minute." I wrote it all down, then told him to go ahead.

" 'I know you need help with you and Little Mommy being on relief and everything, but I told you I would take care of you as soon as I got back into the World.' "

"Who's Little Mommy?"

"That's her daughter. She's real cute," Peewee said. "Earlene was married before, but her husband drove a cab and got kilt in a holdup.

" 'I know it is hard to wait for anybody, but I will try to be worth waiting for, so give it a try. Yours truly, Peewee Gates.' "

"Hey, Peewee," Monaco called over. "You gonna marry her?"

"If she wait," Peewee said.

"I ain't getting married," Monaco said. "I'm playing the field my whole life."

"That's 'cause you so ugly there ain't no pressure on you," Peewee said. "As handsome as I am, I got all kinds of pressure on me to get married."

I finished Peewee's letter and gave it to him.

"You think she's going to wait for you?" I asked.

"No, man, she already married this fat fool."

"Then why are you asking her to wait?"

"Just to break her damn heart," Peewee said.

I saw Peewee put a stamp on the letter and take it out to the mail sack. When he came back, he was quiet. It wasn't like Peewee to be quiet. I left him alone.

Johnson came in, and Brunner opened his mouth to him. Something about being called a name not being a big thing.

"You call me a cootie, and I'm going kick your ass, too," Johnson said.

"You said *what?*" Brunner was about six-three and as bulky as a football player.

"I said I was gonna kick your ass if you call me out my name." Johnson got up and walked over to Brunner.

Brunner looked at Johnson, shook his head, and picked up a magazine. He didn't want any part of Johnson.

I couldn't stand the smell of the insect repellent, and it woke me up in the middle of the night when I put my arms near my head because that's where I put most of it. I looked around and saw Brew kneeling by the side of his bed, praying. It was a good idea. I felt a little guilty about waiting until I got to Nam to think about God. On the other hand I didn't want to not be close to God. I checked Brew out again, and he was praying away. I started out with the Lord's Prayer as best as I could remember it, got messed up with the part about trespassing, and gave it up.

When I was small, Mama used to say a prayer with me before I went to sleep. It was before Kenny was born, and things had been pretty good for us. When I got bigger, she used to say it with Kenny. The night Daddy left she came in and sat on Kenny's bed and started saying it, and Kenny saw her crying and he started crying, too. When she got to the part about dying before you waked I put my head under the cover. I didn't say it in Nam, either.

The sound of incoming choppers woke us up in the morning. A moment later we were being yelled at, whistles were blowing, and the morning cursing had started.

The air outside was still and muggy, but I could smell cordite in the air. Lieutenant Carroll was near a tree, and I went over to him and asked him what was going on.

"Beats the hell out of me," he said. He had coffee in his canteen cup, a cigarette between his fingers, and was leaning against a tree to take a leak. He peed all over his pants. "The next time I join a war I'm going to get circumcised first," he said. "How you doing?"

"Good," I said. "How'd the patrol go yesterday?"

"Bad. Nothing happened, but I don't think we should have been out there."

"Stewart?"

He shrugged and walked away.

We got powdered eggs and cold potatoes for breakfast. Then Lieutenant Berger from Delta Company came over. I thought he had something important to say, but he had the mail, which was pretty important. Nobody in our squad got mail but Johnson. He got a bill from the telephone company.

After breakfast things settled down to a boring normal. Lobel said that he weighed one seventy-three and Walowick said that he should lose weight.

"You should take some of that candy they have," Walowick said.

Lobel and Walowick went through some magazines until they found an ad for the candy that was supposed to make Lobel lose inches from his waistline.

"Perry!" Lieutenant Carroll called me to the front of the hootch. "Bring your gear!"

I got my gear and went outside. He told me that he had to supply one man for a patrol with Charlie Company, and since I had missed one patrol with the squad, it had to be me. He said he was sorry, and that I shouldn't be a hero.

"Don't sweat it," I said.

Chapter 8

WHAT'S YOUR NAME, SOLDIER?"

"Perry, sir."

"Look, Perry, we're going out on a sector patrol. What we want to do is to establish a presence. We're not looking to get into a firefight. We see anything, we call in artillery. You have any questions, you ask me, okay?"

"Yes, sir."

"If we do get into anything, make sure you report any body count. One last thing, you stay close to Scotty over there. Scotty's our machine gunner. You can feed for him."

Lieutenant Doyle was short, nervous. He cupped a cigarette in his hand the way I thought Humphrey Bogart would have. Charlie Company was going out in two sectors. The first platoon went out first, the third and the fourth platoon—the one I was assigned to—were going next, and the second platoon was going to be the backup in case anybody got into trouble.

Scotty was about six-five, with a face that was mostly ashy white. But the eyes were what set him apart. They were dark, and darting. I had seen the look on ballplayers before. They were the kind of eyes that wanted to win.

I was nervous being with these new guys. Scotty must have sensed it, because he came over and told me everything was going to be cool.

"Where you from?"

"New York," I said. "Harlem."

"You a long way from home, man."

"Where you from?"

"Tacoma, Washington," he said. "Doyle tell you about the stand down?"

"No."

"Charlie Company is going to be the first company that stands down," Scotty said. "We'll be standing down for two weeks, maybe even get down to Saigon."

"The whole battalion standing down?"

"From what I hear," Scotty said. "And this boy needs a little vacation. Far as I'm concerned we can stand down till this thing is over."

"I heard it could be over before Christmas."

"Can't be too soon for this boy," Scotty said.

Some guys were getting ready to move out, and Scotty got up and shouldered the .60-caliber machine gun. I crisscrossed two bandoliers of ammunition over my chest and grabbed a boxful. It was heavy as hell.

We went to the pads and then sat down waiting for the choppers.

I liked the idea of standing down. A few weeks away from the combat zone would do me good. If we got to Saigon, maybe we could see what the cities were like before the war was over.

Two black guys came over and asked me if I was new. I said no, that I was on loan from Alpha Company. Then they asked me if I knew a guy named Gifford in Alpha. I didn't.

Scotty introduced me to a couple of other guys, but I forgot their names as soon as I heard them. Lieutenant Doyle was yelling into the radio that the choppers were late. He was asking if the guy on the other end of the phone wanted us to go to the backup position. The best I could figure out, the answer was no.

"You play ball?" Scotty asked.

"Basketball," I said. "Played some baseball but nothing to brag about."

"I played football in high school but couldn't get into a college. You know the only thing I'm good at?"

"What?"

"M-60 machine gun. You know anybody out in the World need a good machine gunner?"

I smiled. My mind shot ahead. What would I do when I got out? I had read some stuff in *Stars and Stripes* about Congress expanding the GI Bill. The paper said it didn't look too hopeful.

The chopper finally came, almost an hour after they were supposed to. We got in and took off.

The LZ was supposed to be secure, but I could see a few muzzle blasts coming from the thick green carpet below me as we came down. I flinched every time I saw one. Scotty and another guy—his name tag read Palumbis—kidded me about the flinching.

"If you see the muzzle blast, it means that the bullet missed."

He had a lot to learn about physics, but we were already landing.

The struts were supposed to take the jolt out of the landing, but I wanted to be out before they hit. Scotty went just as I was thinking of going, and in a moment I was out and running behind him. The ammo box banged against my legs. I felt as if I were carrying a ton of equipment.

We moved out quickly from the LZ and went into some tall grass. The grass cut my hands up so fast I thought I had walked into a booby trap. I couldn't believe it. It was like a thousand paper cuts all over me.

We had to cross a road, and Doyle was telling everybody to look out for mines.

"I don't know why he tells us that," Scotty said. "They don't put the damn mines so you can see them, and we ain't got no detectors."

A picture of Jenkins flashed through my mind. I didn't even look down. I just watched Scotty's back as we crossed the road. We found the area we were supposed to be in and dug in. Scotty had empty sandbags in his ruck-sack, and we filled them with dirt and made ourselves a little nest.

Doyle was twenty meters away. The radio guy was with him, and by the time Scotty and I had finished our nest, Doyle and the radio guy were playing cards.

"We just going to stay here?" I asked.

"Doyle don't go too far," Scotty said. "He don't think this is his war anyway. He's got him a Sunoco service station back in New Jersey."

"He got drafted?"

"He got drafted four years ago, but he changed his name and stayed low," Scotty said. "Then the FBI caught up with him and brought him in. He got big connections and got into Officers Candidate School."

Two jets streaked across the sky. Beautiful. Dark birds in a sweeping arc across a silver sky.

"You join up?" Scotty asked.

"Yeah. Nothing to do in the World."

"Me, either."

"That's why they give these dances," Scotty said.

We sat for a half hour, then Doyle told us we would be moving out in fifteen minutes. Scotty and I had just started to unload the sandbags when the shooting started.

"Four-fifty! Four-fifty!" The shout went down the line. Someone had spotted where the firing was coming from and estimated it to be four hundred and fifty meters in front of us. Scotty was leveling the legs of the tripod, and I jerked open the metal ammo case.

"Get that thing going!" Doyle was yelling at us. I looked up and saw that he was on the radio. The radio man was firing at a line of small trees.

I wasn't scared. For the first time I wasn't scared. I didn't see anybody, no muzzle flashes. I was going to be okay.

Scotty started firing the 60. There were tracers in the belt, and I could see the rounds spit across the distance. Leaves and small branches in front of us seemed to jump into the air. I kept feeding, but I didn't see anything. Doyle let the firing continue for a long time before calling out for us to cease fire.

I watched him. He peered above the dirt mound he was behind.

"You want a squad out?" Scotty called to Doyle.

"I'm calling for Willy Peter!" Doyle called back.

"That's Doyle for you, man," Scotty said. "Whoever started the shooting probably didn't even see anything, but he's still going to call for a couple of rounds of Willy Peter, just in case."

We waited for another minute before a lone round of white phosphorus landed in the distant trees.

"We're too close to be calling in artillery," Scotty said.

One of our machine guns started chattering on our right, and Scotty opened up again. A moment later some more white phosphorus started coming in. The Willy Peter sent streamers of fire into the air. The smell of it was terrible. Terrible and scary. Just the idea of being hit by a white phosphorus barrage sent a chill through me. The barrage lasted for fifteen seconds, then stopped abruptly.

Scotty nudged me and pointed toward Doyle. Doyle had his helmet off and was screaming into the radio. He was gesturing wildly and then he stood up and looked toward the target area. The radio man stood and looked, too.

The machine gun on the right opened up again, and Doyle started screaming.

"Cease fire! Cease fire!" Doyle was jumping around and waving both of his arms over his head.

"Oh, shit!" Scotty turned around and leaned against the sandbags.

"What's up?" I asked.

"I hope not what I think it is," Scotty said.

We waited as Doyle walked a little ahead of his position, hands on his hips, and looked out to the field ahead of us. Behind us I heard choppers. I turned and saw them headed for us. They went by us out to the target zone.

"Hey, Scotty, did we . . . ?"

"Yep, we just shot the shit out of the first platoon."

We walked slowly across the field. There were some kind of crops being grown in between the trees, half of it now burned out or uprooted by the shelling. As we got near the first platoon the smell from the phosphorus grew stronger.

They were loading the guys onto the medevac choppers. Medics were running from guy to guy.

"Look in the bushes!" a captain was shouting.

We looked for wounded. They were all over the place. The medics were so busy they were just tagging guys. The ones they thought they could save they worked on, the others they marked their wounds down. One kid, the angry stain of blood on his T-shirt growing with every breath, watched calmly as the medic wrote up the tag. The medic tied it to his lapel and patted the kid's shoulder. When the medic left, the kid tried to read the tag without taking it off.

If there were time—if the medic had finished with the ones he was fairly sure he could save—he would come back to the kid to see what he could do. I kept looking for other wounded. These were our people.

The first chopper was moving out already. They were so quick. One guy had a plasma bottle strapped to his helmet. He was going through his pockets looking for matches to light his cigarette. He found them but they were soaked through with his own blood. Scotty lit his cigarette.

A sergeant was crying. He was sitting by himself, his rifle cradled in his arms, crying softly.

Nobody was talking. There was nothing to say. More medevacs came in and took away the rest of first platoon. The last one took the body bags. There had to be at least fifteen.

We went back to the LZ an hour later. They had brought in the stand-by platoon to replace us.

A spec four from the first platoon had wandered away from the company and was riding with us. He was a young kid, really good-looking. He had burns on his arms and face. Both eyebrows were gone, but he was still good-looking. He looked so young.

"Where you from?" I asked.

"Charlie Company, sir," he said.

I started to tell him that I wasn't an officer. But it didn't matter.

As soon as we landed I was told to go back to my company. Scotty said that it was nice meeting me.

"You okay?" Lieutenant Carroll was the first to meet me.

"Yeah, sure."

"You know, the way they run this shit over the radio," Lieutenant Carroll shook his head. "You would think all hell was breaking loose."

When I got to the hut, Peewee asked me what had happened.

"We heard that you guys ran into a VC battalion or something," he said. " 'Cause I told them that Perry could handle the shit if it was only one damn battalion."

"I was with their fourth platoon," I said. "We ran into their first platoon and we hit them. They must have lost over a dozen guys."

"You hit our own guys?" Monaco came over to where I was sitting on the bed.

"I didn't hit them! The platoon leader called in artillery on their position."

"Who spotted them?" Monaco asked.

"I don't know."

"Nobody knows nothing. That's why a bunch of guys get nailed for no reason!'"

"Yo, man, I didn't mess them up."

Monaco looked at me and walked away. I watched him lie down on his bunk with his face to the wall.

"They messed up bad?" Peewee asked.

"Yeah, real bad."

Thanksgiving. This year, Kenny's birthday was on Thanksgiving, and I damn near forgot it. I figured it would take three weeks for anything to reach home from Nam. I didn't want to send him money. He could have used the money, but I wanted to send him something more. I asked Lieutenant Carroll if he thought I could get a knife in the mail. I told him it was for Kenny.

Lieutenant Carroll said he had something else, and he gave me a jacket he had bought in Saigon. It was black silk and there was a map in green of Nam on the back. I wanted to pay him for it, but he said no.

I got the jacket in the last mail. Lieutenant Carroll was in the officer's hooch, and I stopped in to see him. He was sitting in his shorts. He was drinking from a bottle of Jack Daniels.

"You know where I got this?"

"Where?"

"We went into a village about six months ago; I guess we surprised some VC. They left their meal, their cards, and this bottle behind. You want a drink?"

I took a drink. It burned like hell going down. It came up easier.

I couldn't sleep. They all started crowding in on me. The guy with the plasma taped to his helmet, the sergeant crying. None of them were together in my mind. They just kept coming, one by one. Short movies. A few seconds of a medic putting a tag on a wounded soldier. A few seconds of a chopper taking off over the trees. A guy cradling his rifle. A body bag.

The guys that our artillery blew away didn't have a reason to die. They hadn't died facing the enemy. They just died because somebody else was scared, maybe careless. They died because they were in Nam, where being scared made you do things you would regret later. We were killing our brothers, ourselves.

Brew was getting ready to go to bed and I went over to his bunk and asked him if he knew where the Lord's Prayer was in the Bible.

"The Bible I got has an index," he said. "You can look up anything you want in the back."

"Hey, that's cool."

"You can borrow mine any time you want," he said, tossing it to me.

"You pray a lot when you in the World?" I asked him.

"Yeah, I prayed a lot," Brew said. "But, man, I didn't pray nowhere near as hard."

Chapter 9

Brunner came into the hooch and told us to saddle up, that we were going on a pacification mission. Monaco asked him who had given the order.

"Just get your ass in gear," Brunner snarled.

"Who the hell elected you God?" Monaco hadn't moved and neither had the rest of us.

"How many stripes you got on your arm, Private Monaco?" Brunner walked to the end of Monaco's bunk.

"Enough to know that I don't have to take any bull from you," Monaco said.

Brunner kicked the end of Monaco's bunk hard enough to knock some magazines onto the wooden pallets that served as a floor. Monaco reached under his bunk, grabbed a grenade, and pulled the pin.

"Now what do you think you're going to do with that, pretty boy?" Brunner said, looking down at Monaco.

Monaco smiled, lifted the armed grenade high over his head, and flipped it toward Brunner.

Everybody dove to the floor, screaming. I tried to pull my bunk down over me. I heard myself screaming, as if the noise I made would somehow cut off the impact of the grenade. Peewee was on the floor near me. He had one hand over his head and his helmet over his rear end.

I didn't stop screaming until I saw Walowick, who had rolled himself into a tight little knot, get up.

Slowly we all got up. Walowick started the cursing, and we joined in. Monaco was on his bunk, laughing.

"The next time I'm going to toss you one with the powder in it," he said to Brunner.

"You're a fucking kid! You're a fucking kid!" Brunner was screaming at the top of his lungs. "You call yourself a fucking soldier, but you're a fucking kid!"

We continued cursing out Monaco. He was called every low-life and every animal we could think of, and then some. Peewee called him a faggot baboon dog, which was different.

When we finished the cursing we all laughed, all except Brunner and

Brew. Brunner was still pissed, and Brew was praying. Brew's praying bothered me. It wasn't that I minded him being religious, it was just that I didn't want him being closer to God than I was.

Everybody was interested in the pacification thing we were going on. It was like the closest thing to a real answer about why we were in Nam. Sergeant Simpson said that the marines had done the bulk of it in the past but that they were digging in up north to establish positions for the Tet truce.

"Keep your eyes open and don't mess with the women folks," Sergeant Simpson said. "Keep your weapons on safe. I don't want none of y'all shooting me."

I thought about my going out with Charlie Company and how we had shot at our own men. Then it left my mind. I noticed that lately there were things I would let myself think about, and things I wouldn't. But every once in a while things would come into my mind, not like a thought but like a picture, and I felt a little strange about that. I wondered if that happened to any of the other guys.

We mounted the choppers and started out. My stomach tensed when I saw the choppers. They were like a trigger. Even when I heard them *putt-putting* into the area I would tense up. It meant that we were leaving the camp, leaving home. At the camp I felt safe. Outside of the camp anything was possible.

It didn't take us long to get to the hamlet. Lieutenant Carroll was showing Sergeant Simpson the map, and I looked at it. It showed all the hills and the streams mostly. That was how we got around, following the hills and streams and paddies. Sometimes there would be a plantation that we would use as a reference, or a field of rice paddies.

The hamlet consisted of a cluster of little huts. They were put together well. Some kids came out to greet us. Most of them were young, four or five, seven at the most. The M-16 I carried felt bigger than it usually did. We came into the village to pacify the people who lived there. Lobel found me and came alongside.

"You know who we are?" he asked.

"Who?"

"You remember those cowboy movies when the bad guys ride into town? You know, the killers?"

"Yeah?"

"That's us," Lobel said.

"I'm not a killer," I said.

He looked at me and smiled. I hated him saying that. I hated his smiling as if he had some dark secret. Sergeant Simpson was up ahead. He didn't walk, he loped. He was cool, simple. I trotted the few steps to catch up with him.

"I wonder what they think of this war?" I said, half to myself and half to Sergeant Simpson. I was looking at a group of Vietnamese kids playing in the mud.

"It ain't so bad for them," he answered.

"How can you say that? They're just kids."

" 'Cause they don't know nothin' else," Simpson said. "You look around at these kids and their mamas and you know they been fighting and getting their asses kicked since way back before I was born. You ain't gonna find ten of these people in all of First Corps know anything about no damn peace."

I started telling him how he was wrong, but he cut me off. He told me not to fall asleep just because I was on a mission of peace.

We had to go into each hut with little gifts. That was to make sure that there weren't any VC hiding out among the civilians. The people were the same. Small, withered women, skin creased over onto itself; dark, life-weary eyes that had seen everything.

I felt huge walking among them. I towered over them. I was huge, and I was armed to the teeth, and these were not my people. Maybe, they did look at me as if I were the killer in Lobel's movie. Then, on the other hand, the hell with Lobel. I wasn't a killer.

The Vietnamese didn't look up at me. They looked down, or at my chest. Sometimes, when they did look directly at us, they would shade their eyes with their hands as if they were looking at something very far away. I smiled at an old man and he nodded his head. I wondered what that meant. I had been trying to be friendly, and he just nodded. Did he know that I wanted him to like me?

Walowick found a place that had jars filled with some kind of paste. He thought they might have been Molotov cocktails and called Lieutenant Carroll over. Carroll smelled the jars and shrugged it off.

"It's some kind of salve," he said. "Maybe it's good for jock itch or something."

We were supposed to smile a lot and treat the people with dignity. They were supposed to think we were the good guys. That bothered me a little. I didn't like having to convince anybody that I was the good guy. That was where we were supposed to start from. We, the Americans, were the good guys. Otherwise it didn't make the kind of sense I wanted it to make.

I saw Brunner pocket a small statue from one of the huts. I told him about it and he gave me the finger.

"Maybe you'll be a better dude when you come back in your next life," I said. "Who knows, cockroaches might be in by then."

He took a step toward me, and Johnson—I hadn't seen him nearby—stepped next to me. Brunner looked at Johnson, then turned on his heel and walked away.

"He ain't spit," Johnson said.

Johnson went off and started looking at a pig that was tied in back of one of the huts. Johnson was different than I thought he was at first. He didn't seem that sharp, but he knew things. He knew when somebody was doing something that he didn't like. He knew when one of the black guys was being messed with. And when he knew something he put his butt on the line. That was Johnson. Maybe back in Savannah he was different. But the war made him a certain somebody. The same way that it made Monaco a certain somebody. Monaco was the point man. Johnson had the pig, the big sixty, the heavy 'chine. Who the hell was I?

I found Peewee trying to play a game with some Vietnamese kids.

"These little fuckers trying to cheat me," Peewee said.

The kids were laughing, having a good time. I told Peewee about the salve that Walowick had found and he wanted to go get some.

"Why, you got jock itch?"

"They got medicine for the stuff they be catching over here," Peewee said. "Right?"

"Right."

"And we over here, right?"

"Right."

We slept in hooches that were surrounded by sandbags. There were vents on both ends, and sometimes they worked. Usually, though, the hooches were hot as anything. We had put straw and leaves on the roof of our hooch back at the base to keep the sun from baking us, but it didn't help that much. The huts that the Vietnamese lived in were made on bamboo frames and covered with woven bamboo slats and dried flat leaves. The joints weren't nailed. They were notched and tied with either rope or wire. Some of the huts had slats that could be adjusted to let the light in. They were cool enough inside, especially the ones with the high ceilings.

Peewee and I found the hut with the salves and went inside. There were two women and a kid sitting on the floor. One of the women was old, the other not much more than a girl. The kid was two at most and didn't have any pants on. The whole place stunk of urine and God knows what.

"What medicine good fo'?" Peewee asked in his best "Let's go talk to the Indians" dialogue.

The two women just looked at us.

"What medicine good fo'?" Peewee asked again.

"My-America number one!" the girl said. "Vietcong number ten!"

"Yeah, I know we number one," Peewee said. "But what the damn medicine good fo'?"

I took a bottle of salve, put some on my finger—the smell of it was awful—and put it near my mouth. I raised my eyebrows.

"No-no," the old woman took the salve from me, took some of it on two bony fingers, and started rubbing it in my hair.

She said something to the younger woman, and she reached up and felt my hair. I remembered in the orientation lecture that you weren't supposed to touch the head of a Vietnamese person.

"If they rubbing our heads for luck I'm gonna burn this mother down," Peewee laughed. He was comfortable with the Vietnamese.

We tried to work out what all the salves were for. The first salve was something that was supposed to make hair grow. We couldn't figure out most of the others, but we did figure that one was to rub on a girl's stomach to either get her pregnant or after she got pregnant, we couldn't figure out which, and the last was to put on your feet.

Peewee paid them three hundred piasters, about three dollars, for four bottles of the hair stuff and the feet stuff. He said that he was going to take the stuff home and make a fortune growing hair. I told him not to mix them up; we didn't want people growing hair between their toes.

A chopper brought in some hot food for us and some grain and a box of chicks for the people in the hamlet.

Brunner told Carroll that he thought that one of the older girls in the hamlet was a VC. Carroll told him not to worry about it.

"We're not playing I Declare War today," Lieutenant Carroll said. "That comes next week. This week you have a choice of stickball, ring-a-levio, and pacification."

There was another outfit doing a pacification project a few kilometers from us, and the chopper that had picked them up was waiting with our chopper. We loaded up and both choppers cut their engines. Then—bingo—they both started up, and we raced back to the base. Our chopper lost by a few seconds.

When we got back there was a lot of yelling in the camp. We were having roast beef, mashed potatoes, carrots, and carrot cake again for supper, and everybody was pissed. An officer wanted to start an investigation and somebody else wanted to frag the cooks.

It wasn't the greatest supper in the world, and the cooks served it in flak jackets.

Lieutenant Carroll said that we were going on another pacification mission the next day, then an hour later he came and told us that we weren't.

"How come?" Brew was trying to increase his vocabulary and was working on a quiz in Reader's Digest.

"That's just the way it is," Carroll said.

Later Monaco heard from Sergeant Simpson that Captain Stewart got us out of it.

"You can't get a body count on a pacification run," Monaco said.

Peewee got a letter from Earlene that said she still loved him even though she married somebody else. She said she was pregnant, and if the baby was a boy she was going to name it Harry after him. Also, Lobel got a letter from his father. The letter was really full of crap. He read it out loud. The whole thing was about how could he go into the war and kill innocent people.

" 'Young men all over the country are burning their draft cards and re-sisting the war machine,' " Lobel read. "He probably got 'war machine' from one of his fifteen-year-old girlfriends."

Lobel didn't make a big thing over it, but I didn't think it was really that cool with him. I sat with him at chow and listened for a while as he talked about movies. Then I asked him about the letter:

"You know why this letter sucks?" he asked.

"How come?"

"Because I joined the friggin' army in the first place so he would stop thinking I was a faggot," Lobel said. "Now he thinks I'm a creep because I'm in the army."

"What the hell does he know?"

"You know what I hope?" Lobel asked. "I hope I get killed over here so he has to fit that shit between his vodka martinis."

"The next time we call for artillery, we'll aim right at your pad at home," I said.

"You know what that jackass doesn't know?" Lobel said, looking away from me. "He don't know that now I can go back home and blow him away. That's what I'm fucking trained for, man. That's what I'm fucking trained for."

Mail call. Got a letter from Kenny. He said a guy is starting a basketball league for kids from nine to eleven. He said he didn't think he was that good in basketball, but he wanted to enter. Everybody on the winning team would get a trophy. He needed ten dollars though, and Mama didn't have the money.

I answered him right away. I told him that he would do just fine in bas-ketball. I put twenty dollars in the letter for him.

It was good having Kenny need me. I almost cried as I thought about him. It had been tough on me not being able to go to college, but things had been tough on him, too. In a neighborhood where you had to be tough just to get to the store with money for a loaf of bread, Kenny wasn't tough at all.

I had been sort of a father to him since our folks split, and I know he missed me.

I thought about what Lobel had said. Here he was with a gun ready to kill people to prove that he wasn't queer, and I was ready to kill people because I wanted to get away from home.

I told myself I would write to Kenny more, and to Mama, too.

"Hey, Perry, what you thinking about?"

"My brother," I said to Peewee.

"Why don't you think about girls so we can get some more sex in the atmosphere?"

"Right on."

Two American Red Cross workers came around and passed out candy and stuff. They were the first American women we had seen in a long while, and the guys just kept looking at them. A funny thing happened. One of them—her name was Sam—asked me what I was going to do when I got home. The question embarrassed me. I was so embarrassed I think she felt bad.

She made a few jokes, and I laughed harder than I should have, and she went off to the next guy.

I remembered sitting in the counselor's office my second week in high school. The counselor, a short, red-haired woman, with blue eyes that bulged slightly from a thin face, had asked me what I had wanted to do in life.

"I'd like to be a philosopher," I had said.

She had started laughing and apologizing at the same time. It was simply not the kind of thing, she explained, that she had expected.

I was hurt. I didn't even know what a philosopher did for sure, but her laughing messed me up. After that I never told anyone I wanted to be a philosopher again, or even a writer. I started telling people in school that I wanted to work on a newspaper. Around the block I told people that I either wanted to play ball or teach. But I was always uncomfortable with the question. Even when Kenny had asked me, I couldn't come up with anything easily.

"Something important?" he had offered.

"Yeah." It was a good answer, and we both had a feel for what it meant.

Bad news. A patrol from Echo Company went out on a pacification thing to the same hamlet we went to, and two guys got hit. They were on their way into the place when it happened. They searched the whole place but didn't find any VC. Everybody felt bad about that. Then we were told we had to go to the hamlet again.

"What the VC do is to go in when we leave and mess up anybody that got help from us. If they see they got some grain from us or some pills that they didn't turn over to them, then they kill the head of the village," Sergeant Simpson said.

"What we got to do," Sergeant Simpson went on, "is to lay an ambush outside the hamlet. If they come in, they got to fight their way out."

"How about the people in the hamlet?" Brew asked.

"We got to show them that we can be peaceful if they peaceful with us, or we can mess them up," Sergeant Simpson said.

"Pacify them to death!" Peewee said.

"Something like that," Sergeant Simpson said.

Chapter 10

It was a platoon thing, but not really a full platoon thing. Our squad was cool, but the other squads were all cut down to four or five men. It was a platoon on paper, but it was just paper, not men. We mounted the choppers an hour before nightfall. We were at the LZ in a little over ten minutes. Sergeant Simpson laid out a new route to the hamlet.

We cut through some dense underbrush for a half hour before we got near the hamlet. Sergeant Simpson laid out the ambush. It was simple enough. We were on one side of a small cemetery. The reports had it that the VC came past the cemetery into the hamlet at night. They terrorized the people in the hamlet, taking what they called a "tax" and killing anybody they thought might have been informing on them. We were supposed to surprise them, to make them pay for coming to the hamlet.

Monaco, as usual, was point. He was about forty meters beyond the cemetery. The way we figured they had to pass him to get to the cemetery. We had claymore mines at the end of the cemetery, and then the rest of the platoon stretched out in a straight line along what we had been told was the path the VC took. Johnson and Brew would be at the end of the line we formed.

We moved in quietly, with Sergeant Simpson placing each of us, and making sure that we knew where the others were.

"Try not to kill each other if you can help it," he said.

We dug in. I had five sandbags, which I filled and put in front of me. Suddenly they weren't big enough, or solid enough. I wanted something else, a wall, maybe. I could rest my piece on the sandbags, but it didn't look very convincing.

Silence. There wasn't to be any communication between us in case the VC had lookouts.

Suppose, I thought, they had spotted us already?

The only radio we had, a PRC-10, or Prick 10 as they called it, was near Lieutenant Carroll. Brew had it. I didn't want the radio. The antenna made you stick out like a sore thumb, and drew a lot of fire.

It got dark. There were bugs. Somewhere in the distance I heard frogs. The night was filled with noises. After a while it dawned on me that I couldn't see anything. There was a moon above us, but it didn't give us enough light. I wanted each VC to have his own light shining right on him.

It was 2230 hours. Back home in Harlem it would have been ten-thirty.

The eight o'clock parties would be just hotting up. Kenny would be fighting with Mama about going to bed. Maybe he would wonder about what I was doing. If he was in bed already, he would be reading comics under the blanket with a flashlight. I wondered if he would feel anything if I got nailed? Would he wake up in the middle of the night, wondering what was wrong? Would he feel uneasy, knowing that halfway around the world his brother was hurting?

Kenny, I love you.

We waited. I told myself that I was bored.

I wondered if Mama was getting the allotment checks. I wondered how she felt about them. Did she think I was doing something for her, or just that it was part of my being in the army? I didn't know myself.

At 2300 hours I had to pee. Actually, I had to do more than that but no way I was taking my pants down out in the boonies. I felt around me to see if I was on an incline, decided I wasn't, and lay on one side and peed as quietly as I could.

It was grave dark and quiet except for the things that crawled in the night. Suppose everyone else was gone? Suppose I was out here by myself? Forget that. Think about something else. Think about Diana Ross waking me up in the morning, begging me not to get out of bed. No, wait, her and Juliet Prowse were secretly sisters trying to get me to make love to them.

The thing was I was a virgin. I didn't tell anybody because I wasn't supposed to be a virgin. I was supposed to be hip. Everybody knew how blacks were, how soldiers were. Everybody knew, and I was still lying in behind a few inches of sand halfway around the world from anything I knew without having loved anything deeply, or spent time with anyone in a bed alone. Maybe it wasn't important.

Insects chirped, moved through the night. There were shadows all around me, laughing, jerking, mocking.

A sound. I raised my head slightly to hear better. Voices. Vietnamese voices. I brought my hand to the weapon, my finger played with the safety. Shadows ahead of me. They were coming out of the cemetery.

They moved about, talking quietly, calm, singsong rhythms. What were they talking about? The lousy chow they got in the army? Their families?

Someone opened up. A scream. We were all firing. It was too dark to aim, I just fired in what I thought was the right direction.

They began to answer fire. I could see faces over the light from the muzzle blasts. I fired faster, trying to space my rounds in a sector. I heard a bullet whine past me and flinched even though I knew it was already gone. A grenade went off, and then another. I kept firing. I didn't know where my rounds were going.

"Cease fire!" Simpson's voice.

"Take cover!" Lieutenant Carroll.

A small pop, and a flare went high into the air. A moment later the entire area was lit up. There was nothing in front of us. I looked from side to side. Then I saw a body, and another. Thin arms not much different in color than mine. A hand waving slowly in the night air, trying to push away the death already there. One body lay facedown. There was a tremendous wound on the back. It's what a blast from an M-16 can do.

We kept shooting at the bodies even though they were already dead.

"Get another flare up!" Sergeant Simpson's voice cracked as he spoke.

Brunner sent another flare into the sky as the rest of us searched the area with our eyes, not moving from the spot we were in.

"What the fuck happened?" Monaco came through the trees.

"They pass by you?"

"No."

"Here!"

Peewee called us over and we went. He had found one of them lying a few feet from the entrance to a tunnel. The tunnel was near the corner of the cemetery, covered by a low, sprawling bush.

Sergeant Simpson took a grenade, pulled the pin, and threw it into the opening as hard as he could. We stepped back, and a moment later the grenade went off.

"Okay, let's hit it!" he said.

We were starting off. Backing out of the village toward the pickup zone. I felt sick. My stomach churned. I looked for Peewee and found him. There was nothing to read in his face.

A pop. Nothing more. A small pop, almost lost in the sounds of the jungle around us. We hit the dirt, the mud. We returned fire. Someone sent up a flare that was defective. It burned for a second and then went out quickly. To my left I heard someone crying out. Not loudly—there was no panic— but a gentle cry of surprise. I turned just as the last of the light from the flare was dying. It was Lieutenant Carroll.

The squad lit up the woods with fire as Sergeant Simpson barked into the radio. We started making our way toward the village. Johnson and Walowick carried Lieutenant Carroll.

Carried him. He was limp. His legs dragged behind him. God have mercy. God have mercy.

I looked toward his face, but he was a silhouette, lost in the darkness of the moment.

Pain. I thought my heart was stopping. I couldn't breathe. We went to the edge of the village and somebody shot off another flare.

"Keep their heads down!" Sergeant Simpson pointed toward the village.

Peewee sent a burst of fire into the village. Johnson had put Lieutenant Carroll down and was setting up the M-60. The sixty—the pig—was hungry, angry that they had hit our man, our leader.

"Cover the trail!" Sergeant Simpson called to Johnson.

Peewee and Monaco kept pumping rounds high into the village while Johnson sprayed the trail behind us.

We didn't see anything. The fire could have come from the village. Lieutenant Carroll, lying behind a wide tree, was a dark silhouette. No one in the squad spoke. We were afraid for Lieutenant Carroll, we were afraid for ourselves, and our only answer to the fear that called each of our names was to fire blindly into the fearful darkness.

It took the chopper another five minutes to get to us. What we hadn't done to the village, it did. It leveled the huts. There were Vietnamese, mostly women and old men, running for their lives. Few of them made it more than a few feet as the chopper guns swept everything in their path. These were the people we had come to save, to pacify. Now it was ourselves that we were saving. God have mercy. God give us peace.

The chopper came down and we handed up Lieutenant Carroll. A burnt offering. We didn't hand him up gently through the chopper doors, we pushed him as hard as we could. It was his life, but it was our lives as well. God have mercy.

We all climbed on and the chopper tilted, jerked, and was off. The door gunner kept spraying the village as we moved off into the night.

A medic on the chopper looked for Lieutenant Carroll's wound, but couldn't find it. Bars of lights passed through us. There were eyes, the outlines of helmets. There was Lieutenant Carroll, unconscious.

"Anybody see where he was hit?" The medic was already putting in the IV.

We hadn't seen. There weren't any signs of blood.

"Maybe he just passed out," Monaco said.

The medic didn't answer, he just shook his head. We didn't land at the base. We went on to Chu Lai. The whole squad made the trip. We got there in what seemed a short time. An ambulance was waiting for us. They took Lieutenant Carroll, and the rest of us went off to one side and sat outside a building.

I was trembling, and I couldn't stop. Peewee put his hand on mine and tried to calm it. I took deep breaths.

A major came by, saw us sitting on the ground, and came over to us.

"What are you men doing here?" he asked.

"I don't know, sir," I heard Monaco say.

"What unit you with?"

Nobody answered. He looked at us, and then said something about either him being in charge or maybe he asked who was in charge, I didn't know.

Sergeant Simpson got to his feet and talked to him, and then we were all headed over to a low building. It was a mess hall, and two cooks sitting listening to the radio got coffee for us.

One of the medics who had been on the chopper came over, and we asked him how Lieutenant Carroll was doing. He said he didn't know, only that he was over in building A-3. We finished the coffee and went over to see him.

"He got hit under the arm," a hawk-faced doctor was saying. "That's why the medics couldn't find the wound. Almost in the armpit. It wouldn't have done any good if they had found it, though."

Monaco knew the prayer.

"Lord, let us feel pity for Lieutenant Carroll, and sorrow for ourselves, and all the angel warriors that fall. Let us fear death, but let it not live within us. Protect us, O Lord, and be merciful unto us."

Amen.

Chapter 11

SHOCK. PAIN. Nobody wanted to look at anybody else. Nobody wanted to talk. There was nothing to say. Lieutenant Carroll's death was close. It hung around our shoulders and filled the spaces between us. Lieutenant Carroll had sat with us, had been afraid with us, had worried about us. Now he was dead.

"It happened so quick," Brunner said.

"That's the way it goes," Monaco said. He shrugged and continued relacing his boots. I looked over at him. His eyes glistened with tears. I started checking my rifle.

At the camp Sergeant Simpson asked me to write a letter to Lieutenant Carroll's family. I said I couldn't do it, and he asked me why.

"I just can't," I said.

"If he was laying out in the boonies, and he was calling to you needing your help, what would you do?"

"He's not laying out in the boonies," I said.

"Yeah, man, he is," Simpson said. "He just in too deep to get out."

I took Lieutenant Carroll's personal stuff from Sergeant Simpson and started looking through it.

There were letters to his wife, Lois, back in Kansas. He wanted to open a bookstore if she could find a place. I read part of one of his letters to her.

> No, I don't think having the bookstore so close to the library is a bad idea. The place on Minnesota Avenue is close enough to the bridge so that we can get customers from Missouri as well. The idea of the bookstore is so comforting to me, Lois. I have this vision of me working behind the counter and you taking care of the baby in the back. Better yet, you work the counter, and I'll take care of the baby. Have you considered Karen as a name if it's a girl? It's your mother's name, and I like it.

There were local newspapers that she had sent him and a Alumnus Bulletin from Emporia State College. There were pictures of his wife—a pretty girl, blonde, dark-rimmed glasses, in a winter coat. There was snow on the street behind her. Another picture of the two of them together in bathing suits. She looked less pretty, but the two of them looked so happy together.

It took me three tries to get the letter even close to something worth saying, and then it was nothing special. In a way I felt real bad just being alive to write it. I could think of her wondering why I didn't do something, why I didn't save him.

> Dear Mrs. Carroll,
>
> My name is Richard Perry, and I had the good fortune to serve under your husband. Last night, we ran into heavy fighting in an area we've been trying to protect for some time. Lieutenant Carroll was in the process of getting us out of there safely despite the fact that we had run into more of the enemy than we had expected to, when he was wounded. The medevac choppers got him down to Chu Lai, to the medical unit there, and they tried their best to save him, but could not.
>
> Mrs. Carroll, I know that it is not much comfort to you that your husband died bravely, or honorably, but he did. All of the guys in the squad who served under him are grateful for his leadership and for having known him.
>
> I am sorry to have to write to you under these circumstances.
>
> > Yours,
> > Richard Perry

I read the letter to Peewee and Walowick and they said it was okay. Then I gave it to Sergeant Simpson to take to HQ.

I thought about Mama getting a letter about me. What would she do with it? Would she put it in the drawer she kept Daddy's papers in? Would she sit on her bed in the middle of the night and take it from the drawer to read like she did his stuff? I wondered how Kenny would feel?

I had to get my mind off of Lieutenant Carroll. The guys in the squad hung out together after we got back to the camp. The conversation was quiet, almost reverent. We got six copies of a book called *Valley of the Dolls*, and Brew hit a rat with one of them. The rat was as big as any I've ever seen.

Lieutenant Carroll stayed on my mind. I knew he would. I thought of his calling Jenkins a warrior angel. It was a gentle thing to say, and he had been a gentle man.

We spent another day lying around. It seemed to be what the war was about. Hours of boredom, seconds of terror.

Morning. The coffee was pretty good. Somebody had found a cache of coffee beans about two months earlier, and they had sent to Saigon for a coffee grinder. I wasn't hungry so I just had coffee in the hooch.

Lobel came over to my bunk. He was really shaken by Carroll's death.

He sat on the edge of my bunk, and I could see he was trying to say something. He finally got it out.

"Hey, Perry, you know . . . I kind of feel that maybe it was my fault."

"What?"

"You know, about Carroll?"

"Wasn't your fault, man."

"Throughout the whole thing I was just lying there, scared out of my mind." There was distress on Lobel's face. "I think I'm a coward."

"Wasn't anybody's fault," I said. "The Congs got him."

"I keep thinking if I had shot more, maybe a lucky shot would have got the guy that . . ." he stopped and shook his head. I thought he was going to cry. "I was so scared I didn't even see them until it was over."

"The Congs?" Peewee had heard Lobel and sat up.

"Yeah." Lobel was wringing his hands.

"You know, I didn't see one till it was over," Peewee said. "I remember what you said about Charlie Company fucking each other up, and I thought we done did the same shit until I seen that Cong laying near that tunnel. I was glad as hell to see him, too."

"You didn't see them during the fight?" Lobel looked up at Peewee.

"The only time I seen a live, straight-money Cong was that guy they was questioning. As far as I'm concerned, the Congs could sneak they asses clear out the damn country, and we'd be here fighting for two more years."

"How about you, Perry?" Lobel looked at me. "Did you see them?"

"During the fight?"

"Yeah."

"I don't know," I said. "Maybe I saw their faces over the muzzle fire. I just fired where I thought they were. I've never aimed at anything. I've never seen anything to shoot at."

Lobel looked down at his hands again.

Sergeant Simpson came in and said that Captain Stewart wanted me over at headquarters.

I went over and there were two colonels there. One was a marine corps guy. I started to salute but the marine corps guy just walked away from me. Stewart motioned for me to sit down.

They had a guy tied up in the middle of the room. I guessed he was VC. A Vietnamese interpreter was talking to him.

I couldn't understand any Vietnamese, but I listened all the same. An orderly had made coffee and passed it around. He brought me a cup and I thanked him with a nod. It was black, and it didn't have any sugar but I didn't want to get up and get the milk and sugar next to the marine colonel.

"What's he talking about, Vinh?" the colonel asked.

"He says he's a fisherman. He says he works on Song Bong River, but he doesn't have an accent like that, he has an accent from the north. Then he say that the VC make him fight with them, but he doesn't want to. He says that if he is killed his people don't get his body from the VC. He doesn't want to be buried under a tree in the forest. That's what the VC do."

"Tell him I don't believe a word he's saying," the marine colonel said. "Tell him that if he doesn't tell me the truth pretty soon I'm going to have to shoot him."

The Vietnamese spoke to the prisoner again. This time his words were harsher. He slapped him a few times, then took his gun out.

The VC was rocking and talking as fast as he could. His voice rose as he spoke. The Vietnamese officer hit the prisoner with his pistol butt.

"Is he saying the same thing?" The army colonel asked. His name tag read Mulig.

"Now he say they make him fight with the Second Division," the interpreter said. "He says he hates army life."

"The Second?" The marine colonel looked at the VC as if he were seeing him for the first time. "He actually said the Second?"

"That's what he said," the interpreter reported.

"That's the fifth one we got from the Second in the last two days. Something's up. Get him over to Chu Lai to intelligence there. Let them work him over for a bit."

The marine colonel and the army colonel both left. Captain Stewart talked to the major who stayed behind for a few minutes and then the major left. The orderly went to Captain Stewart and spoke to him. I heard him mention my name. Stewart, who had been leaning on the edge of a desk, came over to me.

"Your name Perry?"

"Yes, sir."

"You wrote the letter to Lieutenant Carroll's wife?"

"Yes, sir."

"Damn good letter, boy." Captain Stewart wiped away some tobacco juice from his chin with his thumb. "You know how to type? I can use somebody in here who can type and speak English."

"I can't type, sir."

"Well, it's still a damn good letter," he said. He turned and walked away.

I finished the coffee as two guys blindfolded the VC to take him back to Chu Lai. He was trembling.

"They found some tortured marines up near the demilitarized zone," the orderly said. "He probably thinks they're going to do the same thing to him."

"Tortured?"

"They tie them to trees and pull their guts out," the orderly said. "Then they just leave them there. That marine colonel said when they found them they were still alive and begging for somebody to kill them."

"For the marines to kill them? They begged for the marines to kill them?"

"Yeah," the orderly said. "And now they think that a whole regiment of North Vietnamese regulars are coming through Laos and Cambodia now."

"Damn!"

"To say the least," the orderly said.

Back at the hooch I told Peewee what the orderly had said. Peewee asked what had happened to the truce, and I told him I didn't know.

We had a halfhearted volleyball game against some guys from HQ company. They beat us easily and made a lot of noise about how good they were. Peewee wanted to take a shot at one of them. When I got back to the hooch after the game, I saw the Vietnamese house girl putting something on the end of my bunk. I went to see what it was and saw that it was Lieutenant Carroll's pictures. For some reason I put them with my stuff.

The war was different now. Nam was different. Jenkins had been outside of me, even the guys in Charlie Company had been outside. Lieutenant Carroll was inside of me, he was part of me. Part of me was dead with him. I wanted to be sad, to cry for him, maybe bang my fists against the sides of the hooch. But what I felt was numb. I just had these pictures of him walking along with us on patrol or sitting in the mess area, looking down into his coffee cup. It was what I was building in my mind, a series of pictures of things I had seen, of guys I had seen. I found myself trying to push them from my mind, but they seemed more and more a part of me.

We got a new platoon leader, a Lieutenant Gearhart, and he chewed tobacco. He could have been twenty-five, maybe twenty-six, no older. Captain Stewart brought him around and introduced him.

"The first thing Lieutenant Gearhart is going to do is to make sure that we get some gooks for Lieutenant Carroll," Stewart said. "Isn't that right, Lieutenant?"

"Yes, sir," Lieutenant Gearhart answered.

"Where you from?" Monaco asked.

"Wilmington, Delaware," he said.

"What the hell do they have in Delaware?"

"The DuPont company, mostly," he said. "And Delaware State. I played football for Delaware."

"You any good?" Brunner asked.

"Damn straight."

"What position you play?"

"Linebacker."

"You're too small to play linebacker," Monaco said.

"I played it," Gearhart said.

"When you get in country?"

"Two months ago."

"Where you been?" Peewee asked. "Mr. Cong been asking for you."

"Taking reconnaissance training," Lieutenant Gearhart said. "I was supposed to be with the Seventy-fifth's program, but they needed officers here, so here I am."

"How are things going down in the south?"

"Okay. They think we've seen the worst of it."

That afternoon, orders came through for Brunner and Lobel to be promoted to sergeant, and everybody else in the squad moved up to corporal. I didn't even know that Lobel had been a corporal. The word was that everybody was getting short on people.

"Say, Peewee?"

"What?"

"Why you think Lieutenant Carroll got it?"

"The Man dialed his number," Peewee said.

"You really believe that?" I asked.

"Can't handle nothing deeper," Peewee said.

He got up and started fixing his mosquito netting. He had got some new netting from a guy in supply and was tacking it around his bunk.

I wanted to talk to him more about why Lieutenant Carroll had died. I wanted to talk to everybody about it, but nobody could deal with it. Lobel had thought it was his fault. He said if he had shot more maybe he would have got the guy that got Carroll. Maybe. Maybe, even, that was why Carroll got nailed, because somebody didn't shoot enough, or maybe somebody didn't order enough bombs dropped, or enough shells fired into some sector three months ago. But why was Carroll even here? What was he doing so far from Kansas City? So far from his bookstore on Minnesota Avenue?

I hadn't put a reason for his dying in the letter to his wife. I wondered if that had been the reason Captain Stewart had asked me to write it. I started writing a letter to Kenny. What I wanted to put in it was the reason for my dying, if I should die. I knew that I wanted to live because I was afraid of dying, and I knew that I could come up with reasons for wanting to live.

A memory came from so long ago. It was the glow of the light through the spread that I had pulled over my head when Mama got to the part about "If I should die before I wake."

It was another letter that never got finished.

The next afternoon we had to run escort service for a civilian pacification team. These guys wanted to know exactly how to go about winning over the people. That's what they said, anyway. There were four young guys, college types, and one of them had his wife and kid with him. The guy acted sincere as hell, and Brunner was sucking up to him like crazy. I thought the guy was an asshole for bringing his wife and kid to Nam.

"His wife is probably a spook, too," Gearhart said.

"A *what?*" Peewee looked at me.

"The guy's got to be a spook," Gearhart said. "You know, CIA."

"What they do over here?" Monaco asked.

"Below the DMZ they do pacification stuff, look around to see who is infiltrating, that kind of thing. Then they do a lot of stuff above the 'Z. The navy guys slip them in on the west and the Green Berets slip them around the 'Z through Laos. Down here she's probably his cover."

"Is the kid a spook, too?" Monaco asked.

"Who knows?" Gearhart answered. "This is a funny war."

I didn't like the idea of having people who were civilians around. It just didn't seem right somehow.

We took trucks to the hamlet we were going to. If I didn't like choppers that much, I hated trucks. You were in a truck, and you expected bullets coming through the sides any minute. Me, Brew, and Peewee were the only ones wearing flak jackets. The damn things were too hot and too heavy.

We got to the hamlet and just hung around while the civilians set up a screen and started showing Walt Disney movies.

"What the fuck am I doing running around over here protecting Donald Duck?" Peewee complained. "That little dude is three times older'n me and ain't got a scratch on him."

"That's cause he don't wear no pants," Sergeant Simpson said. "You go around with no pants on you got to be cool."

"What kind of freaky mess you talking about?" Peewee asked. "Donald Duck wears pants."

"No he don't."

Peewee and Sergeant Simpson watched the movies with the kids and made notes about who had pants on and who didn't. Sergeant Simpson was right about Donald Duck not having on pants. Peewee got pissed. I think he was really pissed because he thought Simpson was putting down Donald Duck.

Halfway through the movies we heard the sounds of big guns being fired in the distance. Sergeant Simpson said that a lot of it was Cong artillery. It kept up for nearly three hours without letting up. There was a lot of air activity, and we actually saw a jet go down.

The jet was streaking across the sky, and then we saw a rocket go up. I didn't know it was a rocket but Lieutenant Gearhart did. I didn't actually see the rocket hit the jet but I saw the jet twist in the air, hesitate for a long moment, and then start down.

"There's a 'chute!" Monaco spotted it first.

We watched the parachute come down slowly, and the plane streak away. We couldn't figure out what had happened with the plane. Then a heavy stream of smoke came from it, and it disappeared. Sergeant Simpson got on the radio to spot the parachute, but he said it was already on the waves.

All the time we were showing the movies the civilians were talking to the villagers. The woman let some people play with the kid. I got near enough to her to hear her talking Vietnamese.

When it was time to leave, a chopper took the civilians someplace. They thanked us and told us we were doing a good job. They weren't the kind of people that had to be in Vietnam. I wondered just what kind of people they were.

Peewee got a letter. I hoped it was from his woman, but it wasn't.

"Say, Perry, what's your mama's name?"

"I don't play that 'mama' stuff, Peewee," I said.

"No, I ain't running no dozens, man," Peewee said. "I just want to know her name."

"Mabel."

"What's my name?"

"If you don't know, I'm not telling you," I said.

"My name is Peewee Gates," Peewee said. "And what is the name on this letter?"

I looked at the letter. It had his name on it, but it was from Mama.

"How come my mother is sending you a letter?" I asked.

"You must have told her about me."

"Yeah, I did. Open it up."

"Don't be telling me when to open my mail," Peewee said.

Peewee didn't open the letter all day. I tried to figure out what Mama would have to say to Peewee. I had written to her and told her that Lieutenant Carroll had died. Maybe that worried her. Maybe I shouldn't have told her that. People back home didn't want to know about the war, I knew that. But Mama was used to hard times, I thought it would be okay to tell her.

Usually Peewee and I went to chow together, but I told him I wasn't hungry. When he went I looked under his bunk and took Mama's letter out.

Dear Peewee,

Richard has told me all about you and you sound like a very fine boy. I wish you all the luck in the world and hope you get the chance to go home to your family. I do not know why Richard went into the army, because he did not seem to be the type. Only I think he was not happy at home. If something happens to him please tell him that I love him very much. You seem to be his friend and he will believe you. You can write to me if you want to.

Mabel Perry

It made me sad that Mama had written to Peewee to say that she loved me. She hadn't even told me that when I was leaving.

I put the letter back and wrote to Mama. I told her that I loved her very much and missed her very much. I had always had a small war with Mama. I was always the bright one and she always the one that didn't understand what I needed. Now all I could think of was how much I needed her.

Walowick got a rash on the inside of his thigh, his back, and on the inside of his arms. It looked terrible. Everybody took a look at it and offered their opinion on what it might be. Lieutenant Gearhart came in to our hooch and saw it and asked Walowick if he had been having intimate relations with anything with a reptilian background.

"Like a snake or a lizard," Gearhart said with a big smile on his face.

"Go fuck yourself!" Walowick said.

Gearhart didn't like Walowick saying that. You could see it all over his face, but he didn't say anything.

Late that night we watched some television. Security was getting tighter, and we had to cover the windows of the hooch the television was in, which made it just about too hot to watch the thing. We watched *Gunsmoke* and then a Christmas show. I forgot it was almost Christmas. It got me a little sad, and I was just about to go back to our hooch when all of a sudden, there we were, on television. It was the time we had gone out with the television crew.

"There I go," Peewee said. "You know, I sure don't look like no damn soldier."

"What you look like is a VC," Monaco said.

I watched the film with the others. They made little comments about how they had felt walking that day, and how they were surprised at how the cameras made us look.

"Where am I?" I didn't see myself.

"There you go, behind me."

I looked older than I thought I did in real life. Older and sloppier.

The pictures also made it look as if the photographers were leading the patrol. But what the squad wasn't talking about was the guy walking behind Walowick. Lieutenant Carroll turned back to make sure we had kept our distances. He seemed for a moment to look directly into the camera. His eyes were quiet, serious, as they always were. And then, as he had to, he turned away from us.

Chapter 12

I THINK YOU SHOULD MAJOR IN MATH," Peewee said. Walowick had a catalogue from the college he wanted to go to when he got back to the World and Peewee was telling him what to take.

"I'm no good in math," Walowick said. "I think I'll take music or something like that. Something easy."

"Why don't you go to the University of Chicago?" Brunner said. "That's got a good reputation. Who ever heard of Knox College?"

"That sounds like that School of Hard Knocks I been hearing about," Peewee said.

"Knox is good and it's in my hometown," Walowick said. "My cousin went there."

"They got any brothers going to that school?" I asked.

"The first colored senator went to Knox," Walowick said. "The whole town has a good history with helping coloreds and stuff like that. The underground railroad used to go through Galesburg."

"You study math like I told you," Peewee said in a gruff voice. "Then I'll let you come to Chicago and be a big-time numbers man."

"Walowick would rather stay over here than go to Chicago," Sergeant Simpson chimed in. "He figure he stay over here he'll be safer."

"What else you got in the mail?" Monaco asked.

"A newspaper," Walowick said. "Only thing in it is the stuff about guys burning their draft cards."

"Faggots and Commies," Brunner said. "Anybody who wouldn't stand up for their country is either a faggot or a Commie."

"They're doing what they think is right," Monaco said. "Maybe they are right, who knows?"

"That's why we got four- and five-man squads," Brunner said, " 'Cause those jerks are home smoking dope and burning their draft cards. You get blown away because you don't have a full squad, you can thank those creeps."

"I almost went to Canada when I got notice to go down to register," Brew said.

"Yeah, but then you got it together," Brunner said.

"No, man, I didn't have the nerve." Brew had a sheepish grin on his face.

A rat scurried up the side of the hooch, jumped onto Walowick's bunk, and stopped right in the middle of it. We had put some poison around, and we figured he must have been dying. It was about seven to eight inches long and bloated up.

"Brunner, get your piece," Sergeant Simpson said.

Brunner had a twenty-two air rifle. He got it, kneeled down, and shot the rat. It died right on Walowick's bunk, and Walowick got pissed off. He left the hooch and told Brunner he had better have his bunk cleaned up before he got back. The rest of us got up and split and left Brunner and the rat in the hooch.

What Brew had said about not having the nerve to go to Canada shook me. Here he was in Nam, getting shot at every day, afraid of every noise, every step, and yet he had been afraid of going to Canada. It shook me because I knew what he meant. Sometimes standing alone seemed to be the hardest thing in the world to do, even when being in the crowd meant you could be killed.

We got hit by a rocket attack that night. It came on us all of a sudden. I woke up screaming. The sounds of the explosions rattled through the hooches, and we couldn't tell where the rockets were hitting. I grabbed my helmet and rifle and ran for the bunker.

The noise messed me up. I jumped with every explosion, I trembled as the ground shook around me.

"Look for sappers! Look for sappers!"

Sergeant Simpson was calling out for us to look out for sappers, the Vietnamese suicide squads. He had sixty-two days to go and he was trying to stay alive.

"Somebody send up a flare!" Monaco.

"I'm going to get some!" Peewee. The squad had settled down. I was still shaking. I heard somebody screaming for a medic.

The flare went up and there was some firing, but we didn't see any sappers. The rockets stopped, the flares died down, they put out the fires. The night had us again.

Captain Stewart came around to check for casualties. He started talking about how we had to be more aggressive, how we had to go out to get the VC.

"We got to keep them up a few nights," he said. He patted Sergeant Simpson on the shoulder.

When he left I could see that Sergeant Simpson didn't look good.

"You okay, Sarge?" I asked.

"That man bucking for major real bad," he said. "He gonna get somebody killed before he makes it."

I couldn't sleep, and sat outside in the bunker, trying to catch a little breeze. Johnson was there, too.

"This reminds me of a Harlem night," I said. "Sometimes the little apartment we lived in would be so hot you couldn't sleep for days."

"Wish I was anyplace I could call home," Johnson said.

"Wherever it is, I'll think more of it the next time I get there," I said.

"Yeah." He looked away. "What you think about them protesters?"

I was surprised at the question. I looked up and saw that he was leaning back against the sandbags. I could just see his silhouette, helmet pushed back, rifle across his lap.

"I don't know," I said. "You think much about why you were going to fight before you came in?"

"Unh-uh. You?"

"No, but I'm thinking a lot about it now."

" 'Cause they shooting at your ass?"

"Sounds like a good enough reason to be thinking about it," I said.

"You trying to figure out who the good guys, huh?" Johnson spoke slowly. "So what you come up with?"

"I guess somebody back home knows what they're doing," I said. "What it means and everything. You talk about Communists—stuff like that—and it doesn't mean much when you're in school. Then when you get over here the only thing they're talking about is keeping your ass in one piece."

"Vietnam don't mean nothing, man," Johnson said. "We could do the same thing someplace else. We just over here killing people to let everybody know we gonna do it if it got to be done."

"That might be a good reason to be over here," I said.

"That's for people like you to mess with," Johnson said.

"I don't know about that."

"Then why you messin' with it?"

When I turned in, Peewee was still up. He told me he had an idea. He was going to spray the netting with this new repellent we got. I got into my bunk and pulled the mosquito netting around it and then Peewee sprayed the netting, which was supposed to be his good idea.

"Yo, Peewee, I can't breathe in here," I said.

"I wondered if that was going to be a problem," Peewee said.

I fell asleep thinking about what Johnson had said. Maybe the time had passed when anybody could be a good guy.

Chapter 13

D ECEMBER 22, 1967. Three days before Christmas and only ten days left in the whole year. Me and Peewee spent all day talking about whether we should try to have sex with a Vietnamese girl before we got back to the States. He figured it might be our only chance to have sex with a foreign woman.

"Suppose we catch something?" I said.

"That's what combat is all about," he said, looking in the mirror he had nailed on a pole at the end of his bunk. "Taking chances."

"How about Walowick?" I asked.

"He didn't mess with no women," Peewee said. "He just got the Nam Rot."

That was true. Walowick had been sent to the 312th to get his rash treated. Sergeant Simpson said that it usually took a week to clear up a real mean rash. By that time, according to the word going around, the war was going to be over.

Captain Stewart said that the war wasn't over yet, and for us not to get too relaxed.

"We can spend the last weeks of the war kicking a little ass and letting them know who the hell we were," he said.

The way the story was going around was that the Vietnamese had agreed to a truce for their New Year's celebration, which they called Tet. Then the truce would be just extended while the talks went on, and we would all go home. Captain Stewart seemed disappointed.

I wrote Mama telling her that I expected to be home around January or February. I didn't believe all the stories, but I did believe Jamal. Jamal said that all of the South Vietnamese officers were going home for the holidays.

"And they should know," he said, looking like a serious bullfrog.

Then some other stuff started coming down the line. There was a lot of Cong activity and the special forces guys in Cambodia were spotting convoys.

"Them Greenies just don't want to have a truce," Sergeant Simpson said. "If they ain't got them a good war, they don't know what to do with themselves."

Back home the World seemed to be splitting up between people who wanted to make love and people who wanted to tear the cities down. A lot of it was blacks against whites, and we didn't talk about that too much, but we felt it.

Over the summer a kid in Harlem had been killed by a white police sergeant and there had been some riots. I told Mama in a letter to tell Kenny to be careful. Sometimes he had a fresh mouth, and I didn't want him hurt.

Kenny was all Mama had left. She had me, in a way, but not in any real way. Kenny loved her straight up and down. He didn't see any faults in her. I loved her, too, but not like Kenny. When you're young, the way Kenny was, you didn't ask much of people.

Christmas. Depression. We had roast beef, mashed potatoes, peas and carrots, carrot cake, and candy canes.

They were supposed to send in a movie called *Guess Who's Coming to Dinner*, with Sidney Poitier. But when they opened the cans they found the movie with Julie Andrews that we had already seen.

"That other movie don't sound like much anyway," Monaco said. "Some black dude coming to dinner."

"Maybe they were going to have fried chicken, and they were afraid he was going to eat too much," Brunner said.

"Maybe they thought your mama was going to eat too much, too," Peewee said.

That ended that conversation.

Word came in that the marines were catching hell all over the place. Some old-timers said that a piss load of marines were trapped up in the hills of Khe Sanh. The fighting was picking up. Captain Stewart was still saying that the VC were trying to get into place in time for the Tet holiday.

"The only trouble is"—Lieutenant Gearhart sat on an ammo box with his feet up on Brunner's bed—"what they're seeing most of is the NVA, not the VC."

"The NVA ain't nothing but the VC with their pajamas off," Peewee said.

"Bullshit." Gearhart turned and looked toward Peewee with his eyes half closed, as if he were asleep. "The NVA get up to a year of training before they even get to the south. The VC are guerrillas. The NVA is their regular army."

"Don't mean shit to me," Peewee said.

"We're talking about regiment-sized units," Gearhart went on. "They've finally figured out they can't whip us with this little guerrilla action."

"Hey, man," Monaco sat up. "They can't whip us with nothing they got!"

I looked up to see if Monaco was kidding. He wasn't. But he talked about it like it was a volleyball game or something.

The sounds of fighting, the far-off booming of the artillery, the hollow, bass-drum sound of explosions echoing off the mountains became a constant thing. Before, it had been an occasional crackle of gunfire, the steady rhythms of .50-caliber machine guns with the .60's answering in short riffs. Sometimes, just after the gut-shaking boom of a jet, you could see the bombs arc down and, if the wind was just right, the sound would be somewhere in between thunder and a cymbal clash. Peewee said that it sounded like a South Side jazz club when the brothers were right. A death blues for Mr. Cong.

The noises had always scared me. I had gone through basic training just fine until the end when we had to go under live fire. The noises shook you, made you want to stop and hide.

Now it was different. Now the sound swelled in my consciousness like a dull headache. It kept coming and coming, day and night. Sometimes I felt as if the sounds were inside me somehow. And there were times, I never wanted to mention them to anyone else, that I heard the sounds at night when it was very quiet, and no one else heard them.

I was ready for the truce.

Stars and Stripes talked about peace feelers in Paris. Where I was, it was raining. It rained almost every day. The ruts filled with water. There wasn't any place to dry out.

We waited and listened to the stories coming in. They weren't good. When the Tet started, we were put on alert. We kept hearing about truce violations. They kept talking about the body counts we picked up, but the ones they gave at the end of the reports, our own KIAs, Killed in Action, were climbing, too.

All of First Corps went on alert as we found out that all the major cities were being hit. All the way from Saigon north to the DMZ.

Interdiction patrol. That's what they called it, but it sounded like a plain ambush to us. We were being separated from the rest of the outfit, which was supposed to be operating further north above Phuoc Ha. Meanwhile our squad was supposed to stop nighttime traffic between two hamlets.

"*Titi* contact," Gearhart said, using the Vietnamese phrase for little. "All light stuff."

Sergeant Simpson said that, because of Gearhart's training, they were using our squad on long-range reconnaissance. We were packing up to go, when Jamal came by. He told us that Captain Stewart had volunteered us to replace a reconnaissance team that had been wiped out.

Walowick came back just in time for the patrol. He looked okay. The rash was gone. When he found out that we were going on patrol he got really upset. He almost spooked the whole squad.

"C'mon, man, this squad is the best," Monaco said. "Everything within ten kilometers of Tam Ky belongs to us."

"Yeah." Walowick was scared. He had always been kind of even, but being away for a little while must have got to him.

We got six new brothers in the platoon and two were assigned to our squad. One was from the South, a brother named Nate Turner, and the other one, Darren Lewis, was from the Bronx. I couldn't remember exactly where, even though he told me twice.

We went in a chopper with some First Cav guys who were going up to Quang Nam province. The choppers dropped us off first. We went east through a fairly dense stretch of forest and then swung back west until we hit our coordinates. Sergeant Simpson said that we would be picked up in a different zone. He acted worried. It was our first patrol with Gearhart. Simpson told me and Monaco to keep our eyes on Gearhart.

"Just so he don't get me killed," he said. He had twenty-two days left.

This ambush patrol was different than the first one we had been on near the cemetery. This was along a small road going just east of some pretty high hills. We were to take one stretch of the road, and some South Vietnamese regulars—ARVN—were to be up a little way from us.

When we got to the ambush site, Sergeant Simpson didn't like it. The road itself was small and ran along a rice paddy. There were dikes leading from the road, but they didn't look too firm. The other side of the road was a lightly wooded area.

"That sucker's probably mined," Sergeant Simpson said. "We got to go down to the end of the paddy and check that out."

"We'll set up here, Sergeant." Lieutenant Gearhart's voice stiffened.

"We ain't got no cover here, sir." Sergeant Simpson looked at Gearhart.

"There's cover there," Gearhart said. He pointed to a small trench along the side of the paddy. There were thin bushes next to it. Nothing that would stop a bullet. "We'll put sandbags behind the bushes."

"You gonna get some people killed over here!"

"Sergeant, I know what I'm doing." Gearhart took a step toward Simpson. "Now deploy the men."

For a moment the two men stood looking at each other, then Sergeant Simpson turned away. I didn't like it. I knew Simpson, I didn't know Gearhart yet. Simpson got Monaco and took him down the paddy and placed him. Then he came back and got me and Peewee.

"Peewee, you and Perry be our rear security. Monaco got the other end. First noise you hear, light it up! We ain't waiting for nothing to get into no damn killing zone 'cause I don't want it to be my ass that gets killed out here tonight!"

Gearhart came up with a diagram, a little picture of the place we were in. We were to set up an "L" just off the road. The short end of the "L" was the front. Monaco and Lobel had that. The rest of the squad, except me and Peewee, were on the long side of the "L" which paralleled the road. Me and Peewee were off to the rear of the squad line to watch in case the Congs came through the paddies behind the squad.

"Set your claymores out near that paddy dike," Gearhart said to me. The claymores sent fragments of steel in whatever direction you pointed them. They could be set off from a distance. "You see a patrol, you let them into the zone until their rear man gets on a line with that tree over there. You understand that?"

"Suppose it's more than a patrol," Peewee said. "By the time their rear man gets lined up with that tree you could have a hundred of them out there."

"That's okay," Gearhart said. "If it's that large a unit, we'll just open up on their rear and get as many casualties as possible. That'll make them back off until we can retreat. Charlie isn't the only one that can play guerrilla games out here."

He clicked his tongue at Peewee and left.

"What the fuck does that mean?" Peewee looked at me.

"I guess he means we'll hit and run, I guess."

"No, man, what he sucking his tongue at me fo'?" Peewee's eyes narrowed. "That man definitely need his ass kicked."

"I hope we get back to base to kick it," I said. "If somebody's spotted us out here, we got a world of trouble, or if it rains—"

"Rain don't bother me," Peewee said.

"If it starts raining again, how you going to see who's lined up with what damn tree?"

"I'm doing what Sarge said," Peewee said. "If I see a damn dog out here, I'm blasting away."

Johnson was in the center of the squad with the sixty. Brunner had the radio, and the rest of the squad were to one side or the other.

I had the claymores and three dozen grenades. The claymores were the baddest things going. They could be aimed to cover a target area and wasted anything within sixty meters in front of them.

"Peewee, you got your switchblade?"

"Damn straight," came the quick answer.

"Why do you always carry that thing?"

"Case this war get serious," Peewee said.

"Perry, you put out the claymores?" Walowick's voice.

"Damn!" I forgot them. "Cover me!"

I couldn't believe I hadn't put out the claymores. I started off as quickly as I could, keeping a low profile. The moon seemed to float in a curtain of fog over the field. I was praying for rain. I went out and started putting in the first claymore.

There was nothing to attach a tripwire to that looked like it would cover anything. Maybe I could have figured out something if I had stayed out a little longer, but I heard a double click coming from Peewee's direction. I set the mine for remote detonation and got back to Peewee as soon as I could.

"What's up?" I whispered.

"I just heard two clicks from somebody, so I passed them on," Peewee said.

Two clicks were our signal on the first go around. Then it would be one click, and then one and two. I made sure the grenade launcher was ready.

"Psst!"

Lobel was crawling toward us.

"What's up?"

"Gearhart wants to know if you set the claymores for remote?"

"Yeah. He saw me on the Scope?"

You could see almost as well with the Starlight Scope at night as you could see in the daylight.

"Yeah," Peewee said. "He got Brunner on the remote."

It got dark quickly. I was glad for the darkness and afraid of it. Whatever was terrible I thought about. Suppose I was hit, and they didn't notice it in the darkness? No, Peewee would notice it. I just knew he would. Peewee or Monaco. Brew came down the line and checked everybody.

The wet ground soon had my fatigues soaked. I was getting cold. I wondered if they had actually started sending outfits home. I thought about Hawaii.

The war was a thousand miles away. We could hear its rumbling, but all we were doing was waiting for the word to get back to the base. It wasn't our war, I told myself. Not tonight.

There was a faint odor that I recognized. Rotting bamboo. They used it along the paddy dikes for footing.

I tried to think of something to think about. I didn't want to think about Mama. If I thought about her I would get too involved. Same thing with Kenny. Same thing with Lieutenant Carroll. What to think about?

Faye Jackson. Light-skinned, sweet-voiced girl from the Virgin Islands. I think I could have had sex with her before I left. You couldn't tell about the girls from the Virgin Islands. I knew three, Faye and her sister and another girl named Darlene. They all swung their hips when they walked and filled my head with fantasies. I decided to have a fantasy about Faye.

Phloop! Somebody in the squad set off a flare. We were all exposed.

For a moment we all watched it in fascination. Then Monaco started yelling.

"Right side! Right side! Blow the mines!"

"No! No!" Sergeant Simpson jumped up and started waving his hands. I looked at where I had put the claymore and saw a figure moving away from it. "He turned it!"

The claymore went off and we all hit the dirt. I could hear bullets whining by me. I stuck my head up and saw a tracer come at me. I ducked down again. Peewee was firing. I could hear the sixty. I stuck my head up again, and the tracers kept coming at me. I ducked down again. I couldn't believe I wasn't hit.

Peewee took the launcher from me and was firing it, snatching grenades from my rucksack and off my suspenders. I shook my head, trying to clear it. I put my head up again, and the tracers were headed toward the center of the squad. But they were high. They had looked like they were coming toward me, but they were high. There were dozens of muzzle blasts. More than I had ever seen before. It looked like a whole company. We were outnumbered! My stomach cramped and my mouth went dry.

I got Peewee's sixteen and started firing. Peewee had his pistol out. He let off a shot near my head that burned my ear and made my whole head ring.

We fired and fired. I couldn't see a thing except an occasional muzzle blast, and they seemed to be moving away.

"Move it out! Move it out!" Sergeant Simpson was crawling along the ground. We started crawling after him.

"Go through the paddy!" Lieutenant Gearhart said, hoarsely.

"Hell, no!" Sergeant Simpson answered.

We followed Sergeant Simpson until we hit the wood line. He took the Starlight from Gearhart and looked back toward the paddies. Then he signaled us to follow him.

It was a good twenty minutes to the pickup zone if we were fast. We were fast.

Brunner called in the pickup chopper, and we waited and prayed. We didn't hear anything. Then we heard small arms fire to our left.

"They hearing noises in the dark," Sergeant Simpson said.

We waited; it started to rain. I thanked God for the rain. The moon drifted in and out of the clouds. I thought that maybe the Congs wouldn't look for us. The rain dripped down from the branches above us. I was cold, my knee ached, I was scared.

A half hour passed and no chopper.

We heard mortar rounds going off. They seemed close. We all held our breaths, but they landed off from us. The Congs didn't know where we were. They were throwing mortars into the field behind us.

Voices. Vietnamese. I couldn't tell how many, or where they came from. I had taped some of the grenades to my belt. Now I pulled some of the tape off and put it over my tags, sticking them to my chest.

"Where's the fucking chopper?" Monaco whispered.

"Maybe the rain's too hard," Lobel said.

I cursed the rain. Why the hell did it have to rain?

The voices were closer. We were bunched, too scared to move, to spread out.

A noise to the right.

We tried pressing against the trees, keeping our heads down. The moon came out partially. It was one Cong. He had his piece by his side. He looked around then put it down near a tree. He couldn't have been more than the distance from home plate to the pitcher's mound. Then he took his pants down, and squatted.

Lieutenant Gearhart stood and started toward the Cong. Monaco raised his rifle to cover Gearhart. For a few seconds I couldn't see Gearhart at all. Then I saw him just as the Cong saw him, but it was too late. Gearhart was on him. Monaco went toward them. By the time he got there, it was all over. Gearhart had wasted the Cong.

The chopper. We heard it, but we couldn't see it.

"Sweet Mother . . . Density One," Brunner spoke into the phone. "Can you spot yellow?"

Brunner got an affirmative answer, and Brew threw a yellow signal flare toward the clearing in front of us. It flared up briefly and died, but the chopper had seen it. It came down quickly and we started for it.

"Come on!"

Peewee was on first with Monaco on his back. There was firing from behind us. They hadn't spotted us yet. I got on the chopper and twisted to help the next guy on. It was Walowick. Walowick's piece went off and ricocheted around the inside of the chopper and got one of the crew.

"Asshole!" The pilot kicked Walowick as Brew and Johnson got on.

There was a scream. Not just a scream, but a sound that was like something awful and almost inhuman.

"Man down!"

The chopper machine guns raked the wood line.

"Lights!"

Simpson and Gearhart were going back. Monaco was out the door and I followed him. The chopper's guns were sweeping everything and I ran in a crouched position. The lights went on, and I saw Gearhart and Simpson helping one of the new guys. Simpson waved at the chopper and the lights went off. We got back into the chopper, and everybody grabbed something and held on tight as it pulled away.

"Who set the first flare off?" Monaco asked. "We got somebody here working for charlie?"

"It just . . . I made a mistake," Gearhart said.

"Don't be making no more mistakes, man, because I'll frag your ass in a hot damn minute!" Monaco spat on the ground.

"Where the medic? Where the medic?" Sergeant Simpson's voice was high and frantic. "Who the medic?"

"You just shot the fucking medic," the door gunner said.

"I'm okay." The medic was a long shadow in the dark interior of the chopper. I could just see flashes of his face as he started examining the wounded man. A moment later a red light came on. The medic looked deathly white with dark shadows under his eyes.

The wounded man screamed for a while, then begged for a while, then went back to screaming. We turned away from him, tried to shut him out of our minds.

The medic fumbled briefly with the wounded man's fatigues, then cut them away from his chest. It was Turner, the new guy from the South. His eyes were wild and his chest heaving. He started to vomit and clutch at the arms of the medic. The medic pushed his hands away. He sprinkled some powder on the wound and taped a square bandage to his chest. He patted him on the shoulder and gave him the thumbs-up sign.

"Anybody else hit?" He closed the fatigues.

"My arm's hurt." The other new guy.

The medic put a flashlight on the arm. It was swollen, probably broken. He looked at the guy's eyes, then put the flashlight out.

"You'll be okay," he said. Then he slumped backward.

"You okay, Smitty?" the door gunner asked him.

"Light shit, man," he said.

By the time we got to the camp, Turner was dead. We got some guys to first aid the medic and the other new guy and then the chopper took them away.

"We got to kick your lieutenant's ass," Peewee said when Simpson came into the hooch later.

"We'll see about him," Simpson said. "But we got something else to deal with, too. When that flare went up, Perry, you know what I seen?"

"What?"

"I seen with my own two eyes the charlie run up to that claymore you set, turn it around, and run before Monaco got him."

"Yeah?"

"Well, if he turned it around and it went off and it didn't get none of us, how did you have the damn thing facing to begin with?"

"Oh, shit."

Chapter 14

WHAT HAD HAPPENED? The squad had been in a firefight, and we had been almost overrun. For the first time since I reached Nam we had been in the middle of it. Turner had been killed. And not by some faceless enemy, some random shot from far away, but by an enemy I could see and hear. And what about me? I had stood trembling in fear and waiting, and had run in near panic for the choppers and hoped and prayed for a few minutes more of life. The war was not a long way from where we were; we were in the middle of it, and it was deeply within us.

We didn't talk about the wounded man or about Turner, who had died. I think we were glad that we hadn't known him better. Maybe, even, that if somebody had to die from the squad, it was better that it was a new guy. It was always better that it was someone else.

"Hey, everybody listen to this!" Monaco was in his shorts, sitting on his bed with the letter in his lap. " 'Dear Sonny, I have been thinking more and more about you every day. I know that you are a long way away, and have a lot on your mind and everything. But, Sonny, I wanted to ask you this. Will you marry me when you get home? Please think about it a lot, as I think you and I would make a nice couple. I got the idea while I was down at the mall on Route 440 yesterday. If you don't think you want to marry me, please don't put it in a letter. Just don't say anything and I will know. Yours, Julie.' "

"She pregnant?" Peewee asked.

"No, she just loves me, man," Monaco said. "This chick has been in love with me since before I even knew what love was."

"You going to marry her?" Walowick asked.

"I don't know, what do you guys think?"

"What she look like?" Peewee asked.

"She's five-two, maybe five-three," Monaco said. "Kind of fine, but she ain't really the foxy type, you know what I mean? She's an athlete, too. She played softball for St. Dominick's in Jersey City."

"We got to vote on it," Johnson said. "I vote against it."

"Why?" Monaco looked over at where Johnson was cleaning his machine gun.

"She a nice girl?"

"Yeah."

"Then why she want to marry you?" Johnson ran the swab through the barrel of his piece. "You ain't even got no job."

"I'll get a job when I get home," Monaco said. "You see these hands? These hands can do anything in the damn world. I can make stuff, I can fix stuff, I can do anything. Maybe I'll even be a cop or a fireman, something like that."

"What she do?" Johnson asked.

"She got a good job," Monaco said. "She works for Western Electric."

"I vote for the marriage," Peewee said.

"Marry her," Brunner said.

"Monaco, do you love this girl?" Brew said.

"Yeah," Monaco said. "I love the shit out of her."

"You go to the same church?"

"Yeah."

"Then Reverend Brew pronounces y'all man and wife," Peewee said.

"I think you should marry her." Brew spoke for himself but he looked like he didn't mind Peewee calling him Reverend Brew.

The final vote was five to two in favor of Monaco marrying the girl. Walowick didn't think we should vote at all, that it was a sacred decision. Johnson thought that Monaco should get a job first before he made plans to marry her, and Lobel said that he should wait until he got back to the World before he made a decision.

"You got to see her again," Lobel said. "I can't even think of seeing my father again and being the same guy I was when I left home. And if I'm not the same guy, he's not the same, either."

"He got to marry her," Peewee said. "We done voted on it now."

"Okay, you guys are all invited to the wedding. I'll plan it so that the wedding will be after the last guy in the squad leaves Nam."

"How about me?" Johnson asked. "You inviting me, too?"

"Yeah, all of us."

We started talking about weddings. Walowick said he hated weddings and funerals because all of his relatives got together and fought.

"First they dance and hug for about a half an hour," Walowick said. "Then they drink for two hours, then they fight."

"That's cause they white," Peewee said. "If they was black they could slip in some signifying along with the laughing and dancing and then skip right to the fighting before the drinking even started."

Jamal came over from HQ and said that Captain Stewart wanted to see me.

"About my profile?"

"What profile?"

"I'm not supposed to wear boots," I said.

"I don't know nothing about no profile," Jamal said. "I think it's about Gearhart."

I went over to HQ hut, and Captain Stewart was watching Phil Silvers on television.

"You want to tell me what happened last night?" he asked.

"About what?"

"Your patrol lost two men." He was drinking from a cup. I was about four feet away, but I could still smell it was booze. "One killed, one wounded."

"We were waiting for the chopper and—"

"Medevac? You waiting for a medevac?"

"No, sir, we hadn't been hit yet," I said. "We were hoping to get away without being hit."

"Lieutenant Gearhart mess up?"

"He shot off a flare, we got exposed," I said. "But I think they knew we were there."

"You're a good man, Perry," he said. "Why don't you see what you can do with this letter. Give it back to me before it's sent."

"Yes, sir."

"Let me ask you something else, too. How many of the enemy do you think were there?"

"Seemed like the place was crawling with them, sir."

"And you guys laid down a pretty good line of fire?"

"Best we could."

"How many you think we got?" he asked. "I know you can't be sure, just give me a number."

I didn't know what to say. A picture of the paddies came into my mind.

"Twenty? Thirty?"

"Maybe not that many, sir?"

"Maybe, but it could have been."

"It could have been, sir."

"Good enough," Captain Stewart nodded. "See what you can do with that letter."

I read the letter. It was Lieutenant Gearhart to Turner's folks. It said that it was his fault that their son was dead, and he was sorry. There was a lot of pain in the letter. It said that Turner was hit in the back after our position had been exposed to the enemy.

I rewrote the letter. I said that Turner was fighting off the enemy, trying to let the rest of us escape, when he was killed. Gearhart was in the mess hall, slumped over a cup of coffee when I found him and showed him the letter. He read it slowly, and shook his head.

"Captain Stewart told me to write it," I said.

"If I hadn't set off that damned flare. . . ." His voice trailed off.

"He still might have got it," I said. "You can't tell."

"You know, I never thought much about black people before I got into the army. I don't think I was prejudiced or anything—I just didn't think much about black people."

"Well, we're here," I said.

"I think I should let his parents know what happened," Gearhart said. "I don't want to be let off the hook."

"The letter I wrote," I said, "is going to sit better with his family. You might feel bad, like you need to get something off your chest, but don't drop it on his folks. It's going to be hard enough just having him dead."

He looked at me, then pushed the letter across the table. "Yeah, I guess you're right."

I wanted to be pissed at him. I wanted to think that he was crap because of what he said about black people. But the only thing I could think about was that I was glad it was Turner, and not me. It wasn't what I wanted to feel, or what I thought I was supposed to feel.

Jamal came by and showed me the body-count figures. Stewart had listed twenty-eight of the enemy as killed.

We got the word that the first hamlet we had worked on the pacification patrol was being harassed by the VC. A Major Leff was giving us the rundown about what was going on. He seemed to know what he was talking about.

"We've seen the infiltration over the last two months or so," he said. "We thought it was in response to the peace talks. They've been stalling in the talks, and the thinking was that they wanted to get into a favorable position before the talks get under way so they can claim more territory than they actually had. But now we're not sure. Intelligence reports a lot of movement just north of the DMZ and in Cambodia and Laos.

"The harassment of the hamlets and villages is part of the whole movement. If they can terrorize the villages, then they can create a hostile atmosphere in them for us. You have to remember that there's as much of a psychological war going on over here as there is a physical war. I have the feeling that we could win the real war and still lose the psychological war.

"What I want from you men is as much vigilance as possible until the situation is clearer. Your officers have all been briefed, but it's up to you guys to do the job. God be with each and every one of you."

An intelligence report said that our village was going to be hit by the VC at 1800 hours the next day. Eighteen hundred hours was a hell of a time. It would still be daylight, and if they showed up in the daylight, they would be demonstrating that they weren't afraid of us, that we couldn't protect the village.

Captain Stewart sent all of Alpha Company to the village. We were supposed to link up with a company from the 173rd Airborne. They had the 173rd hopping all over the place, and they were really doing a job, from what we heard. They were supposed to go in first and secure the village and then we were to protect it overnight or until it was decided that the VC in the area weren't a threat.

"This mess sounds good," Sergeant Simpson said. "We sit in the village until the truce and maybe we be sitting out the rest of the damn war."

Gearhart was quiet. Sergeant Simpson, who had been bumped up to top sergeant, was more or less leading the whole platoon.

As soon as I heard the sound of the chopper engines I had to pee. I found a tree and peed and then went toward our chopper. Walowick was already in the door of the Huey and gave me a hand up. My stomach was tight as I found a spot to squat.

"Get them weapons on safe!" Simpson called out.

Gearhart was checking gear. He had Peewee carrying a shotgun for the first time.

Peewee, Walowick, Sergeant Simpson, and Brunner were opposite me. Brew, Monaco, Johnson, Lobel, and Gearhart were on my side. We started off with the other choppers. I was scared again. Wasn't there ever going to be a time when I wasn't scared?

Monaco was reading the letter from his girl.

"You know," he said. "It takes balls for a chick to propose to a guy."

"Yeah."

I wondered if anybody else had the feeling of being scared. I looked over at Peewee. He was looking at a manual that had been on the floor of the Huey.

The artillery fire was more frightening now. Puffs of smoke around us meant that they were shooting at the chopper. If they hit us while we were in the air, we didn't have a chance.

Our Father who art in heaven, Hallowed be thy name . . . I thought the words. Would God think I was a hypocrite, praying every time I was scared?

A guy from the chopper crew turned, looked at us, and asked who Gearhart was. Gearhart raised his hand, and the chopper guy handed him the headset.

We all watched Gearhart, trying to figure out what was being said, trying to read his face, his gestures.

He nodded once, again. He handed back the headset.

"We're securing the village instead of the 173rd," he said.

"Where the hell's the 173rd?" Simpson asked.

Gearhart shrugged. Sergeant Simpson wiped his palm on his pants leg. I had heard him say to Peewee that Stewart had asked him to extend. He had less than two weeks left in Nam.

The chopper stopped in midair, then made a violent maneuver. I thought we were hit. I looked up at the chopper crew; they were calm. We picked up speed. There was a whine above the other sounds. Were we hit?

The chopper stopped again. The crew opened the door. The machine gunner started firing even before he looked out. The killers had arrived.

We jumped from the chopper. It was faster now. One foot on the ski, then down. Move. Move. The other squads in our company had landed at the same time. We moved toward the village. We could see fires up ahead.

"Spread left! Spread left! Keep your distances!" Sergeant Simpson barked orders.

We moved straight ahead until we came within forty meters of the village. Several of the huts were on fire; there were people milling about. Even from where we were we could hear the wailing.

"Let's move!" Gearhart went first.

We followed. The VC had already struck. There were bodies all around. Some twisted awkwardly, others looking as if they were just resting, their legs bent for comfort. We started checking out the huts. Empty except for the villagers. Some were hurt bad.

"Two platoon, on perimeter!" I turned and saw Captain Stewart. He must have been in one of the other choppers.

The village looked like the one they had constructed for practice at Fort Devens. Only here there were real people. An old woman stumbled into the open space in front of her hut. Her face was covered with blood. She fell. I went over to her, looked at her, and saw the bones in her face where the flesh had been cut away. Turn away.

There was a sense of panic in the air. We had our weapons ready. Sergeant Simpson was telling us not to kill the civilians. I didn't consciously want to kill anybody, anything. But I felt strange. The sight of all the bodies lying around, the smell of blood and puke and urine, made my head spin, pushed me to a different place. I wanted to fire my weapon, to destroy the nightmare around me. I didn't want it to be real, this much death, this much dying, this waste of human life. I didn't want it. I looked around until I found Monaco. There were tears in his eyes, but his mouth was twisted in hate and anguish and confusion. I turned away from Monaco's pain. It wasn't the time for comforting each other.

The heat from the burning huts was intense; the shimmering air creating phantom figures all around us.

There was a burst of fire behind me. I turned. Walowick was firing toward a steel drum that lay on its side. I reached for a grenade just as Simpson ran past me. He grabbed Walowick and threw both arms around him.

"Easy, man! Easy!"

I stood with the grenade in my hand. My hand on the pin, ready to pull it out and arm it. I watched Simpson holding Walowick. Around us, the other guys went on with their searching.

I looked back at Walowick. He had freaked out. He was breathing hard, and Sergeant Simpson was still holding him. Walowick was a rock, a fucking rock, and he had freaked out. I turned away. I was going to be cool, I had to be.

We went from hut to hut. They were all empty. Some guys formed a bucket brigade and started trying to put the fire out of the huts that were still burning.

The company was calming down. We bandaged some of the wounds. Captain Stewart called in some medevacs to take out the wounded Vietnamese.

We began coming down, but it wasn't easy: stepping around the bodies, turning away from the stench, from the reality of the death around us. I stopped for a moment to look at the bodies of two old men, their arms around each other in death. I saw them even after I turned away.

We could have killed as easily as we mourned. We could have burned as easily as we put out the fires. We were scared, on the very edge of control, at once trying to think of what was right to do and hating the scene about us.

I think, if Simpson hadn't been there, it would have been worse. Much worse. He calmed us down, brought us back to ourselves. He let us be human again; in all the inhumanity about us, he let us be human again.

"They messed up at least one person from each hut," Peewee said.

"They cut a baby's head off." Monaco spoke slowly. His face was dark, his mouth quivered between words. "How the hell do you kill a friggin' baby?"

"Like the major say," Peewee said. "They showin' the people we can't protect them so they might as well be on charlie's side. You know what this is like?"

"Like a trip to friggin' hell," Monaco said.

"No, man, this is like the projects in Chicago," Peewee said. "The police can't protect your ass from the muggers and shit, and the muggers don't protect your ass from the police."

"This ain't like Chicago," Monaco said. "They don't kill babies in no Chicago."

Stewart told us to go to each hut and pick out the wounded who looked most like they were going to live and get them ready for evacuation.

"If you see anybody who looks like a VC make a note of it," he said.

Body counts. I looked over at Simpson, but he was looking away.

I thought I remembered where An Linh lived and I went to look for her. I found her and an old woman who looked like she could have been her great-grandmother. They looked okay. When An Linh saw me, she started crying and tried to get behind the old woman. Okay, I could dig where she was coming from.

I looked around for An Linh's mother. I didn't see her. I tried once or twice to ask the old woman, but I couldn't get through to her. She was squatting against the wall, one thin brown arm raised, the hand over her forehead. She looked as if she might have been still in shock.

I was glad to see that An Linh was all right. It was what it was getting to be: hoping that what you liked, what you had seen before, remained whole.

I didn't have anything to give to An Linh, so I gave her a dollar. I knew there wasn't much she could do with it in the boonies, but I gave it to her anyway. As I left she followed me with her eyes, and I wondered what she saw.

The next hut looked empty. There were two bowls on the table. One still had some kind of food—it looked like a thick soup—in it. The VC must have caught them by surprise, in the middle of a meal, maybe saying grace.

There were pictures on a small wicker chest. I went to see them. A thin Vietnamese man in shirtsleeves stood squinting at the camera. On one side of him was a woman and on the other side a bicycle. He had both of his hands on the bicycle.

A click! Another!

I turned to look at the muzzle of a gun.

Click! Click!

I couldn't move. It was like a dream. I was watching it, but I couldn't move. It was a dream of my death. A gun was pointed at my chest. A small brown man was pumping the bolt frantically to get it to work.

Click! Click! Click!

He came at me and swung the butt of the rifle toward my head. I blocked it with my arm and backed away. He swung again and hit my shoulder, the rifle glancing up from my shoulder into the side of my face. I pulled the trigger of my rifle without lifting it. He went down on one knee. Then it was as if I were suddenly awake. I lifted the M-16 and started firing it in his face. I emptied the clip. I snatched another one from my belt, slammed it in, and fired that point-blank.

"Don't move!" I screamed at him. "Don't move!"

"Perry! Back away!"

Sergeant Simpson's voice snapped at me from the doorway.

"Back away, man!"

I backed away, keeping my rifle pointed at the VC. Sergeant Simpson went over to him. Then he lowered his rifle.

"He ain't in this war no more," he said.

By that time a couple of other guys had shown up. I thought my hands were bleeding, but I went to check out the VC before I put my piece down.

There was no face. Just an angry mass of red flesh where the face had been. Part of an eyeball dangled from one side of the head. At the top there were masses of different-colored flesh. The white parts were the worst. There was a tooth, a bit of skull. I turned away. I vomited.

My hands weren't bleeding. It was that much sweat, pouring down my arms and forearms and from my palms. I heard Sergeant Simpson tell Peewee to stay with me. Peewee put his arm around my waist and told me to come on. We left the hut and went to the next one. "They got some tea on the stove in there," Peewee said.

I went in with Peewee, then pulled myself together. I didn't want the tea. Maybe I was afraid of it. Peewee said that we should go outside and sit down. I said okay.

We had just left the hut when Peewee stopped and turned around.

"Wait a minute," he said. His voice was lower than usual, almost a rumble from his throat. He started back toward the hut.

I went after him. We walked into the hut, and he went over toward the corner. There was a rattan throw mat on the floor. One corner of it was around a bamboo pole that was about six feet high. Peewee aimed at the mat and fired twice.

"I just thought that could have been a breathing tube or somethin'," Peewee said.

I tried to move the mat with my foot. It didn't move. I looked around until I saw a piece of string. I tied it to the mat and went across the room.

"I'll jerk the string," I said. "You cover it."

I jerked it and the mat came up. Even from where we stood, we could see the body. He wasn't dead. Captain Stewart came in and asked what was going on. Peewee pointed toward the wounded Cong. Captain Stewart finished him off.

The company surrounded the hamlet. Captain Stewart called in evacuation helicopters. We loaded up the villagers who were still there. He didn't know how many more Congs were hiding in the huts, half buried under furniture or mats, but he wasn't going to risk any of us to find out. We moved the rest of the people out to the landing zone and burned the whole place down.

Two VC came out from one hut that we were burning. They had their hands up. A woman from the village went over and stabbed one in the side. He tried to get her knife away from her, and two guys lit him up. His body jerked around like a rag puppet being dragged by a dog.

I had killed a man. I thought about how he looked, how I had felt. I remembered looking down at him, the M-16 in my hands, my forearms aching from the tension of holding it. I remembered looking down at him and feeling my own face torn apart.

I thought of the other one, too. It was a nightmare. A nightmare of me crouching somewhere listening to the enemy above. Maybe they wouldn't see me, just take a shot to see if I was there.

The wounded were taken out first. Our squad was on perimeter patrol while others lifted the litters onto the choppers. The throaty sound of the mortars could still be heard, and the incoming fire was getting closer. They were calling in artillery to shut down the incoming mortars even though it was estimated that the mortars were almost on top of us.

The first choppers lifted off and the others started coming in. I couldn't believe they would come in with all the heat in the area, but they came. Great insects, angry and buzzing over the steaming jungle, ignoring the fact that every hostile in the area was trying to bring them down. Any direct hit would bring death to the entire crew, and they all had to know it, and still they came.

I looked over my shoulder at the choppers as they landed, blowing away the loose grass and debris on the ground. A glassine bandage wrapping danced across the area between the huts, flattened itself momentarily against the small, still body of a dead NVA soldier, and then flew off into the jungle.

The chopper crews. They were the stuff of heroes. Swooping from the skies like great heavenly birds gathering the angels who had fallen below.

When we got back to the compound, Peewee couldn't walk. He jumped from the chopper and his legs gave way under him. Johnson had to carry him to the hooch. They got him back to our hut, and Gearhart got a medic over.

"Get the fuck away from me," Peewee told the medic.

"Let him look at your legs, soldier." Captain Stewart was in our hooch.

"Ain't nothing wrong with my damn legs," Peewee said. "All I need is a cigarette."

Captain Stewart gave him a cigarette and he lit up.

The medic told Peewee again to relax while he took his pants off. Peewee took his own pants off. He was right, there wasn't anything wrong with his legs.

I laughed and Peewee laughed and we were all laughing. Then Peewee started coughing from the cigarette, and the medic gave him some water.

Stewart left after saying something about how good we had done.

Gearhart came over and talked with us for a while. Just small talk. He was shaken from what we had been through. Nobody got used to it. Good.

Brew's hand began to jerk and that scared him. We were all jumpy. It wasn't that we were hurt. It was just that we couldn't get down. We had been shooting and screaming and scared that somebody, that something, was going to kill us. We just couldn't get down that easily. It didn't stop when they blew the whistle. I didn't know if it would ever stop.

After a while Johnson noticed that we were all whispering. He laughed a quiet little laugh, and we all laughed about that.

"How the hell do you smoke a cigarette with half of it in your mouth?" Gearhart asked Peewee.

"You know what this is?" Peewee asked. "This is the first cigarette I've ever smoked."

Later we went to the recreation hooch and watched the news. It was all about President Johnson trying to get a bill passed to help the urban poor, and then something about the *Pueblo*, which had been taken over by the North Koreans. Then there was a big thing on the Super Bowl, and whether or not the Packers had a dynasty going. It wasn't real that people were thinking about things like that when all this shit was going on. It just wasn't real.

Sleeping didn't come hard; it didn't come at all. I was asleep, in a way, and yet I wasn't.

"Peewee?"

"What?"

"How you doing?"

"Okay, how you doing?"

"Okay," I said. "You know what happened today in the hut?"

"What?"

"That VC popped up from no damn where," I said. "First thing I heard was him trying to blow me away. His weapon didn't work. If it had, he would have got me, Peewee. He would have got me!"

I started crying, and Peewee got up and came to my bunk. He put his arms around me and held me until we both fell asleep.

We got word that we were moving again, some place near Tam Ky. The whole outfit was going, but Alpha was going first. Captain Stewart told us we were supposed to act as advisers to the ARVN troops. Nobody trusted him.

Lobel got a map and we figured out exactly where Tam Ky was and figured we didn't want to be there. The marines were at Chu Lai, which was pretty safe. They were also up north fighting their rear ends off. Tam Ky was being hit a lot, and Lobel figured that if the VC wanted to hit someplace near there, the ARVN base would be easier than the marines.

"You got too big a base for them to hit at Chu Lai," he said. "They're already fighting like crazy up north, so they hit the ARVNs at Tam Ky. It figures."

"Hey, Lobel?" Sergeant Simpson was packing up his gear and his personal supply of ammunition. He had all of these clips that he had checked round by round, and he was taking it all with him.

"You don't agree?" Lobel asked.

"Why don't you go back to your damn movies, because I only got eight days left and that's too damn short to be listening to your war theories."

Jamal came over to tell us that he was going to be with our squad from now on. He looked scared.

"You think you're man enough to go out with us?" Brunner said.

"No, I don't think so," Jamal said. "But they're sending me, anyway."

Mail call.

Brunner got a letter from his wife in Seattle. She was a waitress in a coffee shop down near the waterfront, and the coffee urn blew up. It burned her arm and her right leg, but it wasn't serious, she said. Brunner went out of his mind over it. He couldn't understand how a damn coffee urn could blow up.

I got a letter from Mama. She told me that Peewee wrote her and he seemed like the nicest boy. She wrote that she was glad that he and I were friends. I hoped she would get to meet him one day. I thought they would have got along just fine.

The thing was, I needed the people in the World to be okay, and to be the same as when I left them. I was holding on, now, and I needed something to hold on to. I had come into the army at seventeen, and I remembered who I was, and who I was had been a kid. The war hadn't meant anything to me then, maybe because I had never gone through anything like it before. All I had thought about combat was that I would never die, that our side would win, and that we would all go home somehow satisfied. And now all the dying around me, and all the killing, was making me look at myself again, hoping to find something more than the kid I was. Maybe I could sift through the kid's stuff, the basketball, the Harlem streets, and find the man I would be. I hoped I did it before I got killed.

The rain came down in buckets. We watched a newscast that said that a guy had got a heart transplant. They had actually taken the heart out of one guy who had been in an accident and put it in another guy, a dentist. Brunner and Walowick thought it was cool, but Peewee didn't believe it, and Monaco wondered how the guy lived between the time they took his heart out and the time they put the other guy's in.

"The whole thing is going to be in *Life* next week," Brew said. "You wait and see."

I dreamt about being in the hut, and hearing the VC trying to get his rifle to work. In the dream he smiled as he worked it and I stood there crying, knowing that eventually it would work and that he would kill me. He would blow my face away the way I had blown his away in real life. I kept waking up in a kind of terror and then falling to sleep again and having the same dream.

In the morning we were roused early for the trip. Peewee was messed up, really messed up.

"What the hell happened to you?" I asked. He looked like he had been in a fight and been beaten up bad. His whole face was puffed up badly. His upper lip was so swollen he could hardly get his mouth shut.

"Nothing," he said.

Gearhart had heard about how Peewee looked, and he came over and asked what had happened. Peewee said nothing had happened, and turned away.

"Gates, can you make it to the new base?" Gearhart asked.

"Yuh," Peewee said. He could hardly talk. He kept packing his gear.

"Look man, we got to know what happened." Sergeant Simpson said. "We a squad, we ain't no strangers."

"You know that stuff I got from that woman?" Peewee said.

"What?"

"That hair stuff?"

"Yeah?"

"I put some on my lip to grow me a mustache," he said. He put his head down. "Guess it don't work too cool."

Chapter 15

I STARTED WRITING A LETTER to Kenny. At first I thought I wanted to tell him about the war, about how I felt about the fighting. Then I knew I wanted to tell him about my killing the Cong. I started the letter off really cool, hoping that he was okay and taking care of Mama, stuff like that. Then I told him I wanted to tell him about a typical day that I had here in the Nam. Then I changed it to special day instead of typical.

Then I tried to tell him about the killing.

I started off saying that war was about destroying the enemy. Then I remembered about the news guys asking us why we were fighting in Vietnam. It wasn't the same. Saying that you were trying to stop Communism or stuff like that was different than shooting somebody. It was different than being scared and looking at somebody who was maybe as scared as you were.

In a way I wanted him to know about me killing the Cong. In another way I didn't. I wanted him to think I was a good soldier. Being a good soldier meant doing your job. For the guys in the squad, it meant killing the enemy. Before I went into the army I had thought about being a writer. Teachers said I used words well. But writing that I had done a good job killing just didn't work.

"Yo, Peewee?"

"What's shakin'?"

"You know that Cong I killed?"

"Yeah?"

"How come I killed him?"

"'Cause he was gonna kill you ass if you didn't kill his," Peewee said.

"That's the only reason?"

"Ain't that good enough?"

"I don't know, is it?"

"It better be till you get your ass home," Peewee said.

"Man, this ain't even Boonieville," Sergeant Simpson said, "This is the *suburbs* of Boonieville." He threw his gear on the small folding cot in the hooch that was our new home outside of Tam Ky.

"You should have known this place was going to be garbage," Brunner said. "We were right outside of Chu Lai and that wasn't that hot."

Brunner was right. The base at Chu Lai was almost like the old section of Fort Devens. The barracks were neat and clean, and there was even a post exchange. Where we had been bivouacked, west of Chu Lai, had been cool, too. Our new area was something else again.

It looked like the other firebases, with barbed wire and mine fields around it. But I didn't see anything that looked like a major generator, which meant that it was going to be dark as hell at night. The hooches were half underground and didn't look as if they could take much in the way of direct hits. If we got incoming mortar, we would have to roll out of the hooches into the sandbag-lined trenches around them. I didn't like it at all.

"The streams around here are a little murky," Lieutenant Gearhart said. "Make sure you take your malaria pills."

"I'm taking every kind of pill I can get my hands on," Peewee said. "I'd take some birth control pills if I could find me some."

There were a few guys there from a boat outfit, the 159th Transportation Battalion. We asked them what they were doing so far away from the water if they were supposed to be boat people. They said that they were teaching the ARVN troops, the Vietnamese friendlies, how to maintain the engines on their landing craft.

"They any good?" I asked.

"They don't seem to get the hang of how we do things," a sergeant said. "They don't expect stuff to work, so when it doesn't, it's no big deal. They don't believe in maintenance at all."

What it looked like to me was that we were going to beat down the Congs and then turn over the last part of the effort to the ARVN troops. That sounded just okay with me.

We went on night patrol. Night patrol from our last base was scary. Night patrol from the new base was something else.

We were picked up at 2000 hours. The LZ was in tall grass, which made us all feel uneasy. Somebody said that an ARVN captain had selected it. The only thing I really knew about ARVNs was what Sergeant Simpson said, and that wasn't good. He said that some units were good, as good as anything we had to offer. Other units were crap, and would bug out on you in a moment.

What we were supposed to be doing was what they called an interdiction number. Which meant that we were supposed to be cutting off the routes the Congs could use to cut off First Corps from the rest of the war. The area just north of Chu Lai was what they seemed to want.

The Congs we were after had been probing along our defenses, looking for soft spots. They would set up a mortar attack from somewhere within the jungle, raise a little hell, and then split before anyone could get to them. HQ figured the Cong operation to be a squad-sized unit. We had two squads from Alpha Company and two ARVN squads to clear them out.

What we were supposed to do was to set up an ambush on what we figured to be their route.

We hit the LZ at 2035 hours. We went in first and cleared the LZ, and then the ARVNs came in. We had four squads, but only twenty-five, maybe twenty-six, guys. All of the squads were short except ours. Simpson said that they kept our squad up to par because the battalion commander liked him.

Near Chu Lai the patrols had been serious, but away from Chu Lai, in the deep boonies, they were dead serious. There was no talking from the time we hit the LZ.

Once we hit the wood line the ARVNs broke off from us and went ahead. We were supposed to set up a company-sized "L" trap. Sergeant Simpson didn't like it because it was too big, and we didn't know how the ARVNs would react. I just hoped and prayed we weren't walking into one.

Walowick was on point. Brunner was in the rear and Johnson was left flank. I was in the middle again, right behind Brew. In the darkness you couldn't keep the proper distance. You were always afraid that you would lose the dude in front of you, that you would suddenly find yourself walking through the woods alone. We had signals, but they didn't help when it was really dark.

"Don't think about anything," Sergeant Simpson had said. "Don't think about your mama, don't think about your girlfriends, nothing. Just look around and be alert."

Sergeant Simpson had six days left in Nam. Brunner said that Captain Stewart had been on his case to extend for three months. The squad said that we would try to watch out for him, but we knew it didn't mean much.

I looked around. I couldn't see anything. I listened for Brew's footsteps. He sounded like a cat, moving through the night. I heard the cat.

We reached the ambush site. The two ARVN squads formed the short end of the "L." The two Alpha Company squads were the long side. Lieutenant Gearhart set out the claymores. He had the detonating wires, too. We waited.

I was lying on my stomach. I tried not to think of anything that would get my mind off of what I was doing. I tried to control my imagination, to keep the shadows from becoming things they weren't.

Something crawled across my wrist. I jumped, and just managed not to cry out. It was too dark to see what it was, but it was still there. I tried to brush it off, but it didn't move. I felt it. I thought it was a finger. For a crazy-ass minute I thought there was a Cong behind me and he had just dropped a finger on me. I grabbed it and squeezed. It was soft and mushy. My heart was pounding. Every Cong in the world had to hear it. I wanted to turn over and look behind me. I wanted to cry.

I remembered something. It was a picture of a guy with his hands on a bicycle. It was the picture that I had seen in the hut. I tried to picture the guy's face that I had shot. Was it the same guy? Could it have been his hut? I wondered what he would have said if he had killed me. Would he have said that he was trying to stop the spread of whatever the hell he thought I stood for? What did he think I stood for? What did the bullets feel like going into his face?

Don't think. Stop thinking. Stop. Look ahead of me. Don't think, don't daydream. Look.

Quiet. Suppose everybody had left except me? I didn't hear anybody. Why was I so afraid of being left alone? It was possible. I knew it was possible.

Look.

I couldn't see anything. Once in a while the moon would be bright enough to cast a shadow. Somebody had the Starlight Scope. Probably Sergeant Simpson. In the moonlight I looked at my wrist. A fucking leech. I got my bayonet out and cut it in half, then scraped it off my wrist. It stung like crazy.

Ignore it. Sure.

We waited for an hour that seemed like four hours. We waited for another hour that seemed like four more hours.

Voices. Charlie. They were supposed to be so quiet, so cool. I moved my hand up to the trigger.

The first charlies were in the killing zone. I waited. I wanted to pull the trigger. I knew they were passing the claymores. I heard them talking. My hands were sweating. We had the upper hand. We had them in the killing zone. I was waiting for Lieutenant Gearhart to open up with the claymores. The claymores would waste them. They were terrible.

Nothing happened. The charlies were going through the killing zone and out the other side. What the hell had happened? Where the hell was the squad? I heard the charlies go off into the night. They must have passed the ARVNs, too.

"What the fuck happened?" Peewee's voice in the darkness.

"Shut up!" Gearhart.

Peewee mumbled something to himself, and was quiet.

Okay, it was cool. We weren't going to do the ambush. We would wait until morning and then split. Maybe Gearhart was scared. He had made a mistake before, and we had lost a man and had one wounded. Now he was playing it safe.

I relaxed. My wrist stung. It felt like the leech was still on it.

Voices. More charlies. They were talking again, taking a stroll through the woods. They entered the killing zone. I kept telling myself not to think about the wrist, and I kept thinking about it.

The voices continued. How many of them were there? The nearly full moon drifted from behind some clouds, and I got my head down. I looked up. There were the charlies. Only instead of the four or five I had imagined there seemed to be an endless line.

I opened my mouth so I could breathe quietly. I had to pee.

Voices behind us. The woods were crawling with charlies.

Our Father, who art in Heaven, Hallowed be thy name. . . .

Don't think. Don't even think of God. I thought. I thought of all the good things I had done in my life. I didn't deserve to die. I didn't want to die.

The voices went on for another ten minutes. If we had sprung the ambush, we wouldn't have stood a chance.

"Let's get out of here!" Brunner.

"Shut up!" Gearhart.

Quiet. More voices. They kept coming.

It lasted nearly fifteen minutes. It was only fifteen minutes, but it seemed like an eternity. Still, we didn't move. A half hour passed after we heard the last one move, before I heard Gearhart calling us together. Simpson went out and got the claymores and we started going back, careful not to take the route the charlies had taken in case they mined it.

Jamal was shaking so badly I wondered how he could have stayed still all that time.

"How you doing, man?"

He didn't answer. I looked at him and he was crying. I made a note to tell Simpson. If Jamal was that shaky, he was going to get us all killed.

There had been too many charlies to pull an ambush; they would have wiped us out. I wasn't sure how many there had been, and I thought that Gearhart was only estimating.

"There had to be at least a battalion." Gearhart was on the radio as soon as we got back to the base.

Peewee was trying to burn what was left of the leech off my wrist with a cigarette. The damn thing was disgusting.

"What did they say?" Sergeant Simpson looked at Gearhart when he put down the phone.

"They wanted to know if we saw any identifying patches on them," Gearhart said.

"How did you figure there were so many?" Walowick asked.

"They were talking too much," Gearhart said. "Too confident."

If it had been me, I thought, I would have screwed it up. I would have.

Sergeant Simpson extended for thirty days. Nobody wanted to look at him, nobody wanted to see him. It was as if he had decided to die. That's what we all felt. They gave him another stripe. He was a Master Sergeant. Big deal.

Most of the guys that extended in Nam did it for the rank, but some had other things in their heads. It was as if the idea that any moment they could be killed excited them. I knew a kid on 119th Street off Eighth Avenue like that. He had run with a gang and was always in a knife fight or something. When he finally got killed—gunned down outside the Showcase Bar on 125th—nobody went to his funeral.

We could tell the action was picking up all over. The air strikes were picking up. The rumble of the big guns started as soon as it was light enough to see and sometimes lasted far into the night. Most of it was outgoing, but not all of it. Once in a while a mortar shell would land near the base, and then we would all run out into the trench built in front of the tent.

We reinforced that sucker with some two-by-fours that Lieutenant Gearhart had had flown all the way up from Saigon. Most of the patrols going out were Vietnamese, and Johnson said that he didn't think most of them were really patrolling.

"They ain't out a kilometer before you hear popping," he said.

He was right. Half the time the ARVNs would go out, especially at night, they would be back within a half hour saying that they had been hit by a company of charlies. Then we would go on alert and send out a few rounds and spend the rest of the night in the trenches.

I won thirty dollars in the football pool. I had Green Bay and a point total of forty-eight, which was closer than anybody else. I sent the money to Mama.

I got a rash or something on my feet. Peewee wanted me to put some of the salve he had bought from the old woman on them but I said no. I remembered how his face had broken out. At the new camp we had been working more in higher ground, and I thought the small cracks between my toes would heal. They didn't. A medic from Tam Ky came by with the pills and gave me some powder for my feet and told me to keep them as dry as possible.

"Your feet get messed up and you're going to end up with a profile."

Yeah, thanks.

Lobel damned near dragged Jamal into our hooch.

"Go ahead, tell him what you heard," Lobel said to Jamal.

"Sergeant Simpson and Captain Stewart got into a fight," Jamal said. "Captain Stewart told Sergeant Simpson that if he didn't shut up and get out he was going to bust him down to private."

"Who the hell does he think he is?" Brunner asked.

"What they fighting about?" Johnson asked.

Brunner got up and walked away.

"He found out that Captain Stewart is volunteering Alpha Company all over the place. He asked him what he's doing that for, and Captain Stewart said that if he didn't want to fight he shouldn't have extended."

What Jamal said went down hard. We didn't mind doing our part because it had to be done, even though we always didn't have answers to why we were doing it.

But nobody wanted to go out and risk their lives so that Stewart could make major.

The mortars started coming in more regularly over the next three days, and the ARVN patrols started staying out shorter and shorter times. We didn't go out for almost a week, but when I saw Captain Stewart talking to Gearhart I figured something was up. I was right. We were headed for another patrol.

The "patrol" turned out to be a company-sized sweep. We were supposed to take off at 1000 hours. At 0930 hours three Hueys, escorted by two Spookies, huge C-47 gunships, came in. It was the rest of our outfit.

Lobel wrote a long letter to his father, telling him that he was sorry about joining the army. He put it in his gear at the hooch before we went on the sweep.

"You really sorry?" I asked.

He shrugged, and I dropped it.

I wondered how my father would take it if I got killed. I told myself that I didn't care. The more I thought of it as we waited to load up, the more I began to understand how Lobel felt. Having people care about you was probably the only thing that made any of it right. Having them not care made your whole life wrong.

The company hit the landing zone at 1117 hours. Some squads from Second Platoon went in first. They didn't get any fire, but they looked confused on the ground. We soon got the word that there were punji sticks in the tall grass we were jumping down into. They were sharpened sticks stuck into the ground or in pits. Usually they were covered with shit, either human shit or animal shit, so when they stuck you, you got infected. No one in our squad hit the punji sticks as we landed, and we started moving out toward the wood line. There was no resistance.

We got into the wood line and formed a skirmish line. Monaco spotted a mine symbol. He called Gearhart over and showed it to him. There were three leaves rolled into the shape of a triangle at the base of a tree. We looked around for the mine but didn't see one. Then Johnson found it. It was one of our C ration cans rigged to a limb that you would have to push out of your way if you were over six feet tall.

Monaco blew the mine, and we went on.

"Look for shells, burnt leaves, anything that says charlie's been here," Captain Stewart said.

"We found the damn mine," Peewee muttered to me. "The tooth fairy didn't leave that sucker."

The wood led up a hill, and the grass was getting taller. I hated it. You couldn't see through the grass and you were scared shit of stepping on a mine.

"Keep your distance! Keep your distance!" Gearhart.

We were going uphill. You had to lean forward and sometimes catch at brushes with your hands. You didn't want to touch anything that you didn't have to, or pull on anything.

I went through a brush and nearly had a heart attack when the thick branches hooked my M-16 and jerked it out of my hand. I turned and saw Peewee. He disentangled my piece and handed it to me. He smiled.

We got a quarter of the way up the hill when a guy in the next squad called out.

"What is it?" Stewart called to him.

"Looks like a spider hole!" It was a corporal, tall, sleeves rolled up, tattoed arms.

Stewart stopped the company and a couple of men approached the hole. A spider hole is a hole dug in the ground that's big enough for one man, sometimes two; but sometimes they're disguised and there's a tunnel entrance in back of them. The corporal fired a few rounds into the hole and then looked in.

"Empty!" he said.

"Look around for more!" Stewart called out. "And be alert!"

Just then the whole damn mountainside opened up. The tall corporal spun around from the impact of the bullets and came flying forward.

"Up the hill! Up the hill!" Gearhart was on his knees and pointing up.

Simpson was firing, and I opened up. We started scrambling up the hill toward where the fire was coming from. I heard the rounds whining and buzzing around my head like angry bees. I was doubled up, firing from a crouched position.

I moved against a tree and aimed at where I thought they had to be.

"This way! This way!" Gearhart was going up first.

I found myself going up after him. Johnson and Lobel were on our left. Johnson got down and started spreading fire. Brew was feeding him. I kept firing, moving under Johnson's cover. We hit a ledge, and I almost fell over a dead Cong.

When we got to the ledge, we were less than thirty meters from the top of the hill. Gearhart had got a M-79 from some place and was shooting grenades to the top. Some guys threw some grenades over the top and Johnson and another sixty raked it over pretty good.

We made the last thirty meters in less than a minute, with everybody throwing grenades over the top. Stewart was on the phone. The choppers and the jets would be in the air already.

We got to the top, and there were three more Congs on the ground. One was only wounded. He was half-sitting up, and I think he was trying to get his hands up. Captain Stewart opened up on him, and his head snapped back and his arms flailed for a moment even after I knew he was dead.

We got to the crest of the hill and started firing down the other side. We didn't see any Congs, but they had to be there somewhere. The fact that we had found four bodies was a miracle.

"Incoming!"

I dove to the ground and bounced up to my knees as the blast hit. I tried to stand, but my legs went out from under me. What the hell was happening?

"To the left! That way! That way!" I heard Gearhart calling out. I saw Johnson; he had a rag or something around the sixty and was shooting it from the hip.

Another round hit, and I saw Johnson go to his knees.

"O Jesus! O Jesus!"

I looked around. It was Brew. There was blood gushing out from the top of his leg. I could see the bone.

"Medic! Medic!"

I tried to get over to Brew. My head was spinning. I thought I was too scared to move. I tried to force myself to move, then I looked down and saw that my pants were ripped open. I saw the flesh already starting to swell. I was hit.

"O Mama, O Mama, please don't let me die!"

"Get the choppers in here!"

I pushed myself over on my stomach and looked for my rifle. The next round lifted me, and I felt something hit my wrist and tear into the flesh, I felt as if somebody was putting a hot iron on my wrist, then dragging it through the flesh.

"O God! O God! O God, please!"

"Back off the fucking hill, they got it zeroed!"

I could get one eye open. I saw Gearhart backing down the hill. He was firing the grenade launcher and looking around. I felt somebody grab me by the collar. I couldn't turn around. My leg twisted under me and there was pain. But more than the pain in my leg, more than my wrist dangling in front of me, was the thought that I was going to die. I was going to die.

"O God. O God, please. Please."

Chapter 16

I WAS TREMBLING. I didn't feel any pain, but I couldn't move. There was stuff going on all around me. I saw guys moving past me. Blurs. I heard cursing. The sounds of automatic weapons seemed to be a rippling that swelled from somewhere.

What was going on? How long was it going to last? What had we run into?

"Howya doing, man? Howya doing?" Jamal was over me. He was opening my shirt.

"I got hit," I said. I couldn't see him too clearly.

"Yeah, I know." He was looking at my chest. He lifted me and looked at my back. Then he laid me back down and started looking at my groin. I just kept looking into his face. Guys were still moving around. I tried to lift my head, but I couldn't. I couldn't because I was too scared to move.

Breathing was hard. I was panting. I wondered if I had been hit in the chest. I couldn't tell.

"Watch the ridge line! Watch the ridge line!" Gearhart's voice.

Everything began to fade except the sound of the sixty. My eyes were closed and I opened them. Jamal moved my leg.

"Ooh!" There was pain. It wasn't too bad, but why couldn't I move? Why couldn't I breathe?

Now there were people over me. Things were getting clearer. I looked up and saw Peewee. His helmet was on the back of his head, his rifle under his arm. He looked down at me. I tried to say something to him, but nothing came out.

Choppers overhead. They were laying down a line of fire. They came down, then back up again. Two other guys were near me. I closed my eyes, and one of them pushed them back open and looked at them. Then he let them close. I opened them again. They were talking to Jamal. One of them was wiping my arm. I tried to turn to see what he was doing, and the other one pushed me back down.

More faces over me; I was being lifted. I was on a litter. My throat was dry.

"How you doing, soldier boy?" A clean-looking dude with a southern accent.

"Okay," I said.

"You gonna stay that way, too," he said.

He patted me on the shoulder. I was on the chopper. The chopper was different now. The straps on the side were huge, the handles were further out from the wall. There was more noise, even, than before.

Smells. Smells of dirt, of sweat, of funk. The smell of blood that I remembered from Jenkins. Bodies gathered around me. The chopper jolted up. There were guys kneeling near me, their backs toward me. I could see their backs.

"I still got a pulse!"

"You ain't got no pulse, man."

"I got a pulse . . . no, maybe not."

There were boots and mud in my face as a guy shifted position. They were moving up and down next to me. I tried lifting my head to see what they were doing. My head swam. I looked between the guys working on somebody next to me. It was Brew. A guy was bent over him, giving him mouth to mouth.

I turned away. There was something over me, it was shining. I thought I was going to pass out. Brew's arm came from between the two guys working on him. I took his hand. It was limp. I squeezed it and I thought that he squeezed back.

"Keep pressure on the wound!"

"It's not helping! It's too open!"

"Just keep the pressure."

"Too many places, we got to try to keep putting it in."

"Okay! Okay! You keep looking! How's the other one?"

The boots scraped against my shoulder as they shifted position.

"Looks like shock, maybe a concussion."

"He breathing?"

A face over mine, lifting my neck, a mouth over mine blowing air into me. I was a balloon, the air pushed into my chest. I gasped.

"He's breathing!"

"Watch him!"

"See if the legs are swelling."

As they started probing my legs, I turned to see Brew again. There were tubes. A medic had what looked like the thing you use to take baby bottles out of hot water. He kept moving it toward Brew's stomach.

The breathing was terrible. Brew's breathing, sucking air. I looked at his face. He wasn't moving. His mouth was closed. Where was the breathing coming from?

The helicopter's engines whined. The medic bent over Brew.

"I got nothing, man! I got nothing."

"Okay! That's it!"

The medic turned to me quickly. He started wiping my face. The corners of my mouth.

"How you doing, big guy?"

I nodded.

"You play basketball?"

Beyond the medic's shoulder I could see them covering Brew.

The medic was checking the bag above me. I tried to move so I could see what they were doing with Brew. The medic saw me. He moved into my line of vision.

"You gonna be okay," he said. "You just got a little concussion, a little steel, a little dirt, the whole thing."

I heard the zipper. I didn't have to see it. I heard the zipper. The medic took my hand. He squeezed it. Then he took the other one and squeezed that one. Then he started on my legs.

"Perry! Perry!"

The voice came to me from a long way away.

"Come on, Perry, wake up, man!"

I opened my eyes. A tall, dark-skinned brother with shades was standing over me. My mouth was dry. I tried to look around. There was a banner on the wall. It read "That Others May Live."

"Where am I?"

"In good hands, my man," the guy said. "You got to pee now."

"Pee?"

"Yeah, that's the routine. You wake up, and we got to bring the thing around so you can get rid of some of the fluids, dig it? Just relax, and I'll take care of it for you."

I started to say something about peeing for myself but then I saw that both of my arms were bandaged. The guy pulled back the sheets and held me while I tried to urinate. At first I couldn't, then I managed a little.

"What happened?"

"When you remember from?"

"I was just inside the wood line . . ." I said.

"I don't know about that part," the brother said. "All I know is that you lucky in a way, and you ain't lucky in a way. You lucky cause you ain't hurt that bad. Then you ain't lucky because you ain't hurt bad enough to go back to the World."

"Where'd I get hit?"

"You had *titi* shrapnel in your side, in your left leg, and a few splinters in your groin. No big thing. You had a bullet wound on your wrist but that just did barely chip your wrist. And you had a concussion. If anything will get you back to the World, it's the concussion. Get what I mean?"

He left.

The right hand was bandaged, and the left hand—which I thought was bandaged—just had an IV stuck in it. Some guys in bathrobes saw me awake and came over.

"How you doing?"

"Okay, I guess."

"Yeah, just take it easy," one guy said; he had sergeant's stripes on his bathrobe. "Where you coming from?"

"I don't know, the valley west of Tam Ky, I think."

"They catching hell up there. They say charlie riding hogs up around Quang Tri."

"Hogs?"

"Tanks, man."

"Really?"

"Where the hell are the tanks coming from?"

"From the north through Cambodia, is the word," he said. "Things are definitely getting heavy."

I thought about the rumors of peace by the end of the holidays. I made myself hope that peace was still on the way.

The medical facility was like heaven. We got to eat good, we went to movies, the day room was cool. Best of all, the doctor said that none of my wounds were bad.

"You had a bad bruise of your breastbone." The guy's name tag read "Haveson." He smiled as he talked, like he enjoyed being a doctor. "Could have been hit by something or could have been just the blast. You were lucky."

Lucky.

They had a recording of a bugle that played in the morning. Everybody was shined and sharp. I hadn't realized that I wasn't until I saw the personnel around the hospital. They even had GIs tending to flowers around some of the barracks and some doing the same kinds of details they would have been doing back in Devens or any stateside base. In the mess hall they had Vietnamese doing KP.

The ward was full of guys. Some were bandaged nearly from head to feet. Some had big lumps of bandage and tape where limbs used to be.

One guy was on a kind of spit. He had been burned really bad, and they came in and turned him every two hours.

Another guy, his name was Joe Derby, asked me to read to him. He wore dark glasses. There were scars, bad scars on his body. He had some books and asked me to read anything I found interesting. The books were cool. I had read one of them, *Platero and I*, in high school. The other books were by T. S. Eliot and Steinbeck.

"Your folks send you these books?" I asked.

"My mom," he said. "I think she has ambition for me."

"What happened to you?"

"We were in a convoy going to Dak To from Kontum. A couple of trucks up front got hit with mines. They set them off from the side of the road. We stopped and then we got hit with everything at the same time. I was trying to get behind a truck when it was hit by a mortar."

"Oh."

"I remember going up, but I don't remember coming down."

"Where you from?"

"Las Vegas."

I didn't ask him about his eyes. I didn't want to know. I read to him from the Jiminez, a small story about what a village looked like on a Sunday morning when everyone had gone to a bullfight. It was a simple story, and it gave you a sense of the author being at peace with the world. Once, when I looked up, I saw that he was crying. I kept on reading.

I wrote Mama a letter. I tried to make it funny. I told her that I had been hit in the leg and the wrist and now I was laying up getting fat. I told her that getting fat was my biggest problem.

I thought of writing her a real letter, but I didn't have anything on my mind that I wanted her to know. I didn't want to say how afraid of dying I had been. I didn't want to say that I had a feeling that I wouldn't get back home.

Brew. I thought about Brew a lot. I felt so sorry for him. I remembered laying on the chopper next to him. I remembered feeling his hand. I wondered if he had felt mine. I thought about his praying and had to push him from my mind.

They moved me from one room in the hospital to a recovery ward. In the new ward there were a lot of guys playing cards, playing dominoes. A spec four asked me if I wanted to play poker. I shook my head no.

"He a boonies rat," a guy said. "You know they ain't right for two or three weeks."

"Yeah?" The spec four looked me up and down. "Maybe he can play later."

On the way to the PX an officer stopped me and asked me why I was out of uniform. The uniform he wore had creases ironed into the shirt. Everything about him was polish and crease. He wanted to know what outfit I was with, and—when he found out I was in the hospital—how long I had been there. He was challenging me, daring me to say something wrong. When he told me I could go on to the PX, I turned around and started back to the hospital. He said he thought I was going to the PX. I told him I had lost my appetite.

"Hey, good-looking!"

I was half asleep. I saw the name tag first, it read "Duncan." It was the nurse I had come to Nam with.

"How you doing?"

"I'm doing okay," she said, sitting on the side of he bed. "How you doing?"

"Okay," I answered. My mouth was dry, and I took some water from the table near the bed.

"I saw your chart," she said. "I was looking in on another guy when I saw you sleeping and thought I recognized you. You been out in the boonies much?"

"Long enough to think this is heaven," I said.

"Sometimes I feel like I would rather be out there myself," she said. "I guess that's stupid, right?"

"Hey, I'm glad to see you," I said. "I'm just a little slow or something."

"Don't sweat it," she said. "You get hurt and it makes you confused. I've seen it a lot of times."

"You been here long?"

"Just transferred in when things started picking up during the Tet," she said.

"How's it going for you? Judy? Right?"

"Right. It's going okay, I guess. Different than I thought it was going to be."

"Different?"

"Well, when I first talked to you in Anchorage and we were headed this way, I imagined myself rushing around and fixing up neat little bullet holes and giving out peppermints. That's not the way it is. You see that."

"Yeah."

"Look, I have to see some other guys. You take care of yourself, Perry. Perry, what's your first name?"

"Richie."

"Richie, you take care of yourself."

She kissed me and left. A couple of guys made comments about her kissing me. One asked me if I was getting over with her. I shrugged him off without answering. He mumbled something about guys from the boonies being strange.

Maybe they were right. I had felt awkward talking to Judy. I was glad to see her, but I couldn't talk to her. The words didn't have the right proportion somehow. There was this feeling that everything I was going to say was either too loud or too strange for a world in which people did normal things.

I thought about Judy. She had seemed so upbeat on the plane. She had come over to me and started talking. Now she seemed tired, sad. I hoped she would be okay.

I cried for Brew. Sometimes, even when I wasn't thinking about him, or at least when I didn't know I was thinking of him, I would find myself crying. And when the tears came, I thought about Brew and the sound the zipper made in the chopper.

Days went by. *Stars and Stripes* had a story about the *Pueblo*, and some guys were talking about the possibility of the U.S. getting involved with Korea again.

The chaplain and a colonel came in and talked to a bunch of us. The chaplain said that everything we did we did for the highest reasons that men knew.

"You are defending freedom," he said. "You are defending the freedom of Americans and of the South Vietnamese. Your acts of heroism and courage are celebrations of life, and all America thanks you."

Then the colonel gave out Purple Hearts to the guys who didn't already have them. I decided to send my medal for being wounded in action to Kenny.

I wrote to Kenny again. I told him that I had read about the garbage strike in New York. I told him that when I got back to the World we would do a lot of things together. Maybe we would go downtown, to the museums. Kenny liked museums. I think, in a way, he felt safe in them. I told him we would go to games at Madison Square Garden, maybe even take Mama if she wanted to go.

I thought about what Peewee had said. That I had better think about killing the Congs before they killed me. That had better be my reason, he had said, until I got back to the World. Maybe it was right. But it meant being some other person than I was when I got to Nam. Maybe that was what I had to be. Somebody else.

When the doctors had finished looking at the wounds, I knew what they would say. They said I looked okay. The shrapnel—small slivers of metal—hadn't hit anything vital. They were pretty sure they had dug out all the pieces. The doctor made a joke about missing a piece that I could tell my grandchildren about. The wrist had healed nicely. The doctor showed me the chip in the bone in the first X ray. Then he showed me a second X ray, it was cloudy, and I didn't make anything of it. He said it showed that the bone was growing back.

They had to come. My orders to rejoin my unit. When the clerk brought them, he made me sign for them. He left, and I threw them on the bed and went to breakfast. When I got back they were still there.

I read all the orders on the page, not just mine. Baines. Jones, Edward. Jones, Nance. Naylor. Perry.

No. I said no to myself. I wouldn't go back. I would go AWOL. I packed my things.

I went to the john and puked my guts out. I was scared. I felt almost the way I had in the chopper. I couldn't breathe, my hands were sweating. What would I do? I had heard of guys running away to Sweden. How the hell did you get to Sweden from Nam? Was there still a Sweden to run to?

The orders said that I was to report back to my outfit, where I would report to my commanding officer.

I went to say good-bye to Joe Derby and some of the other guys. The guy on the spit was gone. I hoped he made it.

"Get back to the World, Perry," Derby said.

"I'm pushing for it, man."

Everything was going too fast. I couldn't handle it. No way.

The plane was full of marines, fresh from Camp LeJeune. They were tough, full of themselves. They seemed so young. They kidded back and forth among themselves. They had weapons. Some of them looked at me, and some asked me questions. Had I been in country long? Had I seen any action? They were itching to get into combat.

I had been in the country four months. I hadn't seen a lot of action, but enough. Lord knows it was enough.

Chapter 17

W<small>E WERE CAMPED</small> at an old landing strip just north of Tam Ky and less than a thousand meters from Highway 1. I was glad to be near the highway. To the west, rice paddies stretched for what seemed miles. The dikes were twisted, uneven. I wondered how many battles had been fought along them. There were guys, mostly ARVN troops, sitting in tight little circles under the trees. I looked around for Americans, and finally found some. I asked them if they knew where Alpha Company was.

"Up the hill a piece," a tired-looking guy said.

I walked up the hill slowly. I could see small clusters of soldiers sitting around. It was less than a company. Maybe a squad or two at the most.

I was afraid again. I had felt it coming when I got my orders. I had felt it on the chopper. Now it sat like a heavy ball in my guts.

The dirt on the hill was soft beneath my feet. Trees once splintered had begun to grow again along the path up. I stepped on the bootprints that were there. The Vietnamese voices below me, ARVN troops, followed me up the hill.

Peewee was standing near a tree, peeing. God bless Peewee.

"Hey, buddy, you see any soldiers around here?"

"Man, you as sneaky as the damn Congs," Peewee said, looking up. "I didn't even hear you coming."

"How's it going?"

"Not too cool," Peewee said. He was rearranging his clothes as he talked. "What's up?"

"First things first," he said. "How the fuck you doing?"

"No big deal," I said. "A couple of scratches."

"I was hoping you were back in the World," Peewee said. "I was hoping you was back in Harlem getting loved up by three big-hipped mamas and wearing you some wing-tipped kicks by now."

"I was kind of hoping myself," I said.

"We ain't done a thing since you been gone but sit out here in this fuck-ing rain and mud," Peewee said. "I been sitting in this shit so long my piles got wrinkles."

"Everybody okay?"

"Yeah, I said we ain't done nothing," Peewee said. "But you see who we with down the way?"

"The ARVNs?"

"Yeah, but that ain't the bad news," Peewee said. "Come on, we got some bar-b-qued pork chops on the fire."

"Where did you get pork chops?"

"Walowick shot a pig and cut the sucker up," Peewee said. "We been eating good since we been out here."

"What's the bad news?" I said, walking alongside of him.

We went over to where Monaco was squatting with a bottle of soda. Monaco looked up, then he stood and threw both arms around me and hugged me. It really touched me. I thought I was going to cry.

"I'm sorry you're back," he said. "But I'm real glad to see you, man. Real glad."

I started to say something about being glad to see him, too, but I felt something wrong in the air. I looked from Monaco to Peewee.

"So what's up?"

"Simpson went back to the World."

Peewee looked up at the sky. I followed his gaze. The skies were a dirty grey. There was a thick cloud cover, heavy and threatening above us. A large bird started into the air as if it had been thrown, then stopped, spread its wings, and glided in a great arc to the west.

"He okay when he left?"

"Yeah," Peewee said. "But I ain't too sure about the new sergeant. He's a first-sergeant and he old."

"How old?"

"Guy's at least thirty-something," Monaco said. "He could even be forty."

"He took Monaco off point and put me on," Peewee said. "I didn't think nothing about it at first until he put me on all the damn time. Then he told Brunner he didn't want him pulling the rear. He put Johnson on the rear *with* the damn pig!"

"Johnson's carrying the sixty in the rear?"

"Yeah."

"What did Johnson say?"

"Johnson asked him to his damn face," Peewee said. "He asked him how come he put a brother on point and another brother in the damn rear with the sixty?"

I looked at Monaco, he looked back at me.

"What did he say?"

"Dongan—that's his name—" Peewee said, "he said he do what he think he should do and it ain't for Johnson to tell him what to do."

"What did Johnson say?"

"Johnson said he gonna mess around and get himself shot in the back of the head."

It rained for seven days straight. We sat in the rain for seven days straight. The mud oozed up into our boots, into our clothes, into our skins. There wasn't any way to get dry.

There was talk about us standing down in Okinawa, but nobody took it seriously. There was a lot of talk about how well the other units in the outfit were doing. But the guys in the squad seemed a little different. Tired. They seemed really tired.

For the first five days after I got back I didn't get to talk to Dongan. He nodded toward me once or twice and that was it. I got an M-16 and a grenade launcher from the armorer and found out that we had to carry more ammunition than I thought we would. Gearhart came around and talked to us a couple of times, but Dongan stayed away. Johnson was getting a thing about him. I went over and talked to Johnson. I wanted to find out more about Dongan, but Johnson wouldn't deal with it. He asked me what I thought about Brew.

"I liked him," I said.

"He probably back home, now," he said.

"Brew?"

"Yeah."

There was something about the way Johnson looked at me. I looked at Lobel, and he shook his head.

"Probably back home," I said.

When Johnson went to chow, I asked Lobel what the hell was going on with him about Brew.

"He's just not accepting the idea that he's dead," Lobel said.

"What's that supposed to mean?"

"It means you ask too many questions," Lobel said.

That's what was going on. The questions kept coming and nobody wanted to deal with them. Johnson didn't want to deal with Brew being dead, and Lobel didn't want to deal with Johnson. Maybe I did ask too many questions.

The first day the weather lifted a little, a chopper came in with a priest. Peewee had made a checkerboard out of some leaves he wove together. He was good at that kind of thing. We played checkers day and night. We were playing checkers when the Huey came in with the chaplain.

The chaplain was Catholic, and the Catholic guys had a mass or something. Then he came around to the rest of us. He didn't look like a chaplain. What he looked like was a middleweight who fought preliminaries in Atlantic City. His name was Father Santora.

"Sometimes," he said, "prayer can be very comforting. I wonder if any of you men would like to pray with me?"

"No," I said.

"Why not?"

"You wouldn't understand if I told you," I said.

"Try me," he said.

"I just don't want to pray," I said.

"Figure you don't want to make your peace if you're not ready to die?"

I smiled. I had to smile. He was right and he knew it. "Something like that."

"I know how you feel," he said. "I'm not quite ready to die just yet, either."

"You ever go into combat?"

"Into combat? Yes. I've never fired a weapon at anyone, though."

"You figure if you don't shoot at anybody, God's going to take care of you?" Peewee asked.

"I don't know," he said. "I sure as hell hope so."

The big guns in the distance kept rumbling. The sound seemed to rumble through the hills and flatten out over the valley.

"If I pray with you, will it keep me alive?" I asked.

"No."

"What will it do for me?"

"I don't know," he said. "I think it can be comforting at times."

"You can't say anything better than that?"

He shrugged.

"You scared being over here?" I asked.

"Yeah," he nodded his head. "I'm scared."

We got the squad together. We told him some of the things that had happened to us. Then he prayed, asking God to take care of us and our loved ones, things like that. I really appreciated it. Then he started asking God to look out for Brew's soul. That's when Johnson walked away. Right in the middle of a prayer, he walked away.

Father Santora looked up at him, and he was puzzled. Or at least I think he was puzzled. When the prayer was over, Father Santora had to split.

"Where you going?" Monaco asked.

"Some place named Khe Sanh," Father Santora said. "How come all these places over here have such foreign-sounding names?"

Johnson and Dongan got into a pretty heavy argument about how Johnson was keeping the sixty. Dongan didn't think the extra barrel that Johnson had to keep was clean enough. Johnson was telling him that he needed a grenade up his ass. They got real close to each other, and Johnson pushed Dongan away from him.

Lieutenant Gearhart got Johnson away from Sergeant Dongan and started pushing him toward the HQ hooch. Peewee told Johnson that if anything funky went down that he could count on him.

"You can count on me, too," I said. I meant it, too.

The squad didn't need any crap to get us separated. I knew that, and I was sure that Peewee did, too. But we didn't have to take any crap, either.

Guard duty. Me, Lobel, Peewee, and Sergeant Dongan. He said that he wanted to pull guard to check us out. When he said that, Peewee opened his pants and told him to check out his crotch.

Sergeant Dongan was from Richmond, Indiana. He sounded southern, he looked southern, and he seemed to think southern. Brunner was sucking up to him, as per usual.

Johnson outlined the problem. "Me, Peewee, Perry, and Monaco is the niggers of this outfit," he said. "We got to keep a serious watch on our asses."

I believed him. Monaco was Italian, but he was the same as the black guys in Dongan's eyes. Maybe because he got along with us so well, I don't know.

We went out on guard duty at 2000 hours. It was my first real duty since I had got back to the squad. I hit the guard position and inspected it. It looked okay. It was a foxhole with sandbags around the top, and boards at the bottom to stand on. The boards were rickety, but they were better than oozing down into the mud. I lifted the boards and dug it down another foot.

Noises.

The crickets and creepy crawlies were out in force. Crickets made a terrible racket. Things slithering through the grass could wake up the dead. The moon, floating above us, scraped against the clouds.

Noises.

My watch's ticking was louder than my heartbeat. There was something out there. No, it was just the darkness. What was out there was me, fearful, crying in the night. I was afraid. I thought of Father Santora.

A noise.

Was it a click? What was it?

Another noise.

I saw Sergeant Dongan move his right arm. He seemed to be groping about in the darkness. He found something. He swung his arm in a tight arc. A grenade.

Thump. It hit. Nothing. It didn't go off. I glanced up. There was movement, what might be a voice.

Sergeant Dongan fired a short burst. There was a muffled scream.

He fired off a flare. It went high into the air, ignited, then parachuted slowly toward the ground, lighting the entire area. There was one dead VC, a sapper with his wire cutters still in his hand, his lifeless body draped across the wire. I looked around, but I didn't see anything else. Slowly the light from the flare died. It was dark. The bogeymen could come out again.

Minutes passed. An hour passed. We were relieved by a crew of grim-faced ARVN marines.

"What a time for a dud grenade," Lobel said.

"Ain't threw no dud," Dongan said. "Threw a damn rock. That gook ducked his head down when he heard it land. Then he wondered why it didn't go off. Stuck his head up and I popped him. Learned that from the Third Marines!"

The man knew what he was doing. He knew how to stay alive.

Back at the hooch Lobel came over and sat on Peewee's bunk. Peewee said that anybody who sat on his bunk had to give him a kiss. Lobel said he wasn't a faggot, and Peewee said he was sorry about that because he could have really used a kiss.

"You guys think we're going to have a race problem over here?" Lobel asked.

"Not as long as everybody over here got them a gun," Peewee said.

Lobel stood up. "Well, just in case we do," he said. "I want you to know you got the Jew on your side."

"Who's the Jew?" Peewee asked.

"Me, I'm a Jew."

"You ain't no Jew," Peewee said. "You too tall."

"Fuck you, Peewee."

"There you go with them promises again," Peewee said.

The rain stopped. We sat. We did nothing. The war was a million miles away. Walowick told me and Peewee that they were talking about progress in the Paris peace talks.

"Perry?" Peewee was hanging over the edge of his bunk directing traffic for an ant traffic jam.

"What?"

"You ever have your black ass in Paris?"

"No."

"Where you been?"

"New York."

"You know where I been?"

"Where?"

"Chicago and Petersburg, Virginia. I got me a cousin in Petersburg. He work in a library down there."

"What he do?"

"He run the whole thing."

"How he get to do that?"

"He just smart as hell," Peewee said.

A joint operation. Captain Stewart came around to tell us how we had to look good because we were going to be working with the marines. He made it sound like a job.

"We'll be going into the Phuoc Ha Valley. The marine unit will move in first and clear the area," he said. "Then we'll secure it and establish an LZ in the valley. Is that clear?"

We didn't do anything. Like half the plans that came down from regiment, this one was canceled. The marines had started a counteroffensive up near Khe Sanh, and moved up there instead of into the Phuoc Ha Valley. We were glad of that, damn glad.

Lobel tried to get up a volleyball game but nobody wanted to play. We got Gearhart to requisition gloves and baseballs from battalion supply.

We got word that General Westmoreland wanted us to "maximize" destruction of the enemy.

"What the fuck does that mean?" Peewee asked. "We get a Cong, we supposed to kill his ass twice?"

"No, monkey face, it means that we're supposed to kill as many of these gooks as we can," Brunner said.

"You going to 'monkey face' your way right to Arlington Cemetery," Peewee said.

Later, lying in the bunk sweltering in the heat, I wondered what it did mean about "maximizing" destruction. Would it mean that we would simply kill more?

But who would we kill? Maybe we would be quicker to shoot in the hamlets. Maybe we would stop pretending that we knew who the enemy was and let ourselves believe that all the Vietnamese were the enemy. That would be the easy way. The women, the babies, the old men with their rounded backs and thin brown legs. They would be the enemy, all of them, and we would be those who killed the enemy.

Okay. I got a letter from Peewee's girlfriend. The first thing she told me is that Peewee said I'm nice-looking and educated. Then she went on to say how she was sorry she couldn't wait for Peewee anymore. Peewee wasn't around when I got the letter so I just burned it.

I got a letter from Kenny, too. He said he had a part-time job working at Kelly's Drugs on the corner of Lenox and 118th Street. For some reason I felt so proud of him, that he would do that. I just hoped Mama was letting him keep all the money he made.

He also said that he heard that Johnny Robinson got killed in the Nam.

Johnny Robinson? The last time I remember seeing him was when we were playing three on three in Morningside Park. Johnny couldn't play that well, but he always tried hard. I had always thought he was younger than me. I didn't know how he could even be in the Nam.

Tuesday. Raining. It promised to be the worst day of the war. We were sitting on the side of the hill. Johnson, Monaco, and Lobel had got some money together, and we were playing poker with some guys from Charlie Company. They called it Charlie Company, but it wasn't really anything more than three squads at best. Three thin squads at that. The ARVNs caught a woman with two children coming along the edge of the paddies. They stopped her and started slapping her around. Some guys from Charlie Company stopped them and brought the woman and the two kids to the HQ hooch.

HQ didn't have an interpreter, and the ARVN interpreter didn't get anything from the woman. They finally let her go. Peewee wanted to give the kids the checkerboard he had made.

"They probably don't even play checkers over here," Sergeant Dongan said.

"No lie?" Peewee said, "Maybe I'll make them a doll or something."

He went over and started grabbing a handful of grass and started making a doll. It was important to him. I could see that, but I didn't know why. He wanted to make those children something, to give them something.

I watched as some guys from Charlie Company started talking to the Vietnamese woman. They were just kidding around with her, talking stupid stuff about how they were looking for some cheerleaders. They followed her to the edge of the camp. Meanwhile Peewee was working hard trying to get his little doll together to give to her kids.

I watched as Peewee stood, putting the last touches on the doll. I thought it was cool when the woman stopped just before she reached the dikes and handed one of the kids to a guy from Charlie Company.

The GI's arms and legs flung apart from the impact of the blast. The damn kid had been mined, had exploded in his arms.

Guys not even near him, guys who had just been watching him take the kid into his arms, fell to the ground as if the very idea of a kid exploding in your arms had its own power, its own killing force.

I saw the woman running across the paddy. I saw her fold backward as the automatic fire ripped her nearly apart. I saw part of her body move in one direction, and her legs in another.

The woman's other child stood for a long moment, knee deep in water and mud, before it, too, was gunned down.

I turned and saw Peewee walking away. The doll he made lay facedown in the endless mud.

It was raining again.

Chapter 18

Peewee skipped his meals the rest of the day. Monaco tried to talk to him, but he wouldn't answer. It was Johnson who finally got him to talk.

"Hey, Peewee?"

"What?"

"You care anything about these damn kids over here, man?"

"They got kids over here?" Peewee asked.

"Naw, man, all they got is Congs," Johnson said. "Congs and mosquitoes."

"And rats," Walowick added.

"Yeah."

"Hey, Peewee," I said. "It's okay to feel bad about what's going on over here, man. It's really okay."

"Me? Feel bad?" Peewee turned over in his bunk and pulled his sheet up around his shoulders. "Never happen."

The first thing in the morning, a guy got hit. Lobel saw it and told me about it. A medic was handing out malaria pills. The guy had just put the pill into his mouth and was getting water from one of the water cans when he got hit in the rear end.

"First the guy turned around because he thought somebody was screwing around with him," Lobel said. "Then he felt his ass and looked at his hand. He saw the blood and knew he had been hit. Then he thought that one of us had shot him and he started looking at us. Then another shot hit the water can and we all dove for cover."

There was no way to find any VC in the area. A shot would come from the woods, and you'd return fire, killing a lot of the vegetation without ever hitting the sniper. If you did hit him, you wouldn't know about it.

The guy that got hit was a private. Everybody was standing around him congratulating him on his wound. He'd have a chance to get back to Chu Lai for a week or so, and it wasn't a bad hit. It was funny. A guy could get hit, be inches from being killed or crippled for life, and make a joke of it. It was all part of Nam. Some parts you could laugh at, like getting hit in the ass. Other parts, like the kid blowing up, you tried to shut out of your mind.

Johnson came over to where I was trying to down some scrambled eggs before the flying bugs got them. What I would do is to wave my fork over the eggs until all the bugs flew away, then grab a forkful before they came back. Johnson sat down on the ground next to me and watched me for a while.

"The officers ain't eating no powdered eggs," Johnson said.

"What are they eating?"

"Dehydrated potatoes."

"How come they get all the good stuff?"

"They having a big fight over at HQ hooch," Johnson said.

"What about?"

"We suppose to go on a joint patrol with the ARVNs and the ARVN colonel wants us to get into position first. Cap'n Stewart wants the ARVNs to go in first."

"Stewart told you that?"

"Gearhart." Johnson grunted the name.

"He say anything else about Dongan?"

"Nothing he can say," Johnson said. "Dongan made them switches too fast. Soon's he got here he looked around and did his thing. He might know how to keep himself together, but I don't want him doing it by getting me killed."

There was something about Johnson that was different than the rest of us. There was a knowing about him, as if he had been here before, as if dying and fighting was something be had been born to. When he talked about Dongan, I listened.

"First thing he done was to sit down and have him a beer with Brunner, then he had him a beer with Walowick. He don't like Lobel because he think Lobel's a faggot. He even ask me if he was a faggot."

It made me feel good to hear Johnson say that. I didn't think he would have said it when he first came into the army, or even when he first got into the squad. But we had all learned something about dying, and about trying to keep each other alive. It was good.

"What did you say?"

"I didn't say nothing," Johnson said. "I don't talk that shit. A man in Nam fighting by my side is a man fighting by my side. I don't care what he doing in bed."

We watched as the guy who had been hit in the rear end came out of the tent. He had a big smile on his face. His boots were unlaced and he was walking with a limp. The medic was just helping him into a jeep when he got hit a second time. It was another *titi* hit, on his hand, but this time somebody saw where the fire had come from.

A squad went out to look for the sniper. He probably could have stayed in his tree or his hole for the rest of the war without being caught, but he elected to fire on the squad. They pinned him down with automatic fire while the mortar squads set up. It must have cost ten thousand dollars to kill him.

"You hear what happened?" Peewee's fatigues hung on him loosely. There were dark stains under the arms that were ringed with salt at the edges.

"What happened?" Johnson looked at Peewee.

"The little Viet colonel gave Stewart a direct order to take some damn hill. Stewart said he wasn't going up first and the colonel called Division."

"Now what going to happen?" Johnson asked.

"Now we going up the damn hill first," Peewee said.

"What it is," Lieutenant Gearhart was saying, "is a small hill overlooking a village called Phuoc Ha Two. There's been activity on the hill, and they want it checked out. The thing is, this colonel is the same one who was leading some ARVN troops that got ambushed along Route 534. Got a whole battalion wasted."

"Let's just not go," Peewee said.

"Division said we had to go, so we're going," Gearhart answered. "We're going to call in artillery to soften up the area, then explore the slopes off the paddies. All we want to do is draw fire if there's any unfriendlies there."

Peewee wrote down the number of the highway that the ARVN colonel's battalion had been ambushed on and said that he was going to send it to his barber, who took numbers back home, and have him play it for the whole month.

"I feel lucky," he said.

It was the first time I had seen Peewee actually smile since I was back. It was funny that he should smile when we might be going into a firefight.

First we choppered into a hot LZ and the pilots jerked us out and took us out of there and into the valley itself, which didn't seem hot. We were getting fire support from Tam Ky, and there was no response from the hill we were supposed to be moving onto. That didn't mean a damn thing. I had heard stories about artillery fire taking off the entire top of a mountain and then having the Congs come out of the ground. Their bunkers were deeper than ours, a lot deeper.

The new LZ was a makeshift number. We were bunched up pretty good, and I was just praying that we hit the wood line before we got fire. The enemy was close enough for us to hear the sounds of their mortars firing. The rounds were going long but, more important, they weren't detonating. You could hear them whistling overhead, but then there wouldn't be an explosion. We figured it was either defective equipment or the Cong mortar squad didn't know how to arm them. That wouldn't last long.

A black lieutenant took Charlie Company to the right of the hill we were supposed to hit and Lieutenant Gearhart took us to the left. We started advancing in as wide a skirmish line as I had seen, but there was still no return fire.

Our squad was on the deep flank and I was far man.

We had to cross a paddy field to get to the wood line that led to the hill we were going to explore. This was why the ARVNs didn't want to go first. The paddy area was at least the size of a football field and exposed.

I breathed a little easier when we reached the wood line. Lieutenant Gearhart picked the route with the most cover for us. We went through a heavy canopy area, and the branches scratched my face and ripped at my hands. I was jumping through bushes, hoping I didn't hit any booby traps, avoiding anything that looked like it might be a step easier. I was struggling to keep up. The two weeks in the hospital had done a number on me. Just two lousy weeks. The M-16 felt like sixteen pounds instead of five.

Jamal carried the radio, and Gearhart was on it. He gave us the signal to stay put, and I got down behind a fallen tree.

Peewee crawled over to me.

"I got a coin back home," he said. "You go in my room and look in the back of the closet on the floor. You find a sneaker there and in the sneaker there's a sock with some stuff in it. Most of the stuff ain't worth nothing, but that coin is real old."

"Yeah?"

"If I don't get out this shit you go get that coin," Peewee said. "My moms might be a little uptight thinking you trying to rip her off or some shit. But if you got to buy it from her you do that. We get out this particular mess, and I'll write her and tell her to save it for you."

That's all he said. Then he started crawling back to his position. It meant he had a bad feeling about this place.

We heard some light fire on the other side of the mountain. The sixty was stuttering. Once in a while I thought I heard the M-16s, but I couldn't be sure.

Some rounds of high explosives came in on top of the hill.

I tensed. I looked over to where Lobel was snuggling up to the base of a tree trunk. I gave him the thumbs-up sign and he returned it.

We waited. I checked my watch and it was 1000 hours. The barrage on the hill stopped. The sounds of a firefight on the other side of the hill picked up. Still, our squad waited. Gearhart was signaling. I looked over at him. He was pointing toward the trees. Okay, look out for snipers.

I tried to make myself smaller.

Don't think, just be alert. Sergeant Simpson used to say it over and over again. But I was thinking.

Gearhart waved his arm in the air. Crap. We started getting up. I had to pee. I'd do it later. I must have had a pee ratio of three to one in Nam versus the amount of times I had peed in Harlem.

We had to move around the base of the hill to another area. Gearhart took us away from the wood line and back toward the paddies.

"What the fuck's he doing?" Peewee asked.

"Trying to draw fire," Walowick said.

We were showing ourselves, being targets. We moved along the edge of the paddy. The ground was muddy, oozing with water.

"Stay away from the dikes!" Sergeant Dongan called out.

"Keep your distances!"

I was wearing a flak jacket. Peewee had found two and had given me one. It weighed a ton. We kept moving. We kept slipping in the mud. Monaco had pushed forward faster than the rest of us. I think he wanted the point. He hit a dry spot and stopped. He held his rifle over his head and we all stopped. He knelt and then stepped off the dry spot into the paddy.

We all followed him into the paddy. When I passed the dry spot I saw how smooth it looked. Maybe it was too smooth. Maybe it was mined. That's what Monaco must have thought.

I thought that if I got killed I would want it to be over quick. I wanted to be hit and not even realize what was happening. I'd be gone, like Lieutenant Carroll. Over. Out. I don't want to lay screaming. I don't want to be carried in a medevac chopper while guys you could be home playing ball with were banging on your chest, trying to get your heart beating again.

Don't think.

The rice paddy seemed forever. The water was up past my ankles, and the stink was something else.

"Johnson, hit that line of trees!" Dongan called out.

Johnson held the sixty at his waist. He leaned into it and fired. I saw that he had something on his left hand. It looked like one of those mittens you used to handle hot pots, only it was silver.

We kept moving. The rice paddy ended. We were crouched, moving forward toward the wood line again. We hadn't drawn fire.

We moved up the hill. It was steep. We slid and fell. I fell, and let myself slide backward. I was afraid to catch on to anything. We fired a few shots, even though we didn't see anything.

We went up thirty, forty meters. Nothing. Gearhart signaled us to stop.

We looked around and found cover.

Wait. It was 1130 hours.

We dug in. Charlie had taught us well. We rested. We sat. Gearhart was on the radio. I tried to read him from where I was. Next to Gearhart, lying exhausted on the ground, was Jamal.

Lobel was sitting against a tree. When I saw him I froze. His eyes were open but there was no expression in them.

"Lobel!" I called to him.

"Wha?"

"You okay?"

"Yeah."

"Shit, I thought you were dead."

He smiled. His face was caked with dirt, and the smile showed his teeth. The blank expression in his eyes never changed.

We waited until almost 1200 hours before Gearhart signaled for us to move out. We moved back down the hill. We backed down the best we could. We got to the bottom and then ran the distance back to the paddy. Then we started back through it. It began to rain lightly.

The trip back through the paddy went faster than it did the other way. We got away from the paddy and started moving toward the LZ. Stewart was already there when we got there. He was pissed.

He told Gearhart to "get over to the command post." Gearhart glanced toward us and then left.

"What was that all about?" Lobel and Walowick came over to where the rest of the squad was already sitting.

"All I know is that Gearhart got the order to regroup here," Jamal said.

"It's my lunch time," Peewee said. "So we had to break."

"Check your weapon," Dongan said to Johnson.

"It's okay," Johnson said, not moving.

"I said check your fucking weapon!"

Johnson looked up at Dongan and then started stripping the sixty.

"What makes you such a hotshot?" Monaco asked Dongan.

"When you were still pissing your pants I was kicking ass, kid," Dongan said. "This ain't no fucking war. These slants can't fight. You go up against the Koreans, then you got your damn hands full."

We listened to Sergeant Dongan talk about how hard things had been in the Korean war, and how tough the Koreans had been. I didn't care. I hadn't been in Korea, and I hadn't been in any other wars. I was in Nam, here and now, and here is where my war was.

Gearhart came back. Brunner, kissing ass as usual, got up from a box he was sitting on so Gearhart could sit on it. Gearhart sat on it. I didn't think Lieutenant Carroll would have done that.

"The Vietnamese officer, Colonel Hai, has changed his mind," Gearhart said. "Now he wants his men to take the hill."

"We was on the damn hill already," Peewee said.

"That's why Stewart is pissed," Gearhart said. "After we reached the hill without drawing fire, Hai thinks it's safe. So he'll send his men up, then he'll write up his report and take credit for the body count."

"What we do, stay here?"

"No, we follow them back up the hill," Gearhart said.

The ARVNs had an ONTOS, an antitank weapon, that was supposed to lead the way. But there was no way the tracked vehicle was going to get through the mud. And if it did get to the base of the hill, there was no way it was going up the hill through the trees unless somebody chopped out a path for it. At least we didn't have to do that.

The ARVNs got into a staging area and started moving out. We sat and watched as what looked like almost a full company of little soldiers moved out. They were bunched too tightly, and they were moving too quickly.

They left a small headquarters contingent behind as they moved out. Charlie Company moved out after the tail end of the ARVNs, which were mostly mortar teams. We followed Charlie Company.

It was 1320 hours.

The first fire came from the flank. Two squads of ARVNs moved out to suppress it.

"I don't like it," Dongan said. "That's about where we were on the first trip. I bet you got the Second over there."

He was talking about the Second North Vietnamese Regiment. I had heard about them. They had been operating in Quang Ngai and just southeast of Tam Ky, but the marines had beaten them pretty badly. If it was the Second Regulars, they would be more disciplined, and better armed than the VCs.

The flank fire seemed to move the whole battalion toward it and toward the paddies. I didn't want to go through the paddies again.

"Incoming!" Monaco yelled and we hit the ground.

The mortar shells landed behind us. They were long again. Long but walking. They had spotters who saw where the shells were landing, and who were directing the fire. They kept shortening up the range to get closer and closer to us. And the shells were coming fast.

The noise was terrible. Every time a mortar went off, I jumped. I couldn't help myself. The noise went into you. It touched parts of you that were small and frightened and wanting your mommy. Being away from the fighting had weakened my stamina. It did even more to my nerves. I was shaking. I had to force myself to keep my eyes open.

The South Vietnamese ahead of us had just cleared the paddies when the whole damned hill seemed to explode with gunfire.

I was thirty meters into the paddies. The shells exploding in the paddy sent water in huge cones into the air. The ARVNs on the far edge of the paddy, and those who were trapped in the open space between the paddy and the hill's wood line were being cut down in waves. Some started to come back into the paddy. Others, in the paddy, were trying to get out to dash across the open space to the wood line.

"Get back! Get back!" Gearhart had turned around and crouched over, one hand holding his helmet.

We started moving back. The ARVNs around us didn't seem to know what to do. I didn't know what to do, either.

I slipped in the mud and went straight down. I tried to hold my piece out of the water, but I wasn't sure if I did or not. Then there was fire from our rear. We were trapped in the paddy! I was on my knees, water up to my waist.

"Stay away from the dikes and work back toward the staging area!" Gearhart called out.

Suddenly there were jets in the skies above us. I watched one as it dove toward the hill, and pulled up just after releasing a bomb. I turned to see the napalm explode and then roll up the hill in a billowing cloud.

An ARVN soldier was struggling to keep moving. He had been hit and the water around him was red with blood. I put my arm under his and lifted him the best I could. Monaco grabbed him by the other side, and we dragged him along.

"Keep going! Keep going!" Lieutenant Gearhart's voice.

We reached the wood line and laid the ARVN guy down. A medic came over, looked at him, and pulled him into a sheltered space.

"Hit that line!" It was Peewee's voice. "Johnson, hit that line!"

I turned to see what he was pointing at. There was a row of bushes that almost completely hid the muzzle flashes coming from their midst. Johnson got down in a prone position and started stitching the bushes. We all went down and started firing.

There were Congs on the hill behind us, and Congs to our flanks. We kept moving toward the line of bushes, and I saw some of them moving out. Johnson cut them down as they ran.

There were stands of trees every hundred yards or so along the rice paddies leading to the hill. We hit the first stand and fought from tree to tree. I got behind a tree and took clips from my belt. They were wet, and I shook them and blew on them to get the water off.

There were hundreds of ARVNs still in the paddies. They were being cut up pretty bad. Many were wounded and screaming. Some of the ARVNs had just stopped where they were and were holding their hands to their heads. They had freaked out completely. Some guys from Charlie Company had tried to get out along the dikes and now lay dead on them. One kept waving his arm in the air. He was still alive.

Another guy from Charlie Company started out after him. I turned away and started firing at the wood line.

"Move it out! Move it out! We'll get pinned here!"

Get pinned shit, we *were* pinned. The wood line was alive with Congs, but we kept moving toward them.

The jet above saw what was going on and came down and raked the wood line. He dropped a bomb that shook the ground. I flinched as the heat from it came over me like a rush. Gearhart was screaming something. I got up and started moving toward the wood line again.

There were fifty, maybe sixty, meters to the next stand of trees. When I got to it, I went down and pushed along on my belly. I saw Lobel pushing along a few meters from me.

The flak jacket caught on everything. I couldn't move with it on. I took it off.

I felt a hundred pounds lighter. We pushed through the wood line until we reached a clearing.

The firing stopped. For a few seconds there was absolute silence, and then everything started up again as heavily as it had been. It was as if somebody had changed channels and then switched back to the war. From the paddies I could hear the screaming of wounded men, mostly Vietnamese. They cried out in high-pitched voices that sounded almost like cats wailing.

We were under cover and held our position.

Gearhart was running by, saw Johnson, and ran to him. He didn't say anything, he just collapsed near him. I saw him feel his chest, and I thought he might have been wounded. Then I saw him pull out a cigarette. His hands were shaking too badly to light the cigarette, and Johnson took it and lit it for him.

Gearhart took a deep draw on the cigarette, then seemed to pull himself together.

I looked around for Peewee and saw him and Monaco together. They had got another sixty from somewhere and were firing it across the clearing.

I looked for the soldier from Charlie Company who had been waving his arm at the dike. I saw him, just his shoulders and an outstretched arm out of the water.

Captain Stewart was coming over toward us. Beyond him I saw guys moving out across the open space. We were getting the hell away from the hill, but I didn't know where we were going. Stewart had blood on his face, but I couldn't see if he was hit or not.

Gearhart waved me over. He told me to keep an eye on Jamal. I said I would.

"This is too hot for a dust-off area," Stewart was saying to Gearhart.

"There's a little village down this road. The VC must have it, but their main force is on the hill. The squad the ARVNs chased went back to the mountain."

"That the Second?"

"I guess so," Stewart said. "But we can't sit out here. We need to get to the village and get picked up from there. We can't hold these positions much longer."

Stewart told Charlie Company to move out first, but when he saw what was left of it he had us all move out together. Jamal had hurt his hand, maybe even broken it, but he was okay except for being winded.

We went on a forced march for ten minutes toward the village. We knew when we reached it as the first men started to fall.

The ARVN troops, still not reorganized, caught up with us as we formed a perimeter and tried to get into the village. Some of them ran past us. We watched them get hit and start running back. I was afraid they would start firing on us. Then I saw that many of them had even dropped their weapons.

I saw the area that Captain Stewart had been talking about. It would make an iffy dust-off area at best. Choppers could get in and out fairly quickly, but it would be easy for the Cong guns on the hill to hit. Maybe our artillery could keep them quiet. But there was no way the choppers could move in if we didn't take the village.

Colonel Hai finally got what was left of his outfit together and attacked the village. They went on what looked like a suicide charge into the village. As they ran they began to fall. They fell according to how they were hit. If they were hit in the head they bent backward or whirled around. Sometimes a man hit in the head would go several more stumbling steps before falling.

If they were hit in the body they would just lean forward, as if they were reaching for the ground, and then collapse.

"Let's go!"

We moved out. Johnson and Monaco were behind us covering us with the sixty. They had given the other sixty to an ARVN squad.

We ran forward, desperately searching for something to get behind as the bullets whined about us kicking up dirt and snapping branches. A fresh company of ARVNs had swung around the flank. We were closing in on the village.

I was on the ground. I was hurting. My arms and shoulders ached. I loaded another clip, and started firing. It was a hamlet, the same thatched roofs, the same smell of burnt bamboo. We fired into the village, trying to chop down anything we could see.

Johnson moved the sixty up and got it into place. Monaco loaded again. It was time for the rest of us to get up, to charge again.

I was tired, so tired. There was nothing to do but to go on. It came to me that we had the hamlet surrounded, so there was nothing for the Congs to do but to defend the village. We were here, and they were here, and the only thing to take care of was the dying.

I ran on. I saw Peewee throwing a grenade. A good idea. I snatched a grenade from my belt and threw it through the window of a hut. Shit. I had forgotten to take the damn pin out. I started firing through the window when I saw the grenade come out. I jumped away, twisting my body as I saw it bounce. It bounced toward me. My hands went up. I tried to turn my chest away. I didn't want to see it, but I couldn't turn away. I looked. It still wasn't armed.

I grabbed it and pulled the pin out, arming it. I threw it again. It went through the same window. This time it exploded.

I was on my feet. Running toward the hut, firing at nothing, at everything.

So tired. I couldn't get my arms up. We went from hut to hut. I wanted to rest. Just for a moment. I saw two ARVNs and a GI go into a hut, their pieces ready. Another GI was outside; he tossed a grenade through the window. The explosion ripped away a side of the hut.

It happened in an instant. A split moment of pain and confusion. A guy had just nailed the two ARVNs and the GI who had walked in the door of the hut. In another instant I swung my rifle toward the soldier who had thrown the grenade. He turned right and moved toward another hut as I lowered my weapon and turned left.

A cart, one wheel blasted off, sat in front of a low building that could have been made out of concrete. A soldier sat on the ground, leaning aginst the wheel. There was an irregular circle of blood spreading over his T-shirt. He seemed to be trying to wipe it away with his hand.

We reached the far end of the hamlet. Monaco was in front when we reached the last hut. I caught up with him. Johnson was lugging the sixty. We flattened ourselves against the sides of the hut, and then Johnson peppered one side of it with the sixty. Monaco took out a cigarette lighter and lit the roof.

"Damn!" Peewee.

I spun around and looked. Peewee was at the far end of the hut toward the wood line trying to get his sixteen to work. It had jammed. Me and Monaco went around the side of the hut and saw two Cong soldiers trying to pull an American into the bushes. Even when we started firing they kept pulling him.

We went after them. Monaco shot one of them and the other stood up and threw his arms into the air.

At his feet the soldier, still alive, was moaning in pain. I looked and saw that they had cut his finger off. I looked up into the face of the Cong soldier. He was young, no more than a teenager. He looked scared and tired, the same as me. I squeezed the trigger of the sixteen and watched him hurtle backward.

Then I sat down on the ground to rest.

"Let's go! Let's go! Get the perimeter!" Lieutenant Gearhart.

"We need a medic," Peewee said, pointing to the wounded soldier.

"Okay. The medevac's on its way."

Somehow I managed to get up. Gearhart went around trying to place guys on the perimeter. It was too much effort to talk. My lips were dry and I was getting cold. I looked over at Monaco. He was sweating.

We waited. It was 1342. I couldn't believe that so little time had passed.

The ARVNs set up a perimeter, and we were told that we could rest. Gearhart said that Sergeant Dongan had been hit. Me and Peewee went over to the medical tent. We found Dongan. They had laid his leg next to him. The other leg was barely attached. But it didn't matter now. His mouth was slightly open and the lower jaw twisted.

"One of you guys got a poncho?" A black spec five asked.

I looked to see if I still had my poncho. I did and gave it to the spec five. He picked up the leg and put it on Sergeant Dongan's chest, then wrapped him in the poncho.

Ten minutes later two gunships came in and cleared everything from around the village. Above them I could see the stack of medevac choppers.

It was 1400 hours.

Chapter 19

T HE ARVNS were the first to start to move out. Word had come that a second North Vietnamese battalion was moving toward the area. We had to get out and get out quickly. We made as many litters as we could to carry out the wounded. The question came up as to what to do with the dead.

Somebody said we should bury them.

"They'll just dig them up," Gearhart said. "We got to strip them and burn them."

Hell. Bodies still warm, limbs that fell as the bodies were moved. Some guys couldn't do it. Some of us had to. We began stripping the Americans. We took their tags, their gear, and took them to a hut. How many were there? There were too many. Everybody took care of their own. We got Dongan and put him in the hut. Some of the bodies were wrapped in ponchos, some weren't.

Guys from Charlie Company saw what we were doing and they got their people in. It was better than having the Congs get them, maybe mutilating the bodies.

"Make sure you get all the tags!" Gearhart was saying.

I was afraid of the dead guys. I saw them, arms limp, faces sometimes twisted in anguish, mostly calm, and I was afraid of them. They were me. We wore the same uniform, were the same height, had the same face. They were me, and they were dead. No one looked into the faces, into the often still-open eyes. We did what we had to do, and turned away.

The ARVNs who hadn't already left watched us impassively. They didn't want any part of what we were doing. They left their dead where they were. They stripped them, took the ammo, and the supplies. They closed their eyes.

"This guy is still alive, man."

Monaco was looking at a guy in the middle of a pile. The poncho he had been wrapped in came away from his face. He was unconscious, but he was still breathing. Two guys from Charlie Company, who recognized him, ran over and started pushing the bodies off him. I watched as the limbs flew off the pile until they reached the guy who was still alive.

When they uncovered his body, I could see bubbles of blood coming from a gaping wound in his throat. The flies around the pile, crawling over the bodies, into and out of the wound, buzzed in delight.

"Somebody get a medic!"

"Jamal!"

Jamal was outside and Monaco got him. Jamal looked at the guy and shook his head. The front of the guy's flak jacket was dark with either sweat or blood. When the sweat mixed with the mud it was hard to tell. Jamal opened it and saw another wound. The flesh was burned and puffed away from a wound big enough to put a fist into. I looked back at the throat wound, the bubble of blood still rose and fell rhythmically. How was he still alive?

"Do something for him!" The guy from Charlie Company's voice was menacing.

"He your friend?" Jamal asked.

"Yeah, he's my friend!" the guy from Charlie Company said.

"Then you do it," Jamal said. He stood and walked away.

A couple of us stood and walked out behind Jamal. A moment later we heard the shot. We went back in and piled the bodies back up on the guy.

They got a flame thrower and we moved away from the hut. The smell of burning flesh came quickly. I knew the smell wouldn't leave me quickly. Maybe it never would.

We started off. I didn't want to look back. I did. The hut was burning furiously.

"Who's got the tags?" Gearhart asked Walowick.

Walowick turned and looked at him. His lips were swollen, one side of his face was puffed. There was blood in the corner of his mouth. He didn't answer Gearhart.

A guy from Charlie Company pointed to another guy from Charlie Company who was supposed to have the tags, and Gearhart went over to him. Then he came back.

"He forgot the tags," Gearhart said. "He left them in the hut."

"How they gonna let their folks know they dead?" Peewee said.

Gearhart didn't answer.

What would they do for a body? Would they send home an empty coffin? Would they scrounge pieces from Graves Registration? What would they say to their parents? Their wives? We lost your son, ma'am. Somewhere in the forests he lies, perhaps behind some rock, some tree?

We burned his body, ma'am. In a rite hurried by fear and panic, we burned what was left of him and ran for our own lives.

Yes, and we're sorry.

Perhaps they would tell them nothing. Not having a body in hand, not having the lifeless form to send with the flag, they would not acknowledge that there was a death at all.

Yes, and we're sorry.

The ARVNs were up ahead of us, pushing through the woods. They were moving quickly. I looked for Peewee and found him. He was behind Gearhart. Gearhart had his head up, his flak jacket was open. We went quickly, stumbling, but somehow in control of ourselves. We were looking out for each other, checking each other out. I stayed with Jamal mostly. I asked how he was doing.

"I don't believe I'm not dead," he said. "You know I'm not made for this kind of life."

The ARVNs were headed for the same pickup zone we were. They cut down along the edge of the paddies, and we took a longer route through the wood line.

The branches ripped at us, vines caught at our feet. It was like a nightmare. The forest itself was our enemy, trying to catch us, trying to hold us in its grip.

Small-arms fire. The ARVNs were under fire. We dove for cover.

"Get up! Get up! Keep moving!"

The voice came from behind us. I saw Captain Stewart look back to see who was talking. I turned. It was Johnson.

"Stay down!" Captain Stewart barked out his order. "Look for the sniper."

"Let's move it!" Johnson started forward.

"I said stay down, damn it!" Stewart yelled.

I was on my feet. Monaco was up. We were moving again, following Johnson. The hell with Stewart. We broke through the underbrush. We kept moving.

I looked around. Stewart was coming, too.

Suddenly I wasn't there. It was as if I were out of my body and looking down at us. And then I was back. What the hell was going on? I shook my head. Everything seemed okay again.

We kept moving. I hoped like hell that somebody knew where we were going.

Monaco was up ahead. He held his hand up, and we dropped where we were. I could feel my heart beating in my temples. I was gasping for air, sucking in tiny fleets of flying bugs. Spitting them out. Sucking in another fleet.

Movement to my right. We were moving again. Peewee was trying to get Jamal up. I went over to them.

"He hit?"

"No," Peewee said.

Jamal was shaking, tears were running down his face. He was ugly. God, a man could be ugly when he cried. Peewee punched him in the face and started pulling him up. I got his other arm and started pulling him.

Gearhart was over. He jerked Jamal by the collar.

"Move it, soldier!" he spat the words in Jamal's face.

Jamal was moving again. He was okay. He was one of us again.

Suddenly I wasn't there. There was somebody running in my boots, but it wasn't me. The legs moved mechanically, the weapon stayed in front of the body. I could almost see myself running. I could feel myself running, but it wasn't me running. What the hell was going on? I stopped.

"Move it, Perry!" Gearhart's voice.

The ground was passing me faster, but it wasn't me running. It was someone else, perhaps even some thing else. It was a body moving through a nightmare, a nightmare in which everything knew everything, where the ground pushed your feet away and the vines clutched at your legs while the trees chortled and shook with silent laughter.

We stopped. The sweat was cold against my body. Up ahead Monaco was sitting with his back to a tree. His chest was heaving. He gave hand signals. Gearhart moved up. Johnson moved up. Where did they get the strength? I looked at Peewee. Peewee, my main man. Peewee's face was dark, there were shadows where his eyes should have been.

The shadows moved, Peewee moved. He was getting up. I didn't want to get up, I wanted to sit there forever. Where the hell was the popcorn machine? Couldn't I just watch the rest of this damned war? Couldn't I just be out of it for a few hours, a few minutes?

We moved up. There were voices, Vietnamese. We moved up. The soft pop-pops of the grenade launchers went off. There was screaming, high-pitched whines that died slowly as the life drained from the body. We pushed up. There was a clearing and nearly a platoon of NVAs. We had them in the open. I couldn't believe it.

We fired as they started scrambling away.

Suddenly I wasn't there. There was a sight in front of me, and I stared at bodies trying to move across an open field. There was the sensation of vibration in my hands, against my face, and the distant sound of an M-16 firing. I felt a shoulder moving, perhaps mine, reversing clips I had taped together. There were soldiers trying to move away from the forward sights of a sixteen. They weren't moving nearly fast enough.

"Get the perimeter!" Captain Stewart again. "You two men get to the other side of this clearing, the sixty will cover you."

"Never happen!" Peewee dug in.

"Soldier!" Captain Stewart swung a forty-five on Peewee.

I didn't see the sixty move. I heard the impact of the bullets in the ground in front of Captain Stewart's feet, I saw him leap backward. I saw him dive for cover. The forty-five went back into its case. I looked over my shoulder. Johnson was on his knees, a menacing silhouette.

The sixty swung toward the clearing and raked the far side. Suddenly a figure popped out of the underbrush carrying a tube.

"Get him! Get him!"

The sixty barked. The figure started at first to collapse, and then to expand. It was as if it drew in on itself, gathered the momentum it needed, and then began to grow. The arms flung apart. But it had already fired the RPG.

Down. Sweet Jesus. *Please.*

Dirt all over me. There was more firing. I looked up. There was something near me. It was flesh. I pushed it away, I wanted to get away from it. I stood and started to run from it.

The ARVNs were on the left. I saw them. I fired in their direction. I don't know why. I stopped and tried to pull myself together.

The charlies were still ahead of us. They had backed themselves into a tight knot in the middle of the field. There must have been sixty, maybe seventy of them. We fired at them, and fired at them, and fired at them. Bodies once alive, then lifeless, seemed to live again as the bullets tore into the dead flesh and made it dance in the afternoon sun. I breathed in some bugs without bothering to spit them out.

"Cease fire! Cease fire!" Gearhart.

The other side of the clearing was burning. The sudden darkness of a jet surprised me. Surprised all of us. One guy opened up. The jet roared and dropped a bomb just over the clearing. Napalm.

It burst into the trees, rolling, rushing, a gale of fire through the trees.

Couldn't breathe. I went down. Guys were dropping around me as the heat from the napalm sucked up the air. The trees above us caught fire. My skin was full of tiny pin pricks. The napalm was too close. We started moving into the clearing.

A Cong, maybe the one who had fired the RPG, was lying on top of a pile of bodies. His chest and stomach were open. There were tubes and organs and the redness of working parts that no longer worked.

"Perry!" It was Peewee.

"Wha?"

He pointed. I looked. It was a soldier. He had been white, round-faced. Now the bottom of one leg was off. Most of the flesh from the thigh was off, too. The white, twisted bone angled out oddly from the hip. His eyes were open, his mouth was open as wide as it would go, the teeth bared.

"Look at his hands, man."

The hands were around the neck of a NVA soldier. There were no other wounds on the NVA. The GI had killed him from the other side of death.

I walked away. People were not supposed to be made like that. People were not supposed to be twisted bone and tubes that popped out at crazy kid's-toys angles. People were supposed to be sitting and talking and doing. Yes, doing.

Chapter 20

WHEN THE ARVN TROOPS first reached us we didn't notice anything unusual. Then we heard one of their officers yelling and motioning for us to move back toward the hamlet.

"What the hell is this?" Peewee reached for his rifle.

Gearhart saw that the ARVN troops were surrounding us. I almost freaked out. I thought the ARVN troops must have been Congs in disguise.

"What the fuck is this all about?" Gearhart was asking.

Then we saw. The choppers started down. The ARVN officer simply wanted to get out first.

"Put your hands up! Put your hands up!" Gearhart shouted.

He threw down his weapon and put his hands high over his head. Peewee lifted the muzzle of his rifle.

"No, put your hands up high," Gearhart shouted. "Like this!"

He put his hands up even higher.

We finally figured out what Gearhart had in mind and put our hands up. He was letting the guys in the choppers know what was up. The door gunners on the choppers opened up on the knot of ARVNs behind us. We got our pieces and started firing into them. They broke it off quickly and moved away.

We started scrambling to the choppers, fighting off any ARVNs that tried to get on before us. The chopper I was trying to get on dipped down and almost knocked me off. Then it seemed to leap into the air with me hanging onto one side. Somebody pulled me in. I felt something slip by me, clutch at my ass, my leg, hold onto my ankle for a long second, and then let it go. I thought my ankle was broken. I twisted to see who was behind me. There was nobody, nothing but the empty space of the door. Somebody had fallen out.

It was forever getting back to the base. We were jumbled over each other, our bodies aching and too tired to move.

We got to the base, and somebody came up with some coffee. I had never been a coffee drinker in the World, but now I wanted it. Now I needed it, anything that promised to get me to the next minute. Gearhart told us to get some rest.

"Sleep," he said.

Sleep. Rest. The words had lost their meaning. Trying to reach sleep, any kind of real sleep, was hard. It was as if I just faded out sometimes, and then faded back in when we got called. Most of it wasn't rest, either. You had to be away from the boonies for three, maybe four days before you felt rested. It wasn't so much the running around, or the fighting, it was the tension.

Monaco's screaming woke me with a start. I jumped up reaching for my rifle.

"There they are! There they are!" he was screaming. He fell to the floor and shot a burst toward the door of the hooch.

"Cease fire! Cease fire!" Walowick was yelling.

Lobel and Johnson jumped on Monaco and wrestled his weapon away from him. I was behind my bunk looking toward the door.

"Be cool! Be cool!" Johnson called out.

"Oh, God!" Monaco had his hands to his head. They were helping him up.

"What the fuck is going on?" I looked toward Peewee, who was standing flat against the wall.

"I swore I thought I saw some Congs dragging a guy through the bushes," Monaco said. "I saw it just as plain as anything."

"You were probably dreaming," I said, getting up from the floor.

"No, man, I was awake," Monaco said. "I saw these two Congs dragging a guy into the bushes."

Monaco shook his head and sat down on his bunk. Everybody else cooled out. Some guys from another squad came over to find out what the shooting was about, and Walowick told them a guy was working on his rifle and it went off.

When they saw that Monaco was okay, Lobel and Brunner walked him over to the mess tent to get some coffee.

"Hey, Perry," Walowick sat on the edge of the bunk.

"What?"

"You know what happened to Monaco?"

"No, what?"

"I mean, you know what he just did? Thought he was seeing something he had seen before?"

"Yeah?"

"That happened to me once," he said. "I was on guard and some VC tried to get through the barbed wire. We were firing on them, and out of the corner of my eye I saw one that had already got through. He came at me and I turned and got him, and then I went back to firing on the other guys trying to get through. We stopped them, and I didn't think much of it. But the next day I was playing volleyball and just as I turned. . . ."

Walowick paused as if he were trying to remember exactly what had happened.

"You thought you saw guys coming through the wire again?"

"No, not coming through the wire," he said. "I thought I saw the guy that had broken through. I screamed and dove for the ground. It was pretty embarrassing."

"It's understandable, though."

"You understand it?"

"No."

Monaco was cool by the next day. He made a lot of jokes about what had happened, but I thought he was worried about it.

It was a dreary Friday, the rain beat down on the tin roof of the hooch all morning, and we were all down. Jamal was typing up a report on Brew and noticed it was his birthday. If Brew had made it he would have been nineteen on the twenty-sixth.

"We could have had a birthday party for the guy," Peewee said. He was cleaning his gear.

I had been trying to get the mud from my boots, gave it up, and went to the mess tent. I asked the cook if he had any cake or anything and he came up with some pound cake and some fruit cocktail. I took it back to the hooch and we celebrated Brew's birthday.

Gearhart wrote three letters to his wife. He gave one to me, one to Walowick, and he kept one.

Gearhart said that if we got back to someplace we could mail the letter to go on and mail it. The letters were all the same he said, more or less.

"Just in case I don't get a chance to mail it myself." He said. "You know. . . ."

Nobody answered him. He nodded and left.

"Who the hell is he to lay this shit on us?" Lobel asked. He seemed really mad.

Peewee told Walowick to open the letter.

"That's not right," Walowick said.

"I didn't say the shit was right," Peewee said. "I just said open the damn letter!"

Walowick opened it and Lobel read it.

Dear Sandra,

I have finally made a decision on the storm doors. I think we should go on and have the glass-paneled doors the way you want. We'll put my den in that room, and I'll put a good strong door that we can lock between that and the hallway leading to the bedrooms. That way it'll be safe even if someone does try to break in, and you can still have the doors the way you want them.

I don't know what you should do about the paper boy. If he insists upon being a wise guy tell him not to deliver the damn paper anymore. The only reason to get the paper from him is to have something to read while you're having breakfast.

Tell the kids I said hello. You were always better with words than me. Could you please tell them how much I love them? Try to explain that I love them as much as I love you and you know how much that is.

Things are going okay over here. I'm with some okay guys.

Love,
Ricky

I wished I had a wife and kids. I mean I really wished I had a wife and kids, somebody somewhere that loved me in a way I could look forward to going back to the World to. I knew Mama loved me, but I also knew when I got back, she would expect me to be the same person, but it could never happen. She hadn't been to Nam. She hadn't given her poncho to anybody to wrap a body in, or stepped over a dying kid.

Maybe she was worried about me the same way a wife would. I didn't even know how a wife would worry. Gearhart wasn't talking about her worrying, he was just talking about the paper boy. It was like she was away, and going through the crap. Maybe she was, in a way.

"Peewee!" I called over to where he was reading a paper. "You think I should tell my little brother about how things are over here?"

"You ain't told him yet?"

"I keep trying to, but I can't get it out right. You know, I don't want him to think about it like you do when you go to the movies."

"You gotta tell him it's just the way things are in the movies," Lobel called out from across the aisle. "You tell people what this is really like, and who's going to come to the next war? They'll have all the announcements out and everything, and nobody'll show up."

"Yeah, but you know what I'm thinking? I'm thinking that whatever I tell him he's going to start thinking about heroes and stuff like that."

"Heroes?"

"You know, to a kid if you kill somebody and the somebody is supposed to be a bad guy, you're a hero."

"You ain't killed nobody yet," Peewee said. "They gots to be people before you can kill them. You think these Congs is people?"

"Yeah, sure they are."

"What they names?"

"How the hell would I know their names?"

"What they like to eat?"

"I don't know."

"See, they ain't people to you yet. You figure out all that shit, what they names is, what they like to eat, who do the dishes and shit like that, then they people. Then you shoot them you killing somebody."

"You're talking technical stuff," Lobel said. "You shoot some guy and he falls down, you've killed him. Pure and simple."

"Hey, Lobel, if they was people to your ugly, overweight ass, you couldn't kill them because you wouldn't have the heart."

"You couldn't, either," I said.

"Yeah, I could," Peewee said. "I'm a damn animal, man."

"Old Peewee is going to fight the next war all by himself." Monaco was putting powder on his crotch.

"No, I'm going to go out get me some more seventeen-year-olds like us that don't know nothing and turn them all into animals," Peewee said. "And if I catch some dude putting face powder on his crotch like you doing, I'm gonna put him on point cause I know he ain't got no sense."

"This is supposed to keep the jock itch down," Monaco said.

They argued about whether or not Monaco was enough of a jock to have jock itch with Peewee saying that Monaco was just about enough man to have jock tickle but not near enough man to have jock itch. I started writing to Kenny.

I just told him that the war was about us killing people and about people killing us, and I couldn't see much more to it. Maybe there were times when it was right. I had thought that this war was right, but it was only right from a distance. Maybe when we all got back to the World and everybody thought we were heroes for winning it, then it would seem right from there. Or maybe if I made it back and I got old I would think back on it and it would seem right from there. But when the killing started, there was no right or wrong except in the way you did your job, except in the way that you were part of the killing.

What you thought about, what filled you up more than anything, was the being scared and hearing your heart thumping in your temples and all the noises, the terrible noises, the screeches and the booms and the guys crying for their mothers or for their wives.

And exciting. It was exciting, too. Sometimes, when we were waiting to make a move, to go into some area where we hadn't been before, it was as if the time would never come soon enough. That's what kept it going somehow, that and the idea that we were better than the Congs. It was that, the knowing that we would win, and the excitement that overcame the being scared. If we just did our job, we would be all right. But I didn't think it was going to last forever. I was growing too tired. It was good that we were only in Nam for a year.

"Y'all children can relax now," Peewee said as he stood in the doorway to the hooch. "This war only gonna last about three more days. We got us a body count of four hundred and thirty-three Congs in the last fight."

"Four hundred and thirty-three?" Johnson looked up to see if Peewee was kidding.

"Yeah, every time we shoot one of them his cousin and his uncle die, too," Peewee said.

Walowick and Monaco made jokes about the body count, but they ended when Captain Stewart told us that afternoon that we were going out again.

"This area is secure," Captain Stewart was saying, "so they're moving the First Cav up to the DMZ, and we're going to be patrolling the region east of the firebase at the edge of the valley. The marines still control the firebase, so we just have to check on any buildups in the area."

"Yo, do the Congs know that shit?" Peewee asked.

"The Congs know everything," Johnson said.

"Yeah, but do they know they moving out the First Cav and putting us in there?"

"Two things, soldier," Captain Stewart's voice hardened. "The first was that I've already told you that the area is secure and the second is a question. Are you saying that the First Cav are better soldiers than we are?"

"Fucking A right!" Peewee said.

Captain Stewart's face turned whiter as he went over to Peewee. "Where the hell is your pride, soldier?"

"In Chicago, sir. Can I go get it?"

Chapter 21

CAPTAIN STEWART put Jamal back into medical again. Peewee said that he did it just so that Jamal could serve him coffee anytime he wanted him to. With Sergeant Dongan gone the squad was down to seven guys again. Gearhart was commanding our squad and two others. The other squads were down to five men each.

"You guys want to switch squads so they're all equal?" he asked. "If you don't you'll probably be out more than the others."

"We don't want to switch, sir," Monaco said.

"That goes for all of us," Peewee said.

"You talking for the squad now, Peewee?" Gearhart was cleaning his piece.

"Yeah," Peewee nodded. "I guess so."

Gearhart wanted to combine the other two squads, but they wouldn't let him do it. They said that we had to have so many squads in the field, even if it was only on paper.

Brunner got a bad case of hemorrhoids. Gearhart wanted to send him to Chu Lai, but his time was short and he wanted to stay. Gearhart told me and Johnson that Brunner wanted to make Sergeant, First Class.

"Captain going to give it to him?" Johnson asked.

"Could be," Gearhart said.

"Sucker get through a calendar, you ought to give it to him," Johnson said.

"I didn't think you liked him," Gearhart said.

"You got to like a man make it through a whole calendar over here," Johnson said.

Things were quiet for a few days, even boring. We heard all kinds of stories about how we were beating back the North Vietnamese.

"Somebody better send them a telegram so they know about it," Peewee said.

From what I heard from guys from other outfits I thought we were winning, too, but that it was going to be a long time before it was over.

We played Pitty Pat and Dirty Hearts every day. Then Monaco came up with a new game. He found some paper and put down the names of all the movie stars and singers he could think of. Then he passed them around and we played for them. That didn't last long. Walowick won Mary Wells from Peewee and Peewee wouldn't give her up. Walowick called Peewee a welcher.

"A what?" Peewee threw down his cards.

"You're a welcher!" Walowick said.

"How you spell that?"

"And you're dumb, too," Walowick added.

"Perry, how you spell it?"

"W-E-L-C-H-E-R," I said. "It means you don't pay your debts."

"What else it mean?"

I didn't know if it meant anything else. That's when Peewee said he was going to HQ hooch where they kept a dictionary.

"If they got anything in there about race I'm gonna come back here and shove a grenade up your ass!"

Peewee stormed out of our hooch. Brunner was shaking his head.

"Guy's a moron," he said.

"Suppose it does have another meaning?" Walowick said.

"Then you got a grenade up your butt," Johnson said.

Walowick left the hooch and went looking for a dictionary so he would know if he was going to have to look out for Peewee. I found Peewee drinking a soda behind the water tank.

"You find the dictionary?" I asked.

"Yeah, but I still ain't giving up Mary Wells."

That night, though, Mary Wells mysteriously disappeared from under Peewee's pillow.

Sunday. The chaplain came around and asked if we wanted to come to nondenominational services. We said we would all be at the services. Only me, Walowick, and Peewee went.

It was good. The chaplain said nice things. He asked God to bless all the guys that had been killed and wounded, and to protect all of us. We sang a hymn and ended the services holding hands and saying the Twenty-third Psalm. It made me feel good.

I went back to our hooch and hit the nets. Ramsey Lewis was on the radio and I really got into it. I could almost imagine being home. The squad had just got some new barrels for the sixties and two new M-79's. They were sitting around a tin can full of carbon tet cleaning the cosmoline off the weapons. The whole hooch smelled of the carbon tet and the guys were getting a little giddy.

"Hey, y'all hear about the dudes collecting ears from dead Congs and wearing them around their necks?" Monaco asked.

"That's rough stuff," Lobel said.

"It ain't nothing to mess with a Cong once he dead," Johnson said. "You cut the mother's ears off while he still alive and kicking—then you doing something."

"And what you gonna say to Mr. Cong when he catch your ass with them damn ears?" Peewee said. " 'Scuse me, Mr. Cong, I just taking these here ears to the lost and found?"

"I don't know." Monaco sighted down the sixty barrel. "You got to be like the Cong to get him."

"They just selling wolf tickets to themselves," Johnson said. "They see them ears round their necks and tell themselves they ain't scared."

"You ain't scared over here, you a fool," Peewee said. "Ain't that right Perry?"

"You guys better open the hooch door and let some of those carbon tet fumes out before we're all high," I said.

"That's why they give us carbon tet," Lobel said. "To get high."

I wanted to get up and open the hooch door myself but just then Brunner came in. As soon as we saw him whipping out his notebook we knew we were going on patrol.

"There was some activity down near a stream about four kilometers away," Brunner said. "We're going to check it out to make sure that no charlies are slipping through."

"What stream?" Monaco asked.

"The Song Nha Ngu River," Brunner said.

Peewee had been drinking a Coke; he started with a fit of laughter, and snorted the Coke out through his nose and all down the front of his T-shirt. He started laughing and trying to wipe the snot off his chin at the same time.

"Is he high?" Brunner put on his pissed-off face.

"Naw, he ain't high," Johnson said. "Go on with what you got to say, man."

Brunner shot Johnson a look and went on talking about how Intelligence had got wind of heavier than usual traffic near the stream. Peewee kept giggling.

"What the hell is so funny?" Brunner turned to him and asked.

"You say we going to the Sha Na Na River?" Peewee asked. "That's what you said."

"I didn't say anything about no Sha Na Na River," Brunner said, checking his notes.

"That's right next to the 'Del Valleys,' " Monaco said.

"All you guys have to worry about is identifying and killing charlies," Brunner snapped. He stood and stormed out of the hooch.

"How we gonna identify them when they don't even know who they are?" Peewee said. "You catch you a Vietnamese and ask him what he is, and he got to check out your piece. You got an American weapon and he say GI number one. You got one of them Russian AK-47's, and he say VC number one."

Bad news. Gearhart was going with the other squads to patrol another sector. That made Brunner the squad leader. All we were supposed to do, according to Brunner, was to check out the river. The rivers in the area were small, almost drying out in the dry season, and swelling in the rainy season. This one crossed a road, Route 586, and it was there that the main activity had been seen.

"If they've seen so much activity, how come we're going out by ourselves?" I asked Brunner.

"We're not supposed to engage any large units," Brunner said. "Stewart said we should try to get some prisoners."

"How long he got to go over here?" Peewee asked.

"I don't know," Brunner said. "Maybe a month at the most. They just turned down his extension."

"Then we making the last big push for his promotion," Johnson said.

The choppers did the same thing to my stomach. Just the sound of them coming in put me in a panic. My arms and legs felt heavy. My palms were sweating. I didn't want to go out anymore. I had had enough.

"Let's go!"

I went. Again. Don't think, react.

The landing zone spooked me. It was supposed to be near an ARVN ranger outpost, but I didn't see any of the South Vietnamese elite troops around.

It took us an hour of cautious walking before we spotted the stream. We stopped a distance from it, maybe the distance from home plate to the left field fence in a regular stadium. On a good day I could have hit a ball that far. How long had it been since I had hit a baseball? I figured it was only sixteen months. It seemed a different lifetime.

We spread out and started looking around. Nothing. I turned and looked back toward the skies. The choppers were already distant silhouettes against the darkening skies.

"Move out!" There was something about Brunner's voice I didn't like. He was trying to make it sound like he had more confidence than he did.

There was a ridge off to our left about three hundred meters. It was bad news. It looked down on the stream and made good cover for anybody who might be up there.

We didn't want to go along the stream with the ridge on our flank. Nobody wanted to go up on the ridge, either. Brunner sent Lobel and Walowick to check out the ridge while the rest of us covered them.

Covered them. Big joke. If there were any Congs there they would get wasted, and all we would be able to do is to chase the Congs off while we picked up the bodies. If we were lucky.

Walowick and Lobel waded across the stream. The waist-deep water was moving slowly, and flecks of white foam caught the last rays of sunset. I was glad to see them climb out on the other side. They started up the ridge. It was rough going, and even slower than I thought it would be. We watched as they climbed slowly toward the top. I prayed that it would be clear. I asked God to let it be clear, just this once.

Walowick looked, then stood, then signaled. It was clear. I hoped I hadn't used up a prayer I didn't have to.

Walowick and Lobel came back and we started sweeping the stream. There was a saddle, a low section in the ridge a hundred meters downstream that was about as scary as anything I had seen. If Walowick and Lobel had missed the Cong on the ridge, the saddle would be the perfect spot for an ambush. I wondered how many prayers I had left. I wondered if Buddha was answering prayers on the other side.

We didn't see anything for the first kilometer out.

"Let's get back," Johnson said. "It's going to start raining."

"We got another kilometer to go," Brunner said.

Lobel was the first. He turned and looked at Johnson. What was Johnson going to do? Nobody had said anything about Johnson, but we all knew he was taking over the squad. The hell with Brunner's stripes, Johnson was taking over.

Johnson shrugged, shouldered the sixty, and kept on. Brunner was visibly relieved.

Monaco was on point. I was rear man. We went out a quarter of a mile more, until we could just about see Route 586, when Monaco halted us and pointed toward the ridge line. I looked up, checked my safety to make sure it was off, and waited.

"I don't see nothing!" Brunner called out.

Monaco leaned forward, and pointed again.

Brunner had glasses and he checked out the ridge line. I saw that Monaco was edging back toward us. He was motioning to one side of the stream and we started moving toward it. He had seen something, but it wasn't necessarily on the ridge. We backed toward what we hoped was enough cover for a firefight.

"I don't see anything up there!" Brunner shouted. He looked nervous.

Monaco spun back toward the direction he had been going in and opened up, shooting into the water. We froze as we saw the rounds kicking up the water. There was nothing there. I thought Monaco was wrong. Then there was a splash and a figure. It looked, in the dim light of evening, as if he were standing in the water, masturbating. Then I saw that it was a Cong, trying to get his wet weapon to work.

Johnson opened up and blew him away.

"Reeds!" Monaco shouted. "They're in the water!"

We got to the sides of the stream and opened up on the reeds. Suddenly the reeds became people, trying to get out of the water, returning our fire. There was fire from the sides of the stream as well. We moved back fifty meters and set up. Walowick had the grenade launcher and was sending them into the bushes at the side of the stream.

"Watch the ridge! Watch the ridge!" Lobel called out.

We were all watching it already. It could have been a trap. We fired and fired until there was no return. I wanted to move out, so did the rest of the guys, but Brunner gave the order to move forward.

The water the reeds floated in was stained dark with blood. There were four bodies on the side of the stream, one we could see just under the water. Lobel put a shot into it and it jerked up. The guy was still alive! He tried to run, and Lobel hit him with a short burst that sent him whirling, his arms over his head as if he were dancing.

"I killed him!" Lobel turned toward us. His eyes were wild. He looked back at the body that now floated faceup in the water, that now slid below the surface into the darkness.

"I killed him!"

Lobel was shaking. He had killed his first man up close. He had seen him die. It was personal. The shit was real. He was a killer.

Brunner called our position in and requested that our present position be our pickup zone. It was denied. We started back.

Problem. It was nearly dark. The sides of the stream were clear for twenty to forty meters on both sides. On the side of the stream that we were on, away from the ridge, there was a rice paddy that we had to cross. We had passed it coming, but going back was another thing. They knew we were there now, knew we were headed back. If we got Congs on the ridge when we were passing the paddies, it would be hard going.

Monaco led the way. It rained for a few minutes, a cold, driving rain that chilled you in ways you wouldn't forget very soon. Then it stopped. A slight wind picked up and made the trees that grew in sullen clusters along the ridge sway menacingly. The moon came up. We were almost back to the LZ.

I wanted to get back quickly. Lobel was just about holding it together. We had to get him back, give him some peace. Let him get the knots out of his nerves again.

We got almost back to the cutoff point where we would move to the LZ. We had to pass the saddle again.

"Peewee, you and Perry check the ridge," Brunner said.

"Keep your asses down," Johnson said.

Me and Peewee started across the stream. It was fairly deep. I remembered I couldn't swim.

"Peewee," I whispered, hoarsely. "You swim?"

"No."

Damn. It took us forever to get across the stream. We got across just as the moon went behind the clouds. I looked back over the stream, but I couldn't see a damn thing. My testicles shriveled up in a hard knot and turned to ice. I was low, I was moving forward.

We started up the saddle. It sloped more than the ridge did and we got to the top fairly quickly. Peewee put his hand up. It was getting dark quickly.

Whick! Whick!

Two shots hit the rock near me, sending chips into the air. Behind me I could hear the sixty open up.

Whick! Whick! Whick!

"Where the fuck's the fire coming from?" Peewee asked.

"I don't know!"

We raced to the top of the ridge. I climbed the last few meters, breathing through my mouth, and started firing over the other side. Nothing. I didn't see anything.

"What you see? What you see?" Peewee's frantic voice.

"Nothing! I don't see anything!"

We hit the ground and turned back toward the stream. There was a firefight below us. We could see tracers, and muzzle blasts. It was all on the other side of the stream. The sixty was sweeping the banks of the stream. The popping of the M-79 sounded like champagne being opened. The squad was turning loose. Then everything was quiet.

Chapter 22

Silence. It was dark and getting darker. Soon even the few silhouettes against the sky would disappear into the blackness. There were the sounds of insects, a constant chirping. The night belonged to them. It belonged to little things with green and black bodies that knew their way through the tall grass.

I listened for the sounds of a firefight. I listened for the sounds of voices. What had happened? Were the Congs gone? Were our guys down?

The sounds replayed through my head. There had been fire in our direction then the sound of a sixty. Was it Johnson's sixty or something they had? Were both sides waiting for the other to make a move?

"Perry!" Peewee's voice in the darkness nearly stopped my heart.

"Here!"

"What's going on?"

"I don't know."

Silence.

Were the Congs creeping up on us? Could they see in the dark? Could they wrap the shadows around themselves and make themselves invisible?

"Peewee!"

"Wha?"

"Let's open up, let the squad know we're still here."

"They got to know already." Peewee was closer. I was glad he was closer. I wanted to touch him.

"How do you know that?"

"They know we ain't there, we got to be someplace," Peewee said.

"Yeah."

"Let's just keep quiet and shoot the shit out of anything that come near us."

"Okay."

I touched the safety. Changed clips. I put a frag grenade in front of me. I had three. I'd use two and save one for myself if it came to that. I remember hearing stories about what the Congs did to prisoners.

I thought about Kenny. He was afraid of the dark. We were all afraid of the dark.

Peewee put his hand on my wrist.

"What is it?" I whispered.

"Nothing," he whispered back.

He kept his hand on my wrist. I moved my hand and took his. We held hands in the darkness.

I tried to get the possibilities straight in my mind. Maybe the squad had called in reinforcements. No way they overran the squad. No way. You didn't overrun Johnson. Johnson was the man. Johnson would kick some ass. Him and his sixty would sing.

Yea, though I walk through the valley . . .

Then where were they? They had to know we were over here. They wouldn't leave us.

Voices. Vietnamese voices. Peewee let go my hand and I knew he was checking out his piece.

"Peewee, we get the direction of the voices, then go the other way."

"Bet!"

The voices were coming up from the stream. We weren't going away from the stream, no way. They were coming nearer. Think. Think. Don't think, react.

I opened up toward the voices. Peewee followed me.

"Skirmish spray!" he called to me.

In the darkness he had moved a little away from me. I did what he said. I sprayed fire down toward the stream in as even a line as I could.

There was some confusion. I could hear a number of voices. Then they returned our fire. They were Cong.

"Perry! I see them!" Peewee was making his way over toward me.

"How many?"

"A million of them!"

"Damn!"

We started moving backward. Maybe they had overrun the squad. We moved down the long side of the ridge, trying to keep our balance, hoping we wouldn't step on a mine or pull a trip wire.

The voices were coming closer.

A flare! We hit the dirt. We were on the other side of the ridge and their line was coming up. They wouldn't come up too fast. They didn't know how many of us were on the ridge. I hoped to God that they didn't know how many of us were on the ridge.

I got off the ground as soon as I saw that they hadn't reached the top of the ridge. We had to get the hell out of there. There were paddies off to the left. They must have used the stream to water them. We'd never make it across the paddies. There was an overhang on the side of the ridge. I pointed toward it and Peewee caught on.

We reached the overhang and tried to back against it. It went deeper than we thought and Peewee turned to me. I couldn't see his face, but I knew what he was thinking. We were backing into a Cong spider hole.

Peewee turned and rammed his rifle into the hole. Nothing. He moved into it and I heard him flail around.

"Yo," he said. "It's cool."

It's cool. Bullshit it was cool. He knew it wasn't cool and so did I. If it was a Cong hole then they knew about it. It was better than the paddies, but it definitely wasn't cool.

The spider hole was about a meter and a half all around and a meter deep. Once we climbed in it we were just below ground level. It might have been cozy for one little Cong but it wasn't made for me and Peewee. The grass in front of it was high. We had knocked some of it down and Peewee was trying to get it to stand up. I felt around the hole. It felt like an open grave.

"Peewee, maybe we should try to work our way back across the stream," I said.

"No way, man," Peewee said. "There's a million of them out there."

"Oh, God."

"They ain't taking me alive," Peewee said.

"Me, either,"

We waited. There weren't any voices at first. Then there were. The high, sing-song grunting that was Vietnamese. What were they saying?

A flare. The light terrified me. Peewee was in front of me, and I could feel his body tense. I had to force myself to keep my eyes open. We could see the light from the flare through the grass in front of the spider hole. If they had the guts to send up a flare it had to be a damn battalion of them. I pulled myself into as tight a ball as I could. More voices. Hide-and-go-seek.

They were looking for us. Were they confused?

I could see them walking down the ridge. If I were a sniper, I could pick one of them off easily. They were looking toward the paddies. Most of them didn't even crouch. They knew they had the numbers.

As the light from the flare died, the darkness seemed to eat their bodies. Black.

The voices went past.

What had happened to the squad? Were they on the bank of the stream? Were they down?

I had one arm around Peewee. I held him close. There was nothing to talk about. We couldn't tell where the voices were coming from. We couldn't leave.

My right leg had gone to sleep. I flexed the muscles in it, moved it a little.

I wondered what time it was. A thought flashed through my mind. The Congs would take watches and rings from dead soldiers. They would cut the rings off. Suppose I wasn't dead? Suppose I just lay wounded, trying to fake it, and some Cong came to take the watch?

I slipped my watch off in the darkness. Then I put it back on. Stop thinking; it didn't help.

Thoughts came. What would Morningside Avenue look like now? It would be day and the park would be filled with kids, their screaming and laughter would slide along the light beams into the helter skelter world of monkey bars and swings. On the courts there would be a tough game. Black bodies sweating and grunting to get the points that would let them sweat and grunt in the sun for another game. It wasn't real. None of it was real. The only thing that was real was me and Peewee, sitting in this spider's grave, waiting for death.

Artillery off in the distance. Outgoing? Maybe, maybe not. Somebody had to know that the squad wasn't back. Somebody had to know something.

Pray.

God. . . . What to pray? What to tell God? That I'm scared? That I'm so scared that my heart might stop any moment? That my heart might stop without the fragments of metal that would rip it apart?

God. . . . What to tell God? That I didn't want to die? That I was like everybody else over here, trying to cling to a few more days of life?

Peewee moved, adjusted position.

"I got to shit," he said.

It was funny. It was funny as hell. We both started giggling. I buried my head in his shoulder. We were both a glance from dying, and he had to shit and it was just so damn funny.

The Congs wouldn't understand that. Not at all. They wouldn't understand two Americans giggling in a spider hole in the middle of their country. They'd stop us from giggling, too.

Be alert, don't think. Don't think.

I think that time is passing and they haven't found us. I'm thinking that if daylight comes we might live. We might be able to crawl out of this mother and see some Cong dressed like a farmer, his rifle hidden in a bush somewhere, working in the paddies.

We might be able to see the stream and get across. The helicopters might swoop us up from the ridge and save us a trip back to the hooch. All that and life, too, if daylight came.

Thou preparest a table for me in the presence of mine enemies. . . .

It came. The insects noticed it first. The chirping picked up. There were birds. The distant boom of artillery switched from its sporadic night rhythm to the purposeful daylight pounding.

We hadn't heard voices all night. Now they were there again. The Congs were awake. The voices didn't seem too close.

"I'm going to look outside," Peewee said.

"Okay."

He stuck his head out and looked around. When he got back in he unhooked a frag grenade from his belt. I gripped his shoulder.

"They look like they getting ready to move out," he said.

"They headed this way?"

"No, but if any of them do. . . ."

No more voices. Peewee was between me and the front of the hole. Our sixteens were at our side, too jammed between us and the walls of the hole to use. My legs ached. I couldn't have run if I had wanted to.

Peewee patted me on the leg, and started to look out again. He jerked back in.

"One coming this way, the others headed away from here."

I tensed. I flexed my hand twice, quickly. Got it back on the sixteen.

Outside the hole. Something had stopped just outside the hole.

A voice. Movement in the grass. I could see the feet. They wore thick black-soled sandals. A rifle poked in. Peewee put his hand on mine, moved my fingers off the trigger.

He moved his hand away, and my finger went back onto the trigger.

The voice again. We had disturbed the grass in front of the spider hole and the guy wasn't sure. The feet turned and moved away.

Peewee didn't say anything. He pushed up and looked out. A long moment passed. Peewee moved back against me.

"Most of them gone. This dude went a little way after them then stopped," Peewee said.

"He coming back?"

"I don't know," Peewee said. "I think this his hole."

The feet again. The rifle came into the hole. A voice. Peewee was right. He was nervous about the hole. Then a pole came in. On the end of the pole was a knife. It went near Peewee, then into the wall near me. The Cong above us shifted his position, then pushed the pole in again. Peewee was pushing it aside with his hand. I saw blood on Peewee's hand. Then the pole went into the dirt near my head. It came out clean. Then it was gone.

Then a rifle was thrown into the hole. Peewee grabbed it and pulled it in. The Cong's feet followed. I pushed the sixteen into the small brown body and pulled the trigger. The body jerked backward once.

Peewee was frantically trying to pull him in on top of us.

"Get his arms!"

I could hardly move before; with the Cong in the hole I couldn't move at all. I couldn't reach the arms and just grabbed a piece of his shirt and pulled on that. We got him in and for a moment he was still. I thought he was dead. Then the shock of being shot must have worn off and he began to struggle.

"Don't shoot again!" Peewee was saying.

I got one arm free and was pulling at the Cong's hair. Peewee was trying to strangle him with one hand. The Cong was desperately trying to push his way out of the hole. Me and Peewee were desperately trying to hold him.

He got one arm out of the hole.

"Shoot him!" Peewee said.

I couldn't find the trigger of the sixteen. Peewee had one hand around the Cong's neck. We pulled until he stopped struggling.

We waited. The Cong was dead. I knew he was dead. The smell of death filled our small grave. The Cong's body growled and let off gases.

"Peewee, we got to get out of here!"

Peewee started to push on the Cong. He was halfway wedged between the front of the spider hole and Peewee.

"Can't move his ass," Peewee was saying.

"Wait, let me pull him."

I searched around until I found his arm. Then I pulled on it. He came down in the hole. His knees were on either side of Peewee. The three of us were wrapped around each other. I kept pulling. His head slipped past Peewee's shoulder.

A kid. He was a damned kid. The blood stained the smooth chin. The eyes weren't completely closed.

"Pull, man!"

I pulled. Peewee got his elbow on the Cong's side and pushed him enough to get his arms out of the hole. He pushed up and went out.

"C'mon!"

I pushed past the dead Cong out into the open air.

I had to reach back in and get my sixteen. I felt around for the grenades, felt the Cong's body, and left them.

I sucked in the fresh air as hard as I could. The day was clear, the sky brilliant. There were fields of rice paddies before us and in one of them a Vietnamese farmer stood. He turned toward us, still kneeling in the knee-deep water. Maybe it was his son in the hole. He stood and Peewee lifted his rifle. He ducked down into the water again.

We left him and got to the top of the ridge. There was nobody around.

"Watch the stream," Peewee said.

We ran down the side of the ridge until we got to the stream. There were some reeds in the water. I didn't remember if they had been there the night before or not. I hoped they had been as we started across the stream.

Peewee was slightly ahead of me. The water turned bright crimson around him as he went through it.

"You bleeding?"

"Ain't shit," he said.

We were on the other side of the stream. We started moving along the stream as fast as we could. We ran for five minutes before Peewee stopped and fell to one side.

"Peewee!'

"Go on, man, I can't make it," he said.

"Never happen, man. I'm not leaving you, Peewee."

"Go on, man."

"No way, Peewee."

I looked around for a stick or something he could use as a crutch. I didn't see anything. My mind wasn't working anyway. Nothing made sense. I looked at Peewee to see how he was doing. He was looking at me through the oldest eyes I had ever seen.

"Get my neck!"

He threw his arm around my neck and I pulled him to his feet. We started off again.

It took another five minutes to find the pickup zone. When we got there, it was more trouble.

It was Monaco. He was sitting against a tree. He had his head in his hands. His piece was about ten meters in front of him. I wanted to go to him, but Peewee stopped me.

"He ain't sitting there for nothing," he said.

I looked around. Nothing. What the hell was wrong with this damn war? You never saw anything. There was never anything there, until it was on top of your ass, and you were screaming and shooting and too scared to figure out anything.

Me and Peewee found some cover and watched Monaco.

"Maybe he's dead," I said.

"Could be."

Monaco moved. He straightened his legs out and then brought them back up again.

Voices. We looked to see where they came from. There was a clump of bushes off to one side. It was just a little thicker than the rest, but I could still see one branch that was a little too straight. It was the barrel of a gun pointed at Monaco.

"They got him covered. He move and he dead. They waiting for a chopper to come in and get him," Peewee said.

We looked around, trying to spot anything else we could find. There was another suspicious clump of bushes on the other side of the pickup zone.

"Let's get the one on this side when the chopper come," Peewee said.

"Right."

He wanted to fight back. That was Peewee. He was hurt, maybe hurt bad, but he was still thinking about fighting back. Who the hell were these people? These soldiers? Was I really one of them? If I was, could I ever be anything else again?

Wait. Always. Wait. We waited. Across from us, no more than sixty to seventy meters, Monaco sat, looking at his hands. His helmet was pushed back on his head.

He was sitting in the shadow of death. We were all sitting in the shadow of death. I wondered what he was thinking about. Maybe he was thinking about his girl. I even hoped he was thinking about her.

We heard the chopper. It came in from behind us, like a great, angry hornet, swinging its tail. Me and Peewee opened upon the first clump of bushes.

We surprised them. It took them a while to return fire, but the chopper had them spotted. The moment the chopper opened up on the first machine gun, we started shooting at the second.

The chopper came down fast. We thought it had been hit. It landed and guys started piling out. Me and Peewee came out and started heading for the chopper. Monaco was up and had his piece.

He came running over to us and grabbed Peewee's other side. We got to the chopper, the damn thing bounced up a foot and almost knocked Peewee's head off. Me and Monaco grabbed his legs and threw him into the chopper. A crewman pulled him in. I thought about putting my piece on safety before crawling in.

Monaco was up and in and the other guys who had come in with the chopper were piling back in.

"Move your ass!"

I lost the little strength I had left. The wind from the chopper sent pieces of sand and dirt into my face, and I just wanted to lay down. I got my rifle in the door and reached for something to grab hold of. Somebody, I didn't know who, was pulling on me as we started moving. The floor of the chopper smelled of oil.

Pain! God! A sudden, searing pain in my right leg. I was hit again! The pain took my breath away and I tried to twist to look at the leg. Somebody pulled it around, and I screamed. Somebody else was screaming, too. Or maybe it was me. The chopper was in the air. I couldn't breathe. Somebody was laying on top of me.

The guy on top of me was trying to get off. I heard myself yelling as his weight came down on my leg.

The chopper veered crazily to one side, and I was struggling to hold on. My leg was burning, bursting with the pain, but I was able to hold on. The dark interior of the chopper began to spin. I called to Peewee.

"Peewee!"

"I'm making it, man," he said, weakly.

"Monaco?"

"Hanging in, baby," Monaco was near me and put his hand on my shoulder. "Hanging in."

A short burst of rounds hit the side of the medevac, and I clenched my teeth and grabbed for the sides. It spun in the air, and then I felt the floor lift into me as we started away. There were bodies around me, some crying out in pain, others shaking in fear, others trying to help the wounded. One thought filled my whole being. I was still alive. Alive.

Chapter 23

So WE OPENED UP ON THE GUYS WE SAW," Monaco was saying. The smell of disinfectant, mingled with that of insect repellent, hung in the air. "We cut down a few of them, and then we looked upstream and saw the whole damn Cong army coming at us. The way we figured we had to split or die right there. Yo, man, Johnson wanted to go down right there."

"How did they get you?" The morphine wasn't helping the leg at all. I kept having flashes of me in a wheelchair or on crutches.

"We laid down a few bursts, threw some grenades, and made a run for it," Monaco said. "They took cover, but they didn't return fire. I think they thought we were an advance patrol or something. They didn't know if they should come after us or bug out. Brunner figured that they thought we knew their size.

"They sent out a couple of squads after us. I got hit with something and went down just when the choppers landed. I got stunned or something, then I look up and see the choppers leaving, and I know I've had it, right?"

"You must have really freaked out."

"I started praying to God and to Saint Jude," Monaco said. "I mean some heavy praying. I'm making all kinds of promises, too. You know, get me out of this one and I'm going to be so cool for the rest of my life it won't be funny."

"I thought I was the only one making all the promises," I said.

"If God gets even half the promises we've been laying down, the U.S.A. is going to be holier than the Vatican," Monaco said. "Anyway, I stayed near the pickup zone all night in case they came back for me. Maybe I dozed off, I don't even remember. When it got light I hear this noise, and then I saw the machine guns and I know the Congs got my ass. Every time I move a finger they lay down a burst right near me. The Congs started talking to me in English. I was so scared I couldn't even think of nothing except dying."

"What they say to you?"

"They said 'Hey, GI, how about some Cheu Hoi . . .' " Monaco started to cry. "Then I just sat there waiting for them to kill me."

The dust-off choppers had taken us to Chu Lai. They had rushed Peewee right into surgery, and I was waiting to go in. A medic had come in and examined my leg. I had asked him how it looked, and he said I would be okay. I imagined him saying the same thing a hundred times a day to a hundred guys.

I was in the hospital. There were guys on both sides of the corridor. A guy across from me was twisting and screaming. The right side of his head was bandaged and so was the lower part of his face. We all had tags, and the doctors would come out, check our tags, and then take us into surgery.

"What's my tag say?" I asked Monaco.

He got up and looked at it. " 'Fracture wound, simple projectile, type O.' "

"It doesn't say anything about amputation, does it?"

"Nah."

"That's good," I said, straining to see Monaco's face to see if he was telling the truth.

"Hey, Perry, I got to split," he said. He was crying again. "I been sitting here trying to think of something to say about . . . you know . . . you and Peewee saving my life and all. . . ."

"No big deal, man," I said. "We all got lucky."

"No, I was dead, Perry. I was actually sitting there with that Cong gun right on my ass and I was dead. You know, when it went down, when you and Peewee opened up on the gun, it was like I was brought back to life. I was dead and I was brought back to life again."

"We're all dead over here, Monaco," I said. "We're all dead and just hoping that we come back to life when we get into the World again."

"Yeah. . . ." He patted me on the arm.

Somebody called my name and I looked up. It was the doctor. He came and started wheeling me into the operating room. Monaco held my hand until the doctor, rolling the gurney I was on, pulled it from his hand. I had never been in love before. Maybe this was what it was like, the way I felt for Monaco and Peewee and Johnson and the rest of my squad. I hoped this was what it was like.

I dreamt about the Apollo Theater. I dreamt that I was in the Apollo and the Shirelles were there. There were a hundred girls in the audience, and they were all going crazy over the Shirelles. Peewee was there, too. He was saying something about the Shirelles not being so hot. I told him he was crazy. He said they had better singers in the projects in Chicago. I told him he was a Chicago fool. We were having a good time, me and Peewee.

Then I heard my name. I looked at Peewee to see if he was calling me, but he had his back toward me. I stood next to him and looked at his face but he was watching the stage. And still I heard my name being called.

"Perry!"

I opened my eyes. There was a nurse. She wasn't pretty. Her eyes were brown, tired.

"Hi!" I said.

"Hi, yourself, soldier," she answered. There was more life to the eyes. "How you feeling?"

"Okay, how's my leg?"

"You won't be dancing on it for a while, but it'll come around."

She gave me something to drink that tasted like orange juice and castor oil. She fixed my pillow and asked me where I was from.

"New York," I said. "Where you from?"

"Puerto Rico," she said, smiling. When she smiled she was very pretty. "Santurce. You know where it is?"

I didn't. She started to leave and I called her back.

"Look, you see a guy named Gates? Harold Gates?"

"Could be around here," she said. "You get any pain in the leg, you call the nurse. Try not to ask for painkillers unless you really need them, though, okay?"

"Sure."

My mouth was dry and tasted like gasoline residue. The nurse wheeled me out into a small room. There was another guy there, he was bandaged around his chest. He was staring at the wall.

"How you doing?" he said.

"Okay. How do my legs look?"

He looked down at them. "They're there," he said.

Peewee found me two days later. He was in a wheelchair and came up alongside the bed like gangbusters.

"I got full charge of the numbers racket in this hospital," he said. "What you want to play?"

"How the hell you doing, Peewee?"

"What number you want to play?" he insisted.

"How about 3-1-2?" I said.

"That's too long for me to write down," he said. "I'm out of here in two weeks."

"Back to the States?"

"Where else I'm going to go?"

"How's your wound?"

"Nothing to it," Peewee said. "He cut enough to make me have to have another damn operation when I get back to the States, that's all."

"Is it serious?"

"Serious enough to get my ass home," Peewee said. "I'm gonna say a prayer to Buddha for the boy who done it soon's I get a chance."

"They didn't tell me anything yet," I said.

"If they say you ain't hurt bad enough to go home you got to play crazy.

Tell them you keep seeing pink-ass zebras running around the room and you want to catch one of them and eat him."

"I'll tell them something," I said.

"They ain't getting me back in this war. We been in this shit too long, man"—Peewee shook his head—"and it's too damn heavy."

The nurse from Santurce was named Celia Vilas. She got us some beer, and me and Monaco drank it on the night before Monaco had to go back to the boonies. Peewee couldn't drink anything except plain water and a little warm milk. We did a lot of drinking and a lot of crying. Me and Peewee didn't want Monaco to have to go back. Monaco didn't want to go, either. But he didn't feel it was right to leave the squad unless he had to.

Peewee got sick, threw up, and busted all his stitches. The doctors had to sew him up again, and I realized that Peewee was hurt worse than I thought he was. Monaco said he would come by in the morning before his plane left and say good-bye. He didn't. He left a note at the desk, and Celia gave it to me. It said that I had to wear a tux to his wedding.

I got to sit up in a wheelchair, and the leg felt right in spite of the cast. It felt good. I hoped it wasn't. I could make it with a limp, I just didn't want to go back to the boonies anymore.

We got a call from Lieutenant Gearhart on the ham radio network. He told us the other guys in the squad were all right. It was nice of him to call us, but it wasn't true. Monaco wasn't all right. Monaco was like me and Peewee. We had tasted what it was like being dead. We had rolled it around in our mouths and swallowed it and now the stink from it was coming from us. We weren't all right. We would have to learn to be alive again.

He also told us that Captain Stewart had been promoted.

It was two weeks before they took the cast off. The doctor looked at the X rays and then at the wound.

"How do you feel?"

"Okay," I heard myself saying.

He examined the chart again, then went to the foot of the bed. "You're Richard Perry, right?"

"Yes, sir."

"What was your stateside station?"

"Fort Devens."

"Why were you in combat?" he said. "You've got a medical profile. Did you volunteer?"

A butterfly, maybe a moth, had gotten into the room. It flittered about the ceiling, then landed on the foot of the bed opposite me.

"No, sir. They said the profile from Devens hadn't arrived."

He looked at the record again. "It was here since, oh yes, the eighth of March. I guess it was late. You're going to be sent home. This is your second Purple Heart, isn't it?"

"Yes, sir."

"I hope it's your last, Corporal."

Peewee had another operation on his stomach for something called adhesions, but he was still scheduled to leave with me.

We kept up with the war in *Stars and Stripes*, but it seemed different in the papers. In the papers there didn't seem to be any cost. A hill was taken, or a hamlet, and the only body counts that were given were for the Congs. Once in a while there would be mention of our own killed, but the numbers didn't seem to even match the numbers I saw in the hospital unit.

President Johnson was saying that the United States was willing to stop its bombing if the North Vietnamese were ready to begin serious talks.

We looked for word of our guys, of the squad, but it was as if we weren't even there. The papers mentioned something about the Third NVA, a crack Cong regiment, being pushed out of the Nui Loc Son basin, but it was only that, a mention.

A sergeant I got to play chess with told me that the personnel sergeant would look up friends for you if you gave him a few dollars. I found him and gave him ten bucks to look up Judy Duncan. The guy, a tall red-faced spec four with freckles and a shock of red hair, told me he would look her up and that I could leave my name and come by later.

"You a relative, or just a friend?"

"Just a friend," I said. "But I'm shipping out for the States and. . . ."

He had already turned back to his papers, so I left.

Peewee stayed in his bed for a day and a half. He said he didn't want anything to happen to the wound.

"I'm getting out of here," he said, "if I got to put some Scotch tape on this sucker."

Waiting for word. Monaco was far away now, and so was Johnson. They were already names in my past. I would think of them, worry about them, but for the moment I was just hoping for the Freedom Bird to take me back to the World.

Word came. Me and Peewee had orders to be on the same plane back, but my orders were on a different set of papers than Peewee's. We read them together. I was on crutches, but the leg was feeling stronger. I felt a sharp pain every now and then. I thought it might have been shrapnel, but I wouldn't complain. Not now, not until I was back in the World again.

We were lined up, waiting to get on the plane. The line wasn't that rigid. Half the guys were on crutches or in some kind of bandages. We all talked nervously, not looking at the stack of silver caskets that were being loaded on. They would be going back to the World with us. Me and Peewee kidded a guy from the 159th Transportation Battalion who had lost part of his left hand about how he should have taken one of his boats home when he had the chance.

"Perry?"

The red-haired clerk had a clipboard. It was the guy I had asked about Judy Duncan. The name tag read "Witt." I tensed as he came near me. The stream flashed in my mind. The sound of the crickets in the darkness.

"Yeah?"

"Your friend didn't make it," he said.

"Didn't make it?" I looked at him. "I'm talking about a woman. Her name is Duncan."

"Yeah, Judy Duncan," he said. "She got transferred to a field hospital and it got hit. Sorry."

In the distance there were helicopters headed toward the mountains. Headed toward the hell of an LZ. I turned away.

A plane landed. GIs came tumbling through the doors and out into the hot Vietnamese sun. They lined up and started marching toward us from the other side of the field. A major near us jumped into a jeep and went across the field to meet them. They stopped while the major talked to the officer leading them.

The major returned and sat in his jeep.

Judy Duncan. I forgot what part of Texas she was from. I hadn't known her, not really. I felt sorry for her. I felt sorry that Texas was so far away and that nobody there would know about her, how this part of her life had been, what she had seen, or how she had felt at the end. They would get a telegram, and a body, but they wouldn't know.

The caskets were almost completely loaded into the tail end of the C-47. They were there together, but they had died alone. Maybe some of them had been friends. I turned away.

They finished loading the caskets, and the major drove his jeep around the front of the plane and signaled the officer with the new guys.

They marched them by us to the orientation barracks. They were supposed to be looking straight ahead, but they were looking at us. We tried to straighten up the best we could. It wasn't the wounds that kept us bent, that tugged at our shoulders, so much as it was the fatigue. We were tired of this war.

We got to Osaka and the C-47 picked up some more caskets. The GIs were spread on other planes and me and Peewee talked a lieutenant into putting us both on a flight to Fort Ord, in California. I made him promise he'd take some leave with me in New York. Peewee said he'd go, but he knew Harlem couldn't touch Chicago.

I was telling him about the wonders of Harlem when I noticed he was shaking. I asked if his stomach was bothering him, and he said no, that he just couldn't believe he was out of the Nam. The stewardess came over and offered us Cokes. I think she was embarrassed that we were holding hands.

Slowly, ever so slowly, I began to relax. Peewee fell asleep and turned away from me. The stewardess came by and smiled.

"He looked tired," she said.

I nodded. She went on.

I took the thin magazine from the pouch in front of me and began to thumb through it. I felt self-conscious, as if I shouldn't be there. My mind began to wander, as I knew it would, back to the boonies. I was on patrol again. Monaco was on point. Peewee and Walowick followed him. Lobel and Brunner were next, then Johnson, the sixty cradled in his arm as if it were a child. We were walking the boonies, past rice paddies, toward yet another hill. I was in the rear, and for some reason I turned back. Behind me, trailing the platoon, were the others. Brew, Jenkins, Sergeant Dongan, Turner, and Lewis, the new guys, and Lieutenant Carroll.

I knew I was mixing my prayers, but it didn't matter. I just wanted God to care for them, to keep them whole. I knew they were thinking about me and Peewee.

Peewee stirred in his uneasy sleep. The plane droned on. A fat man complained that they didn't have the wine he wanted. We were headed back to the World.

Related Readings

Denise Kusel

Catharsis

The story of the war in Viet Nam has been told over and over again, but the women who were a part of the American forces in Viet Nam have, to a large extent, been ignored. Glenna Goodacre did something to help those women to obtain recognition and to heal their memories of a terrible yet important part of their lives.

GLENNA GOODACRE sits at a massive desk in the anteroom of her Santa Fe, NM, studio. Nearly five months have gone by since the dedication of the memorial, and this morning she's not exactly dressed for handling clay.

"I haven't really gotten back to work," she admits. "It's not a let-down that I feel, it's not that at all. And these days, I don't think about the project as much. I mean, I have six commissions I need to be working on right now. Plus I have a one-woman show in the summer of 1995. . . ."

She pauses. "You know what I learned? I learned more tolerance, that's what. I'm just amazed at how many lives the sculpture did change."

She gazes absentmindedly into the next room where administrative assistant Dan Anthony is wrapping a small bronze for shipping. The working portion of the 18-foot-high studio is flanked by two 12-foot French doors that allow large sculptures to be moved in and out. But today, Goodacre is not working. As she collects her thoughts, her fingers reach out to straighten small stacks of paper on the desk. "I had no idea this many people . . . this many women . . . would stop and see it," she says in her flat West Texas drawl.

"So many things surprised me. Every ceremony, every face, Washington, DC, three trips to the White House. The letters I've received from people all over the country. The faces . . . there are hundreds of people I will never forget. I am just so proud and in awe of how many lives were touched. . . ."

Her voice trails off and her fingers stop dancing on the papers. As if she has caught herself in a revealing reverie, she quickly changes the subject. "You know, my name was a clue on one of those television game shows. Can you imagine that? I'm getting to be famous."

For the 53-year-old artist, this particular sculpture was a high point in a career that's been peppered with successful nuggets.

Beneath a 50-foot American flag draped over a glass wall in the Mall of America in Bloomington, MN, a man dressed in fatigues pushes his wheelchair to the sculpture and grasps the hand of one of the bronze figures. He bows his head.

This is the first time the statue has been removed from the Federal Express truck, which was specially equipped with a rolling bed and bifold doors so the sculpture may be viewed from all sides.

"I spent a year in anger during the design-approval process in Washington," Goodacre says. "A year in rage. I had lost control of my work. I was the Big Bitch of the West. But you have to get over it. And the end result was worth the grueling process."

Last fall in Santa Fe, while sharing a podium with photographer Barbara Van Cleve, Goodacre talked about the special pressure of creating public art during a program sponsored by Judy Chicago's Through the Flower Society. "You have to remember that the work doesn't belong to you," she said. "You are being paid for it, but it isn't yours. I gave up my copyright to the project. These are times when someone else is making the decisions."

This decision wasn't made all at once, and even after it was made, it was changed and changed again. In the fall of 1990, the Vietnam Women's Memorial group launched an open design competition, eventually drawing 317 entries. Goodacre's original design for the monument was not the initial choice.

"I was runner-up!" Goodacre says with a touch of gleeful irony in her voice. "That should be a word to aspiring artists: Don't give up on the competitions. Second place can rise again! And never say you've already done your best work."

She smiles reflectively. "I put a lot of myself into that piece. I still remember the butterflies in my stomach the day I signed it. I'll probably never do another piece that means so much. . . . There were thousands of people who needed this as a catharsis. People wrote poetry to it. They composed songs for it. They stood there and cried and placed valued objects and flowers on it. They touched it."

In Baltimore, a Navy chaplain arrives to deliver the invocation. He stops suddenly. "Something told me to turn around and look at the statue. I hadn't seen it before, and when I did, I felt a hot, white light move all the way down my spine. I saw my son up there. That soldier, that wounded soldier, that was my Buddy. That was my son. He never came home."

"There is a healing that people can identify with in this bronze," Goodacre says. "I left interpretation open enough so that people can read into it what they want. My intention was that it not all be spelled out."

At the dedication on November 11, Goodacre, flanked by military brass and Vice President Al Gore, stood on the stage and explained that the statue intentionally did not reveal insignia nor branch of service but instead was a tribute to every woman. The echoes of *Stars and Stripes Forever* were still reverberating in the crisp afternoon. "There is no rank," she said, talking about each of the three women depicted in the work. "The woman who is cradling the wounded soldier across her lap is the nurse. I purposely covered the top of the soldier's face so he would be anonymous.

"The standing woman is looking up for help . . . looking for a medevac helicopter. Or perhaps looking for help from God. The kneeling woman many vets think of as the heart and soul of the piece. Women have looked at it and said, 'That was me. That's how I felt.'"

Minutes later, by the time Goodacre fully understood the immensity of what she had accomplished, and while looking at the 7-foot, 8-inch bronze, her voice broke as she was swept up in the moment. "This has been a phenomenal experience for me. To think my hands can shape the clay that heals the heart. I'm proud of my sculpture."

This memorial has given me a sense of peace . . . a sense of great joy. It also gives me the incentive to continue to reach out to my sisters and brothers who have not quite reached that place of peace. —Former Red Cross volunteer viewing the statue in Pentagon City, VA.

The war the women fought in Vietnam was different from the one fought by the men. It was insidious. It didn't explode with action. It crept into the consciousness. It imploded in the psyche. There are no names on the Vietnam Women's Memorial, but the 11,000-pound sculpture vibrates with raw emotion. It never fails to evoke tears.

"The night after the dedication, I went back to see the statue," Goodacre relates. "I wanted to see it by myself, without all the crowds. I wanted to see how it looked. But even at midnight, there were still people standing there and looking at it. I was amazed. A woman walked up to me and said, 'Now, I can come home.'"

Goodacre reaches down to pet her golden retriever, Tesuque. "You know, I and my assistants didn't stop the project abruptly. We had worked on the piece so long that once it was gone from the middle of the floor where we molded it in the studio, we missed it. Looking back, I don't have a derogatory thing to say about the three years it consumed. From a sculptor's standpoint, to get everything done and to just pull that drape. . . . My advice to young sculptors is don't sit on your laurels, which I'm ashamed I've been doing for a few months. It's time to get back to work."

Steve
Hockensmith

The Home Front

*In a time before television, Americans obtained much of
their news about World War II from on-the-spot
newspaper reporters. One of the most famous of these was
Ernie Pyle.*

AFTER WAR CORRESPONDENT ERNIE PYLE was killed by a machine-gun bullet on the tiny Pacific island of Ie Shima 55 years ago, American soldiers put up a sign near the ditch where he died. "At this spot, the 77th Infantry Division lost a buddy—Ernie Pyle," the sign read.

That's how the Army—and all of America—viewed Pyle. He was the G.I.'s buddy, the beloved newspaper columnist who spent his time huddling in foxholes with foot soldiers, not cozying up to the brass behind the lines. And that's how Pyle is still remembered today, 100 years after his birth. (He was born in Dana, Ind., on Aug 3, 1900.) Visit the Ernie Pyle State Historic Site in Dana, for instance, and you'll find that the museum there is as much about World War II as it is about the tiny town's most famous son.

Yet though it is Pyle's dispatches during World War II that made him the most famous correspondent of that—or any other—war, there was another side to the journalist that has been largely forgotten. Before he left the U.S. in 1940 to begin covering the war with a series on the London blitz, Pyle already had begun building his reputation as one of America's most talented newspaper writers. He had spent the previous five years crisscrossing the country in a beaten-up Ford, writing a syndicated column about the people he encountered along the way. An ice-cream salesman in Evansville, Ind.; a female barber in Platinum, Alaska; the patients at Hawaii's Molokai leper colony; the drought-plagued farmers of the Dust Bowl—Pyle wrote about them all, 1,000 words a day, six days a week.

"His chief motivation was boredom," says David Nichols, who edited "Ernie's America," a 1989 collection of Pyle's prewar columns. "He had been the managing editor of the Washington Daily News and he was bored with conventional newspaper work, particularly desk work like writing headlines and editing copy. He wanted to blow out, hit the road, 'strike out for the territory,' as Mark Twain put it."

Pyle's greatest asset during his travel-writing years (aside from his formidable talent as a columnist) was an ability to strike up a conversation with just about anybody anywhere.

"When he went into a small town, he didn't go to the Chamber of Commerce and say, 'What's famous about your town?'" says Evelyn Hobson, who was curator of the Ernie Pyle State Historic Site from 1978 to 1997. "He sat on a park bench and somebody would come along and he'd get to talking to them. And sometimes he would even end up writing a story about the person who sat down beside him."

"People like down-home, friendly folks, and Ernie certainly was one," says the site's current curator, Rich Bray. "He grew up on a little farm in a close-knit community where everybody knew everybody else and they were used to people coming by and helping out. I think those small-town values suited him very well on the road."

They came in handy during the war too. Pyle's easygoing nature—and the years he spent on America's highways and byways—gave him a big advantage over other correspondents.

"In many cases, he had instant rapport with soldiers because he could talk to them about their hometowns. Wherever they were from, he had probably been there," says James Tobin, author of the 1997 book "Ernie Pyle's War: America's Eyewitness to World War II." "That gave him instant access that a lot of other correspondents couldn't get."

Though Pyle's travel column was eventually overshadowed by the war reporting that came after it, it did have a lasting impact. In the early 1960s, Pyle admirer John Steinbeck wrote about his own cross-country ramblings in "Travels With Charley." And throughout the '60s and '70s, CBS television correspondent Charles Kuralt wandered across America filing a series of reports he acknowledged were directly inspired by Pyle. Later, writers like William Least Heat-Moon and Jonathan Raban went on their own American odysseys.

"There's that whole idea that you learn about America by traveling its back roads and talking to people you meet along the way," Tobin says. "Pyle didn't found that tradition—I think you could trace it back to Mark Twain—but he did help shape it."

Writer Rheta Grimsley Johnson helps keep that tradition alive today. Her syndicated column about the people and places of the South appears in more than 80 newspapers. She doesn't look upon Pyle as some prehistoric journalistic ancestor: His travel column provides the standard she still tries to live up to every time she sits down to write.

"We had the book 'Home Country' [an early collection of Pyle's prewar work] around the house when I was growing up, and I always loved the pieces in that book. I didn't even realize he was a famous war correspondent." Johnson says. "I re-read his columns constantly. They are so well-crafted. There's no padding, not an extra word anywhere, and a lot of reporting is evident. It just puts columnists today to shame.

"He did the kind of reporting that's missing these days, just writing about interesting people and things without any kind of trendy, topical angle, and I love that. It's writing that stands the test of time."

Ernie Pyle

Frontlines in Italy

The relationship of an officer to those under his command is dramatized repeatedly in Fallen Angels. *In a report from the Italian frontlines during World War II, Ernie Pyle gives his readers back home a vivid picture of this relationship.*

IN THIS WAR I have known a lot of officers who were loved and respected by the soldiers under them. But never have I crossed the trail of any man as beloved as Capt. Henry T. Waskow, of Belton, Texas.

Captain Waskow was a company commander in the 36th Division. He had led his company since long before it left the States. He was very young, only in his middle 20's, but he carried in him a sincerity and a gentleness that made people want to be guided by him.

"After my own father, he came next," a sergeant told me.

"He always looked after us," a soldier said. "He'd go to bat for us every time."

"I've never known him to do anything unfair," another one said.

I was at the foot of the mule trail the night they brought Capt. Waskow's body down the mountain. The moon was nearly full at the time, and you could see far up the trail, and even part way across the valley. Soldiers made shadows as they walked.

Dead men had been coming down the mountain all evening, lashed onto the backs of mules. They came lying belly-down across wooden pack saddles their heads hanging down on the left side of the mule, their stiffened legs sticking out awkwardly from the other side, bobbing up and down as the mule walked.

The Italian mule-skinners were afraid to walk beside dead men, so Americans had to lead the mules down that night. Even the Americans were reluctant to unlash and lift off the bodies at the bottom, so an officer had to do it himself, and ask others to help.

The first one came early in the evening. They slid him down from the mule and stood him on his feet for a moment. In the half light he might have been merely a sick man standing there, leaning on the others. Then they lay him on the ground in the shadow of the low stone wall alongside the road.

I don't know who that first one was. You feel small in the presence of the dead men, and ashamed at being alive, and you don't ask silly questions.

We left him there beside the road, that first one, and we all went back into the cowshed and sat on water cans or lay on the straw, waiting for the next batch of mules.

Somebody said the dead soldier had been dead for four days, and then nobody said anything more about it. We talked soldier talk for an hour or more. The dead man lay all alone outside, in the shadow of the stone wall.

Then a soldier came into the dark cowshed and said there were some more bodies outside. We went out into the road. Four mules stood there, in the moonlight, in the road where the trail came down off the mountain. The soldiers who led them stood there waiting. "This one is Capt. Waskow," one of them said quietly.

Two men unlashed his body from the mule and lifted it off and lay it in the shadow beside the low stone wall. Other men took the other bodies off. Finally there were five, lying end to end in a long row alongside the road. You don't cover up dead men in the combat zone. They just lie there in the shadows until somebody else comes after them.

The unburdened mules moved off to their olive orchard. The men in the road seemed reluctant to leave. They stood around, and gradually one by one you could sense them moving close to Capt. Waskow's body. Not so much to look, I think, as to say something in finality, to him and to themselves. I stood close by and I could hear. One soldier came and looked down and he said out loud, "Goddammit." That's all he said, and then he walked away. Another one came. He said "Goddammit to hell anyway." He looked down for a few moments, and then he turned and left.

Another man came; I think he was an officer. It was hard to tell officers from men in the half-light, for all were bearded and grimy dirty. The man looked down into the dead captain's face, and then he spoke directly to him, as though he were alive. He said:

"I'm sorry, old man."

Then a soldier came and stood beside the officer, and bent over, and he too spoke to his dead captain, not in a whisper but awfully tenderly, and he said:

"I sure am sorry, sir."

Then the first man squatted down, and he reached down and took the dead hand, and he sat there for five full minutes, holding the dead hand in his own and looking intently into the dead face, and he never uttered a sound all the time he sat there.

And then finally he put the hand down, and then reached up and gently straightened the points of the captain's shirt collar, and then he sort of re-arranged the tattered edges of his uniform around the wound. And then he got up and walked away down the road in the moonlight, all alone.

James Boswell

On War

Why is war so significant a part of the history of nearly all civilizations? In 1777, British author James Boswell offered his theories of wars—why they are fought and the rightness or wrongness of such conflicts.

WHILE VIEWING, as travelers usually do, the remarkable objects of curiosity at Venice, I was conducted through the different departments of the Arsenal; and as I contemplated the great storehouse of mortal engines, in which there is not only a large deposit of arms, but men are continually employed in making more, my thought *rebounded*, if I may use the expression, from what I beheld; and the effect was, that I was first as it were stunned into a state of amazement, and when I recovered from that, my mind expanded itself in reflections upon the horrid irrationality of war.

What those reflections were I do not precisely recollect. But the general impression dwells upon my memory; and however strange it may seem, my opinion of the irrationality of war is still associated with the Arsenal of Venice.

One particular however I well remember. When I saw workingmen engaged with grave assiduity in fashioning weapons of death, I was struck with wonder at the shortsightedness, the *caecae mentes* of human beings, who were thus soberly preparing the instruments of destruction of their own species. I have since found upon a closer study of man, that my wonder might have been spared; because there are very few men whose minds are sufficiently enlarged to comprehend universal or even extensive good. The views of most individuals are limited to their own happiness; and the workmen whom I beheld so busy in the Arsenal of Venice saw nothing but what was good in the labour for which they received such wages as procured them the comforts of life. That their immediate satisfaction was not hindered by a view of the remote consequential and contingent evils for which alone their labours could be at all useful, would not surprise one who has had a tolerable share of experience in life. We must have the telescope of philosophy to make us perceive distant ills; nay, we know that there are individuals of our species to whom the immediate misery of others is nothing in comparison with their own advantage—for we know that in every age there have been found men very willing to perform the office of executioner even for a moderate hire.

To prepare instruments for the destruction of our species at large, is what I now see may very well be done by ordinary men, without starting, when they themselves are to run no risk. But I shall never forget, nor cease to wonder at a most extraordinary instance of thoughtless intrepidity which I had related to me by a cousin of mine, now a lieutenant-colonel in the British army, who was upon guard when it happened. A soldier of one of the regiments in garrison at Minorca, having been found guilty of a capital crime, was brought out to be hanged. They had neglected to have a rope in readiness, and the shocking business was at a stand. The fellow, with a spirit and alertness which in general would, upon a difficult and trying emergency, have been very great presence of mind and conduct, stripped the lace off his hat, said this will do, and actually made it serve as the fatal chord.

The irrationality of war is, I suppose, admitted by almost all men: I almost say all; because I have met myself with men who attempted seriously to maintain that it is an agreeable occupation and one of the chief means of human happiness. I must own that although I use the plural number here, I should have used the dual, had I been writing in Greek; for I never met with but two men who supported such a paradox; and one of them was a tragick poet, and one a Scotch Highlander. The first had his imagination so in a blaze with heroic sentiments, with the 'pride, pomp, and circumstance of glorious war,' that he did not avert to its miseries, as one dazzled with the pageantry of a magnificent funeral thinks not of the pangs of dissolution and the dismal corpse. The second had his attention so eagerly fixed on the advantage which accrued to his *clan* from the 'trade of war,' that he could think only of it as a good.

We are told by some writers, who assume the character of philosophers, that war is necessary to take off the superfluity of the human species, or at least to rid the world of numbers of idle and profligate men who are a burden upon every community, and would grow an insupportable burden, were they to live as long as men do in the usual course of nature. But there is unquestioningly no reason to fear a superfluity of mankind, when we know that although perhaps the time 'when every rood of land maintain'd its man' is a poetical exaggeration, yet vigorous and well directed industry can raise sustenance for such a proportion of people in a certain space of territory, as is astonishing to us who are accustomed to see only moderate effects of labour; and when we also know what immense regions of the terrestrial globe in very good climates are uninhabited. In these there is room for millions to enjoy existence. In cultivating these, the idle and profligate, expelled from their original societies, might be employed and gradually reformed, which would be better surely, than continuing the practice of periodical destruction, which is also indiscriminate, and involves the best equally with the worst of men.

I have often thought that if war should cease over all the face of the earth, for a thousand years, its reality would not be believed at such a distance of time, notwithstanding the faith of authentick records in every nation. Were mankind totally free from every tincture of prejudice in favour of those gallant exertions which could not exist were there not the evil of violence to combat; had they never seen in their own days, or been told by father or grandfathers, of battles, and were there no traces of the *art of war*, I have no doubt that they would treat as fabulous or allegorical, the accounts in history, of prodigious armies being formed, of men who engaged themselves for an unlimited time, under the penalty of immediate death, to obey implicitly the orders of commanders to whom they were not attached either by affection or by interest; that these armies were sometimes led with toilsome expedition over vast tracts of land, sometimes crouded into ships, and obliged to endure tedious, unhealthy, and perilous voyages; and that the purpose of all this toil and danger was not to obtain any comfort or pleasure, but to be in a situation to encounter other armies; and that those opposite multitudes the individuals of which had no cause to quarrel, no ill-will to each other, continued for hours engaged with patient and obstinate perseverance, while thousands were slain, and thousands crushed and mangled by the diversity of wounds.

We who have from our earliest years had our minds filled with scenes of war of which we have read in the books that we most revere and most admire, who have remarked it in every revolving century, and in every country that has been discovered by navigators, even in the gentle and benign regions of the southern oceans; we who have seen all the intelligence, power and ingenuity of our nation employed in war, who have been accustomed to peruse Gazettes, and have had our friends and relations killed or sent home to us wretchedly maimed; we cannot without a steady effort of reflection be sensible of the improbability that rational creatures should act so irrationally as to unite in deliberate plans, which must certainly produce the direful effects which it was known to do. But I have no doubt that if the project for a perpetual peace which the Abbé de St Pierre sketched, and Rousseau improved, were to take place, the incredulity of war would after the lapse of some ages be universal.

Were there any good produced by war which could in any degree compensate its direful effects; were better men to spring up from the ruins of those who fall in battle, as more beautiful material forms sometimes arise from the ashes of others; or were those who escape from its destruction to have an increase of happiness; in short, were there any great beneficial effect to follow it, the notion of its irrationality would be only the notion of narrow comprehension. But we find that war is followed by no general good whatever. The power, the glory, or the wealth of a very few may be enlarged. But the people in general, upon both sides, after all the sufferings are passed, pursue their ordinary occupations, with no difference from their former state. The evils therefore of war, upon a general view of humanity are as the French say, *àpure perte*, a mere loss without any advantage, unless indeed furnishing subjects for history, poetry, and painting. And although it should be allowed that mankind have gained enjoyment in these respects, I suppose it will not be seriously said, that the misery is overbalanced. At any rate, there is already such a store of subjects, that an addition to them would be dearly purchased by more wars.

I am none of those who would set up their notions against the opinion of the world; on the contrary, I have such a respect for that authority, as to doubt my own judgement when it opposes that of numbers probably as wise as I am. But when I maintain the irrationality of war, I am not contradicting the opinion, but the practice of the world. For, as I have already observed, its irrationality is generally admitted. Horace calls Hannibal, *demens*, a madman; and Pope gives the same appellation to Alexander the Great and Charles XII: from Macedonia's madman to the Swede.

How long war will continue to be practised, we have no means of conjecturing. Civilization, which it might have been expected would have abolished it, has only refined its savage rudeness. The irrationality remains, though we have learnt *insanire certa ratione madoque*, to have a method in our madness.

That amiable religion which 'proclaims peace on earth,' hath not as yet made war to cease. The furious passions of men, modified as they are by moral instruction, still operate with much force; and by a perpetual fallacy, even the conscientious in each contending nation think they may join in war, because they each believe they are repelling an aggressor. Were the mild and humane doctrine of those Christians, who are called Quakers, which Mr Jenyns has lately embellished with his elegant pen, to prevail, human felicity would gain more than we can well conceive. But perhaps it is necessary that mankind in this state of existence, the purpose of which is so mysterious, should ever suffer the woes of war.

To relieve my readers from reflections which they may think too abstract, I shall conclude this paper with a few observations upon actual war. In ancient times when a battle was fought man to man, or as somebody has very well expressed it, was a group of duels, there was an opportunity for individuals to distinguish themselves by vigour and bravery. One who was a '*robustus acri militia*, hardy from keen warfare,' could gratify his ambition for fame, by the exercise of his own personal qualities. It was therefore more reasonable then, for individuals to enlist, than it is in modern times; for, a battle now is truly nothing else than a huge conflict of opposite engines worked by men, who are themselves as machines directed by a few; and the event is not so frequently decided by what is actually done, as by accidents happening in the dreadful confusion. It is as if two towns in opposite territories should be set on fire at the same time, and victory should be declared to the inhabitants of that in which the flames were least destructive. We hear much of the conduct of generals; and Addison himself has represented the Duke of Marlborough directing an army in battle, as an 'angel riding in a whirlwind and directing the storm.' Nevertheless I much doubt if upon many occasions the immediate schemes of a commander have had certain effect; and I believe Sir Callaghan O'Bralachan in Mr Macklin's *Love A la-mode* gives a very just account of modern battle: 'There is so much doing every where that we cannot tell what is doing any where.'

John McCrae

In Flanders Fields

At the close of World War I, 368 American military dead were buried in a six-acre cemetery near Flanders in Belgium. John McCrae was a Canadian medical officer who wrote this poem after witnessing the aftermath of a battle.

In Flanders fields the poppies blow
Between the crosses, row on row,
   That mark our place; and in the sky
   The larks, still bravely singing, fly
5   Scarce heard amid the guns below.

We are the Dead. Short days ago
We lived, felt dawn, saw sunset glow,
   Loved and were loved, and now we lie,
    In Flanders fields.

10   Take up our quarrel with the foe:
To you from failing hands we throw
   The torch; be yours to hold it high.
   If ye break faith with us who die
We shall not sleep, though poppies grow
15   In Flanders fields.

The Gift in Wartime

The enormous price of war is the death of many. Like the writer of Fallen Angels, *poet Tran Mong Tu reminds readers that the "many" are made up of individuals.*

I offer you roses
Buried in your new grave
I offer you my wedding gown
To cover your tomb still green with grass

5   You give me medals
Together with silver stars
And the yellow pips on your badge
Unused and still shining

I offer you my youth
10   The days we were still in love
My youth died away
When they told me the bad news

You give me the smell of blood
From your war dress
15   Your blood and your enemy's
So that I may be moved

I offer you clouds
That linger on my eyes on summer days
I offer you cold winters
20   Amid my springtime of life

You give me your lips with no smile
You give me your arms without tenderness
You give me your eyes with no sight
And your motionless body

25   Seriously, I apologize to you
I promise to meet you in our next life
I will hold this shrapnel as a token
By which we will recognize each other

Chaim Potok | Zebra

In this story, Chaim Potok suggests one possible future for veterans like the characters in Fallen Angels.

His NAME WAS Adam Martin Zebrin, but everyone in his neighborhood knew him as Zebra.

He couldn't remember when he began to be called by that name. Perhaps they started to call him Zebra when he first began running. Or maybe he began running when they started to call him Zebra.

He loved the name and he loved to run.

When he was very young, his parents took him to a zoo, where he saw zebras for the first time. They were odd-looking creatures, like stubby horses, short-legged, thick-necked, with dark and white stripes.

Then one day he went with his parents to a movie about Africa, and he saw zebras, hundreds of them, thundering across a grassy plain, dust rising in boiling brown clouds.

Was he already running before he saw that movie, or did he begin to run afterward? No one seemed able to remember.

He would go running through the neighborhood for the sheer joy of feeling the wind on his face. People said that when he ran he arched his head up and back, and his face kind of flattened out. One of his teachers told him it was clever to run that way, his balance was better. But the truth was he ran that way, his head thrown back, because he loved to feel the wind rushing across his neck.

Each time, after only a few minutes of running, his legs would begin to feel wondrously light. He would run past the school and the homes on the street beyond the church. All the neighbors knew him and would wave and call out, "Go, Zebra!" And sometimes one or two of their dogs would run with him awhile, barking.

He would imagine himself a zebra on the African plain. Running.

There was a hill on Franklin Avenue, a steep hill. By the time he reached that hill, he would feel his legs so light it was as if he had no legs at all and was flying. He would begin to descend the hill, certain as he ran that he needed only to give himself the slightest push and off he would go, and instead of a zebra he would become the bird he had once seen in a movie about Alaska, he would swiftly change into an eagle, soaring higher and higher, as light as the gentlest breeze, the cool wind caressing his arms and legs and neck.

Then, a year ago, racing down Franklin Avenue, he had given himself that push and had begun to turn into an eagle, when a huge rushing shadow appeared in his line of vision and crashed into him and plunged him into a darkness from which he emerged very, very slowly. . . .

"Never, never, *never* run down that hill so fast that you can't stop at the corner," his mother had warned him again and again.

His schoolmates and friends kept calling him Zebra even after they all knew that the doctors had told him he would never be able to run like that again.

His leg would heal in time, the doctors said, and perhaps in a year or so the brace would come off. But they were not at all certain about his hand. From time to time his injured hand, which he still wore in a sling, would begin to hurt. The doctors said they could find no cause for the pain.

One morning, during Mr. Morgan's geography class, Zebra's hand began to hurt badly. He sat staring out the window at the sky. Mr. Morgan, a stiff-mannered person in his early fifties, given to smart suits and dapper bow ties, called on him to respond to a question. Zebra stumbled about in vain for the answer. Mr. Morgan told him to pay attention to the geography *inside* the classroom and not to the geography outside.

"In this class, young man, you will concentrate your attention upon the earth, not upon the sky," Mr. Morgan said.

Later, in the schoolyard during the midmorning recess, Zebra stood near the tall fence, looking out at the street and listening to the noises behind him.

His schoolmates were racing about, playing exuberantly, shouting and laughing with full voices. Their joyous sounds went ringing through the quiet street.

Most times Zebra would stand alongside the basketball court or behind the wire screen at home plate and watch the games. That day, because his hand hurt so badly, he stood alone behind the chain-link fence of the schoolyard.

That's how he happened to see the man. And that's how the man happened to see him.

One minute the side street on which the school stood was strangely empty, without people or traffic, without even any of the dogs that often roamed about the neighborhood—vacant and silent, as if it were already in the full heat of summer. The red-brick ranch house that belonged to Mr. Morgan, and the white clapboard two-story house in which Mrs. English lived, and the other homes on the street, with their columned front porches and their back patios, and the tall oaks—all stood curiously still in the warm golden light of the midmorning sun.

Then a man emerged from wide and busy Franklin Avenue at the far end of the street.

Zebra saw the man stop at the corner and stand looking at a public trash can. He watched as the man poked his hand into the can and fished about but seemed to find nothing he wanted. He withdrew the hand and, raising it to shield his eyes from the sunlight, glanced at the street sign on the lamppost.

He started to walk up the street in the direction of the school.

He was tall and wiry, and looked to be about forty years old. In his right hand he carried a bulging brown plastic bag. He wore a khaki army jacket, a blue denim shirt, blue jeans, and brown cowboy boots. His gaunt face and muscular neck were reddened by exposure to the sun. Long brown hair spilled out below his dark-blue farmer's cap. On the front of the cap, in large orange letters, were the words LAND ROVER.

He walked with his eyes on the sidewalk and the curb, as if looking for something, and he went right past Zebra without noticing him.

Zebra's hand hurt very much. He was about to turn away when he saw the man stop and look around and peer up at the red-brick wall of the school. The man set down the bag and took off his cap and stuffed it into a pocket of his jacket. From one of his jeans pockets he removed a handkerchief, with which he then wiped his face. He shoved the handkerchief back into the pocket and put the cap back on his head.

Then he turned and saw Zebra.

He picked up the bag and started down the street to where Zebra was standing. When the man was about ten feet away, Zebra noticed that the left sleeve of his jacket was empty.

The man came up to Zebra and said in a low, friendly, shy voice, "Hello."

Zebra answered with a cautious "Hello," trying not to look at the empty sleeve, which had been tucked into the man's jacket pocket.

The man asked, with a distinct Southern accent, "What's your name, son?"

Zebra said, "Adam."

"What kind of school is this here school, Adam?"

"It's a good school," Zebra answered.

"How long before you-all begin your summer vacation?"

"Three days," Zebra said.

"Anything special happen here during the summer?"

"During the summer? Nothing goes on here. There are no classes."

"What do you-all do during the summer?"

"Some of us go to camp. Some of us hang around. We find things to do."

Zebra's hand had begun to tingle and throb. Why was the man asking all those questions? Zebra thought maybe he shouldn't be talking to him at all. He seemed vaguely menacing in that army jacket, the dark-blue cap with the words LAND ROVER on it in orange letters, and the empty sleeve. Yet there was kindness in his gray eyes and ruddy features.

The man gazed past Zebra at the students playing in the yard. "Adam, do you think your school would be interested in having someone teach an art class during the summer?"

That took Zebra by surprise. "An *art* class?"

"Drawing, sculpting, things like that."

Zebra was trying *very hard* not to look at the man's empty sleeve. "I don't know. . . ."

"Where's the school office, Adam?"

"On Washington Avenue. Go to the end of the street and turn right."

"Thanks," the man said. He hesitated a moment. Then he asked, in a quiet voice, "What happened to you, Adam?"

"A car hit me," Zebra said. "It was my fault."

The man seemed to wince.

For a flash of a second, Zebra thought to ask the man what had happened to *him.* The words were on his tongue. But he kept himself from saying anything.

The man started back up the street, carrying the brown plastic bag.

Zebra suddenly called, "Hey, mister."

The man stopped and turned. "My name is John Wilson," he said softly.

"Mr. Wilson, when you go into the school office, you'll see signs on two doors. One says 'Dr. Winter,' and the other says 'Mrs. English.' Ask for Mrs. English."

Dr. Winter, the principal, was a disciplinarian and a grump. Mrs. English, the assistant principal, was generous and kind. Dr. Winter would probably tell the man to call his secretary for an appointment. Mrs. English might invite him into her office and offer him a cup of coffee and listen to what he had to say.

The man hesitated, looking at Zebra.

"Appreciate the advice," he said.

Zebra watched him walk to the corner.

Under the lamppost was a trash can. Zebra saw the man set down the plastic bag and stick his hand into the can and haul out a battered umbrella.

The man tried to open the umbrella, but its metal ribs were broken. The black fabric dangled flat and limp from the pole. He put the umbrella into the plastic bag and headed for the entrance to the school.

A moment later, Zebra heard the whistle that signaled the end of recess.

He followed his classmates at a distance, careful to avoid anyone's bumping against his hand.

He sat through his algebra class, copying the problems on the blackboard while holding down his notebook with his left elbow. The sling chafed his neck and felt warm and clumsy on his bare arm. There were sharp pains now in the two curled fingers of his hand.

Right after the class he went downstairs to the office of Mrs. Walsh, a cheerful, gray-haired woman in a white nurse's uniform.

She said, "I'm sorry I can't do very much for you, Adam, except give you two Tylenols."

He swallowed the Tylenols down with water.

On his way back up to the second floor, he saw the man with the dark-blue cap emerge from the school office with Mrs. English. He stopped on the stairs and watched as the man and Mrs. English stood talking together. Mrs. English nodded and smiled and shook the man's hand.

The man walked down the corridor, carrying the plastic bag, and left the school building.

Zebra went slowly to his next class.

The class was taught by Mrs. English, who came hurrying into the room some minutes after the bell had rung.

"I apologize for being late," she said, sounding a little out of breath. "There was an important matter I had to attend to."

Mrs. English was a tall, gracious woman in her forties. It was common knowledge that early in her life she had been a journalist on a Chicago newspaper and had written short stories, which she could not get published. Soon after her marriage to a doctor, she had become a teacher.

This was the only class Mrs. English taught.

Ten students from the upper school—seventh and eighth grades—were chosen every year for this class. They met for an hour three times a week and told one another stories. Each story would be discussed and analyzed by Mrs. English and the class.

Mrs. English called it a class in the *imagination*.

Zebra was grateful he did not have to take notes in this class. He had only to listen to the stories.

That day, Andrea, the freckle-faced, redheaded girl with very thick glasses who sat next to Zebra, told about a woman scientist who discovered a method of healing trees that had been blasted apart by lightning.

Mark, who had something wrong with his upper lip, told in his quavery voice about a selfish space cadet who stepped into a time machine and met his future self, who turned out to be a hateful person, and how the cadet then returned to the present and changed himself.

Kevin talked in blurred, high-pitched tones and often related parts of his stories with his hands. Mrs. English would quietly repeat many of his sentences. Today he told about an explorer who set out on a journey through a valley filled with yellow stones and surrounded by red mountains, where he encountered an army of green shadows that had been at war for hundreds of years with an army of purple shadows. The explorer showed them how to make peace.

When it was Zebra's turn, he told a story about a bird that one day crashed against a closed windowpane and broke a wing. A boy tried to heal the wing but couldn't. The bird died, and the boy buried it under a tree on his lawn.

When he had finished, there was silence. Everyone in the class was looking at him.

"You always tell such sad stories," Andrea said.

The bell rang. Mrs. English dismissed the class.

In the hallway, Andrea said to Zebra, "You know, you are a very gloomy life form."

"Andrea, get off my case," Zebra said.

He went out to the schoolyard for the midafternoon recess. On the other side of the chain-link fence was the man in the dark-blue cap.

Zebra went over to him.

"Hello again, Adam," the man said. "I've been waiting for you."

"Hello," said Zebra.

"Thanks much for suggesting I talk to Mrs. English."

"You're welcome."

"Adam, you at all interested in art?"

"No."

"You ever try your hand at it?"

"I've made drawings for class. I don't like it."

"Well, just in case you change your mind, I'm giving an art class in your school during the summer."

"I'm going to camp in August," Zebra said.

"There's the big long month of July."

"I don't think so," Zebra said.

"Well, okay, suit yourself. I'd like to give you something, a little thank-you gift."

He reached into an inside pocket and drew out a small pad and pen. He placed the pad against the fence.

"Adam, you want to help me out a little bit here? Put your fingers through the fence and grab hold of the pad."

Extending the fingers of his right hand, Zebra held the pad to the fence and watched as the man began to work with the pen. He felt the pad move slightly.

"I need you to hold it real still," the man said.

He was standing bent over, very close to Zebra. The words LAND ROVER on his cap shone in the afternoon sunlight. As he worked, he glanced often at Zebra. His tongue kept pushing up against the insides of his cheeks, making tiny hills rise and fall on his face. Wrinkles formed intricate spidery webs in the skin below his gray eyes. On his smooth forehead, in the blue and purple shadows beneath the peak of his cap, lay glistening beads of sweat. And his hand—how dirty it was, the fingers and palm smudged with black ink and encrusted with colors.

Then Zebra glanced down and noticed the plastic bag near the man's feet. It lay partly open. Zebra was able to see a large pink armless doll, a dull metallic object that looked like a dented frying pan, old newspapers, strings of cord, crumpled pieces of red and blue cloth, and the broken umbrella.

"One more minute is all I need," the man said.

He stepped back, looked at the pad, and nodded slowly. He put the pen back into his pocket and tore the top page from the pad. He rolled up the page and pushed it through the fence. Then he took the pad from Zebra.

"See you around, Adam," the man said, picking up the plastic bag.

Zebra unrolled the sheet of paper and saw a line drawing, a perfect image of his face.

He was looking at himself as if in a mirror. His long straight nose and thin lips and sad eyes and gaunt face; his dark hair and smallish ears and the scar on his forehead where he had hurt himself years before while roller skating.

In the lower right-hand corner of the page the man had written: "To ADAM, with thanks. John Wilson."

Zebra raised his eyes from the drawing. The man was walking away.

Zebra called out, "Mr. Wilson, all my friends call me Zebra."

The man turned, looking surprised.

"From my last name," Adam said. "Zebrin. Adam Martin Zebrin. They call me Zebra."

"Is that right?" the man said, starting back toward the fence. "Well, in that case you want to give me back that piece of paper."

He took the pad and pen from his pocket, placed the page on the pad, and, with Zebra holding the pad to the fence, did something to the page and then handed it back.

"You take real good care of yourself, Zebra," the man said.

He went off toward Franklin Avenue.

Zebra looked at the drawing. The man had crossed out ADAM and over it had drawn an animal with a stubby neck and short legs and a striped body.

A zebra!

Its legs were in full gallop. It seemed as if it would gallop right off the page.

A strong breeze rippled across the drawing, causing it to flutter like a flag in Zebra's hand. He looked out at the street.

The man was walking slowly in the shadows of the tall oaks. Zebra had the odd sensation that all the houses on the street had turned toward the man and were watching him as he walked along. How strange that was: the windows and porches and columns and front doors following intently the slow walk of that tall, one-armed man—until he turned into Franklin Avenue and was gone.

The whistle blew, and Zebra went inside. Seated at his desk, he slipped the drawing carefully into one of his notebooks.

From time to time he glanced at it.

Just before the bell signaled the end of the school day, he looked at it again.

Now *that* was strange!

He thought he remembered that the zebra had been drawn directly over his name: the head over the A and the tail over the M. Didn't it seem now to have moved a little beyond the A?

Probably he was running a fever again. He would run mysterious fevers off and on for about three weeks after each operation on his hand. Fevers sometimes did that to him: excited his imagination.

He lived four blocks from the school. The school bus dropped him off at his corner. In his schoolbag he carried his books and the notebook with the drawing.

His mother offered him a snack, but he said he wasn't hungry. Up in his room, he looked again at the drawing and was astonished to discover that the zebra had reached the edge of his name and appeared poised to leap off.

It *had* to be a fever that was causing him to see the zebra that way. And sure enough, when his mother took his temperature, the thermometer registered 102.6 degrees.

She gave him his medicine, but it didn't seem to have much effect, because when he woke at night and switched on his desk light and peered at the drawing, he saw the little zebra galloping across the page, along the contours of his face, over the hills and valleys of his eyes and nose and mouth, and he heard the tiny clickings of its hooves as cloudlets of dust rose in its wake.

He knew he was asleep. He knew it was the fever working upon his imagination.

But it was so real.

The little zebra running. . .

When he woke in the morning the fever was gone, and the zebra was quietly in its place over ADAM.

Later, as he entered the school, he noticed a large sign on the bulletin board in the hallway:

SUMMER ART CLASS
The well-known American artist Mr. John Wilson will conduct an art class during the summer for students in 7th and 8th grades. For details, speak to Mrs. English. There will be no tuition fee for this class.

During the morning, between classes, Zebra ran into Mrs. English in the second-floor hallway.

"Mrs. English, about the summer art class . . . is it okay to ask where—um—where Mr. Wilson is from?"

"He is from a small town in Virginia. Are you thinking of signing up for his class?"

"I can't draw," Zebra said.

"Drawing is something you can learn."

"Mrs. English, is it okay to ask how did Mr. Wilson—um—get hurt?"

The school corridors were always crowded between classes. Zebra and Mrs. English formed a little island in the bustling, student-jammed hallway.

"Mr. Wilson was wounded in the war in Vietnam," Mrs. English said. "I would urge you to join his class. You will get to use your imagination."

For the next hour, Zebra sat impatiently through Mr. Morgan's geography class, and afterward he went up to the teacher.

"Mr. Morgan, could I—um—ask where is Vietnam?"

Mr. Morgan smoothed down the jacket of his beige summer suit, touched his bow tie, rolled down a wall map, picked up his pointer, and cleared his throat.

"Vietnam is this long, narrow country in southeast Asia, bordered by China, Laos, and Cambodia. It is a land of valleys in the north, coastal plains in the center, and marshes in the south. There are barren mountains and tropical rain forests. Its chief crops are rice, rubber, fruits, and vegetables. The population numbers close to seventy million people. Between 1962 and 1973, America fought a terrible war there to prevent the south from falling into the hands of the communist north. We lost the war."

"Thank you."

"I am impressed by your suddenly awakened interest in geography, young man, though I must remind you that your class is studying the Mediterranean," said Mr. Morgan.

During the afternoon recess, Zebra was watching a heated basketball game, when he looked across the yard and saw John Wilson walk by, carrying a laden plastic bag. Some while later, he came back along the street, empty-handed.

Over supper that evening, Zebra told his parents he was thinking of taking a summer art class offered by the school.

His father said, "Well, I think that's a fine idea."

"Wait a minute. I'm not so sure," his mother said.

"It'll get him off the streets," his father said. "He'll become a Matisse instead of a lawyer like his dad. Right, Adam?"

"Just you be very careful," his mother said to Adam. "Don't do anything that might injure your hand."

"How can drawing hurt his left hand, for heaven's sake?" said his father.

That night, Zebra lay in bed looking at his hand. It was a dread and a mystery to him, his own hand. The fingers were all there, but like dead leaves that never fell, the ring and little fingers were rigid and curled, the others barely moved. The doctors said it would take time to bring them back to life. So many broken bones. So many torn muscles and tendons. So many injured nerves. The dark shadow had sprung upon him so suddenly. How stupid, stupid, *stupid* he had been!

He couldn't sleep. He went over to his desk and looked at John Wilson's drawing. The galloping little zebra stood very still over ADAM.

Early the following afternoon, on the last day of school, Zebra went to Mrs. English's office and signed up for John Wilson's summer art class.

"The class will meet every weekday from ten in the morning until one," said Mrs. English. "Starting Monday."

Zebra noticed the three plastic bags in a corner of the office.

"Mrs. English, is it okay to ask what Mr. Wilson—um—did in Vietnam?"

"He told me he was a helicopter pilot," Mrs. English said. "Oh, I neglected to mention that you are to bring an unlined notebook and a pencil to the class."

"That's all? A notebook and a pencil?"

Mrs. English smiled. "And your imagination."

When Zebra entered the art class the next Monday morning, he found about fifteen students there—including Andrea from his class with Mrs. English.

The walls of the room were bare. Everything had been removed for the summer. Zebra noticed two plastic bags on the floor beneath the blackboard.

He sat down at the desk next to Andrea's.

She wore blue jeans and a yellow summer blouse with blue stripes. Her long red hair was tied behind her head with a dark-blue ribbon. She gazed at Zebra through her thick glasses, leaned over, and said, "Are you going to make gloomy drawings, too?"

Just then John Wilson walked in, carrying a plastic bag, which he put down on the floor next to the two others.

He stood alongside the front desk, wearing a light-blue long-sleeved shirt and jeans. The left shirtsleeve had been folded back and pinned to the shirt. The dark-blue cap with the words LAND ROVER sat jauntily on his head.

"Good morning to you-all," he said, with a shy smile. "Mighty glad you're here. We're going to do two things this summer. We're going to make paper into faces and garbage into people. I can see by your expressions that you don't know what I'm talking about, right? Well, I'm about to show you."

He asked everyone to draw the face of someone sitting nearby.

Zebra hesitated, looked around, then made a drawing of Andrea. Andrea carefully drew Zebra.

He showed Andrea his drawing.

"It's awful." She grimaced. "I look like a mouse."

Her drawing of him was good. But was his face really so sad?

John Wilson went from desk to desk, peering intently at the drawings. He paused a long moment over Zebra's drawing. Then he spent more than an hour demonstrating with chalk on the blackboard how they should not be thinking *eyes* or *lips* or *hands* while drawing, but should think only *lines* and *curves* and *shapes*; how they should be looking at where everything was situated in relation to the edge of the paper; and how they should not be looking *directly* at the edges of what they were drawing but at the space *outside* the edges.

Zebra stared in wonder at how fast John Wilson's hand raced across the blackboard, and at the empty sleeve rising and falling lightly against the shirt.

"You-all are going to learn how to *see* in a new way," John Wilson said.

They made another drawing of the same face.

"Now I look like a horse," Andrea said. "Are you going to add stripes?"

"You are one big pain, Andrea," Zebra said.

Shortly before noon, John Wilson laid out on his desk the contents of the plastic bags: a clutter of junked broken objects, including the doll and the umbrella.

Using strips of cloth, some lengths of string, crumpled newspaper, his pen, and his one hand, he swiftly transformed the battered doll into a red-nosed, umbrella-carrying clown, with baggy pants, a tattered coat, a derby hat, and a somber smile. Turning over the battered frying pan, he made it into a pedestal, on which he placed the clown.

"That's a sculpture," John Wilson said, with his shy smile. "Garbage into people."

The class burst into applause. The clown on the frying pan looked as if it might take a bow.

"You-all will be doing that, too, before we're done," John Wilson said. "Now I would like you to sign and date your drawings and give them to me."

When they returned the next morning the drawings were on a wall.

Gradually, in the days that followed, the walls began to fill with drawings. Sculptures made by the students were looked at with care, discussed by John Wilson and the class, and then placed on shelves along the walls: a miniature bicycle made of wire; a parrot made of an old sofa cushion; a cowboy made of rope and string: a fat lady made of a dented metal pitcher; a zebra made of glued-together scraps of cardboard.

"I like your zebra," Andrea said.

"Thanks," Zebra said. "I like your parrot."

One morning John Wilson asked the class members to make a contour drawing of their right or left hand. Zebra felt himself sweating and trembling as he worked.

"That's real nice," John Wilson said, when he saw Andrea's drawing.

He gazed at the drawing made by Zebra.

"You-all were looking at your hand," he said. "You ought to have been looking at the edge of your hand and at the space outside."

Zebra drew his hand again. Strange and ugly, the two fingers lay rigid and curled. But astonishingly, it looked like a hand this time.

One day, a few minutes before the end of class, John Wilson gave everyone an assignment: draw or make something at home, something very special that each person *felt deeply* about. And bring it to class.

Zebra remembered seeing a book titled *Incredible Cross-Sections* on a shelf in the family room at home. He found the book and took it into his room.

There was a color drawing of a rescue helicopter on one of the Contents pages. On pages 30 and 31, the helicopter was shown in pieces, its complicated insides displayed in detailed drawings. Rotor blades, control rods, electronics equipment, radar scanner, tail rotor, engine, lifeline, winch—all its many parts.

Zebra sat at his desk, gazing intently at the space outside the edges of the helicopter on the Contents page.

He made an outline drawing and brought it to class the next morning.

John Wilson looked at it. Was there a stiffening of his muscular neck, a sudden tensing of the hand that held the drawing?

He took the drawing and tacked it to the wall.

The next day he gave them all the same home assignment: draw or make something they *felt very deeply* about.

That afternoon, Zebra went rummaging through the trash bin in his kitchen and the garbage cans that stood near the back door of his home. He found some sardine cans, a broken eggbeater, pieces of cardboard, chipped buttons, bent bobby pins, and other odds and ends.

With the help of epoxy glue, he began to make of those bits of garbage a kind of helicopter. For support, he used his desktop, the floor, his knees, the elbow of his left arm, at one point even his chin. Struggling with the last piece—a button he wanted to position as a wheel—he realized that without thinking he had been using his left hand, and the two curled fingers had straightened slightly to his needs.

His heart beat thunderously. There had been so many hope-filled moments before, all of them ending in bitter disappointment. He would say nothing. Let the therapist or the doctors tell him. . . .

The following morning, he brought the helicopter to the class.

"Eeewwww, what is *that?*" Andrea grimaced.

"Something to eat you with," Zebra said.

"Get human, Zebra. Mr. Wilson will have a laughing fit over that."

But John Wilson didn't laugh. He held the helicopter in his hand a long moment, turning it this way and that, nodded at Zebra, and placed it on a windowsill, where it shimmered in the summer sunlight.

The next day, John Wilson informed everyone that three students would be leaving the class at the end of July. He asked each of those students to make a drawing for him that he would get to keep. Something to remember them by. All their other drawings and sculptures they could take home.

Zebra lay awake a long time that night, staring into the darkness of his room. He could think of nothing to draw for John Wilson.

In the morning, he sat gazing out the classroom window at the sky and at the helicopter on the sill.

"What are you going to draw for him?" Andrea asked.

Zebra shrugged and said he didn't know.

"Use your imagination," she said. Then she said, "Wait, what am I see-ing here? Are you able to move those fingers?"

"I think so."

"You *think* so?"

"The doctors said there was some improvement."

Her eyes glistened behind the thick lenses. She seemed genuinely happy.

He sat looking out the window. Dark birds wheeled and soared. There was the sound of traffic. The helicopter sat on the windowsill, its eggbeater rotor blades ready to move to full throttle.

Later that day, Zebra sat at his desk at home, working on a drawing. He held the large sheet of paper in place by pressing down on it with the palm and fingers of his left hand. He drew a landscape: hills and valleys, forests and flatlands, rivers and plateaus. Oddly, it all seemed to resemble a face.

Racing together over that landscape were a helicopter and a zebra.

It was all he could think to draw. It was not a very good drawing. He signed it: "To JOHN WILSON, with thanks. Zebra."

The next morning, John Wilson looked at the drawing and asked Zebra to write on top of the name "John Wilson" the name "Leon."

"He was an old buddy of mine, an artist. We were in Vietnam together. Would've been a much better artist than I'll ever be."

Zebra wrote in the new name.

"Thank you kindly," John Wilson said, taking the drawing. "Zebra, you have yourself a good time in camp and a good life. It was real nice knowing you."

He shook Zebra's hand. How strong his fingers felt!

"I think I'm going to miss you a little," Andrea said to Zebra after the class.

"I'll only be away a month."

"Can I help you carry some of those drawings?"

"Sure. I'll carry the helicopter."

Zebra went off to camp in the Adirondack Mountains. He hiked and read and watched others playing ball. In the arts and crafts program he made some good drawings and even got to learn a little bit about watercolors. He put to-gether clowns and airplanes and helicopters out of discarded cardboard and wood and clothing. From time to time his hand hurt, but the fingers seemed slowly to be coming back to life.

"Patience, young man," the doctors told him when he returned to the city. "You're getting there."

One or two additional operations were still necessary. But there was no urgency. And he no longer needed the leg brace.

On the first day of school, one of the secretaries found him in the hall-way and told him to report to Mrs. English.

"Did you have a good summer?" Mrs. English asked.

"It was okay," Zebra said.

"This came for you in the mail."

She handed him a large brown envelope. It was addressed to Adam Zebrin, Eighth Grade, at the school. The sender was John Wilson, with a re-turn address in Virginia.

"Adam, I admit I'm very curious to see what's inside," Mrs. English said.

She helped Zebra open the envelope.

Between two pieces of cardboard were a letter and a large color photo-graph.

The photograph showed John Wilson down on his right knee before a glistening dark wall. He wore his army jacket and blue jeans and boots, and the cap with the words LAND ROVER. Leaning against the wall to his right was Zebra's drawing of the helicopter and the zebra racing together across a facelike landscape. The drawing was enclosed in a narrow frame.

The wall behind John Wilson seemed to glitter with a strange black light.

Zebra read the letter and showed it to Mrs. English.

> Dear Zebra,
>   One of the people whose names are on this wall was among my very closest friends. He was an artist named Leon Kellner. Each year I visit him and leave a gift—something very special that someone creates and gives me. I leave it near his name for a few hours, and then I take it to my studio in Virginia, where I keep a collection of those gifts. All year long I work in my studio, but come summer I go looking for another gift to give him.
>   Thank you for your gift.
>
>   Your friend,
>   John Wilson
>
> P.S. I hope your hand is healing.

Mrs. English stood staring awhile at the letter. She turned away and touched her eyes. Then she went to a shelf on the wall behind her, took down a large book, leafed through it quickly, found what she was searching for, and held it out for Zebra to see.

Zebra found himself looking at the glistening black wall of the Vietnam Memorial in Washington, D.C. And at the names on it, the thousands of names. . . .

Later, in the schoolyard during recess, Zebra stood alone at the chain-link fence and gazed down the street toward Franklin Avenue. He thought how strange it was that all the houses on this street had seemed to turn toward John Wilson that day, the windows and porches and columns and doors, as if saluting him.

Had that been only his imagination?

Maybe, Zebra thought, just maybe he could go for a walk to Franklin Avenue on Saturday or Sunday. He had not walked along Franklin Avenue since the accident; had not gone down that steep hill. Yes, he would walk carefully down that hill to the corner and walk back up and past the school and then the four blocks home.

Andrea came over to him.

"We didn't get picked for the story class with Mrs. English," she said. "I won't have to listen to any more of your gloomy stories."

Zebra said nothing.

"You know, I think I'll walk home today instead of taking the school bus," Andrea said.

"Actually, I think I'll walk, too," Zebra said. "I was thinking maybe I could pick up some really neat stuff in the street."

"You are becoming a pleasant life form," Andrea said.